FLYING IN SHADOWS

The Black Creek Series

Book Two

R.T. Wolfe

Photography: S.L. Jones Photography

Cover and Book design by eBook Prep www.ebookprep.com

First Edition, April 2013
ISBN: 978-1-61417-405-9
ePublishing Works!
www.epublishingworks.com

ACKNOWLEDGMENTS

A special thank you to the East Coast Center for Conservation Biology and Operation Migration for your thoughtful time in reviewing Flying in Shadows for authenticity regarding the facts involving eagles and Whooping cranes.

CHAPTER 1

As soon as he heard the chorus of *fight, fight, fight*, Andy knew Rose would likely be in the middle of it. Since she was in the grade below him, her class was kept on the blacktop while his was on the adjacent field. Bolting through damp grass, he maneuvered through the sweaty ring of tightly fit bodies to just under the basketball hoops. It was that damned Devon and his wanna-be gang. Three boys surrounded one small, skinny girl. Stupid boys, Andy thought with a half-grin.

One of the boys was already bent over, holding his bloody nose. Rose was lightning quick and spun into one of her side-kick things, planting her heel right into the jewels of kid number two. Ouch, that had to hurt. Andy preferred more traditional methods.

The recess supervisors noisily made their way through the mass of students. He knew Rose wouldn't make it to boy number three in time. He grabbed the little prick's arm just before his fist connected with her head. Devon grimaced in pain. What a wimp. They always were, as he and Rose knew all too well. Andy recognized the drop in Devon's other shoulder as the wanna-be geared up for the next sucker punch. Using his traditional methods, Andy landed a quick jab to just under Devon's ribs. The kid gasped for air.

Andy turned to Rose. He could see pieces from the wild mass of her strawberry blond hair that were stuck to her sweaty neck.

She turned on him and his gaze met the ice blue of her eyes. Together, they held years of secrets between them. His smile dropped as he recognized the look on her face.

"What are you doing?" she growled as they stood among the chaos. He would be in twice the trouble if he was caught fighting at school. His aunt taught first grade there. She'd been *his* first-grade teacher when he started at Bloom Elementary. In the few seconds their eyes were locked, they held an entire conversation without speaking a word.

Damn it. If Rose would just give him the green light to get her out of this mess...he had a knack for talking his way out of trouble. He always did. Instead he strode, dejected, past Rose and casually ran a hand through the side of his wavy hair. He slid it down into his pocket before disappearing back into the crowd.

A man impatiently searched the Nolan home. He could do a decent sweep through a house this size in just under twenty minutes. Not bad, he thought, even as frustrated nerves bubbled beneath his skin. "But where is the fucking cash?" he ignited, clearing the contents of the kitchen counter in one sweep of his arm.

He was an average-looking man with stringy blond hair. It lay on the golden skin of his shoulders exposed from the tank he wore in the heat. His light blue eyes darted around the room as he worked to contain his temper.

"So, this is where you live now, Mandy baby. Doin' good for yourself."

He looked around at Amanda's house. It was like frigging Mayberry and had to have some dough in it somewhere. Having already tossed around her dressers and closets upstairs, he grew angrier by the minute. Mandy didn't like it when he was angry, he remembered, as he ran his hand down the front of his pants. He knew her from before she had the little house and family. It seemed like she had maybe two daughters from the look of the rooms upstairs. Wasn't that just fucking nice?

"Where do you keep the rich girl money, Mandy?"

He tossed through coffee cans and the wraps in the freezer. Glancing around the kitchen cabinets into the living room, he considered the wall of electronics and had to remind himself he was just here for the money. Keep a low profile. Don't take anything that could be traced. That's what kept him in the game. It had to be here. She always had cash. Maybe it was on her. He could wait. Nice reunion, huh? Took him long enough to find the bitch. This was a long way from Nicaragua, where he first met her.

Hearing the front lock turn, he sneered with anticipation and stepped behind a corner. He looked around just enough to see who came through the front door. An elderly man walked in like he owned the place. Tossing his keys on the base of the entertainment center, the geezer headed straight for the kitchen, whistling some old jazz shit.

The intruder didn't look for a place to hide. Didn't want a place to hide. This was too perfect. He used his lightly gloved hand to skim his knife out from under the cuff of his pants. When the old man noticed him it was too late, of course. He turned to run as the smooth blade went through the thin, wrinkled skin of his back. The intruder closed his eyes and nearly purred as the knife reached soft flesh. Expertly, he moved his arm out of the way of the dripping blood and backed up to let the frail man fall where he stood.

Standing over the old man, he watched the blood begin to seep from his mouth. He could swear the guy had a look of recognition on his face as he gaped. His eyes were open like saucers, but not with the shock of impending death like most of his prey. Huh. If this was Mandy's old man... No, he tilted his head back and forth to judge as he watched him writhe in his blood. Too old. Must be grandpa, he decided. If this was Mandy's gramps, he corrected himself, he'd sure never met him before. He was trying to say something. Bending down, the intruder heard something about a rose before the old man went still with death.

Lucky for Rose, she had Andy sitting in the seat next to her. If not, she knew the ride home wouldn't be such a quiet one. Her mom and stepdad didn't yell at her in front of Andy...usually.

She'd carpooled with him since they started grade school. His house was just across her cul-de-sac and over Black Creek. She would have been much happier in her mom's car. It was an embarrassing olive green minivan, but at least it wasn't a frigging cop car. Rose's stepdad was a detective—Detective Dave Nolan. The American-built sedan they rode in screamed *unmarked cop car* with its tan color, factory hubcaps and searchlight tucked near the driver's side window.

They sat in the deafening quiet of the backseat as they drove from Bloom to Rose's home. The windows were rolled up and the air on. Her fuming mother added to the heat as she sat stock-still in the front passenger seat.

The houses grew larger and the driveways longer as they came closer to their neighborhood. Rose sort of liked how everyone had big yards here, not like the new homes near the school that were so close together.

Northridge, New York, was a comfortable size—not so big that it was crammed with people, yet it was still close enough to Rochester and Binghamton if someone wanted to get away to a bigger city. The aging hickories and maples towered with millions of leaves that were just changing from the light color of spring to a deep summer green.

As they turned onto her street, Rose stealthily cocked her head, glancing at Andy. The waves of his caramel colored hair were just long enough to hide his eyes from the side, yet he must have sensed her gaze because he turned to look at her. Both of their shoulders jiggled slightly with a silent chuckle. She decided it was better to quickly look back out her window rather than get caught laughing in the backseat.

Her house was the smallest one on the short street. It wasn't really even theirs. It belonged to her great-granddad. He had been living in sin down the street with the feisty widow Lucy Melbourne since Rose was five years old. Rose and her anti-nuclear family rented the conservative house from him ever since her mom had married Dave and became Amanda Nolan. Rose kept her mother's maiden name—something about her mom not wanting to search for Rose's dad so that Dave could formally adopt. Name or no name, Detective Nolan was good to her. Hopefully, she would still be able to say that after they had *the talk* about her little disagreement with the boys at school.

Detective Nolan pulled in the drive and shifted the car into park.

Here we go, Andy thought, as he took a deep breath.

He cringed as Rose's mom turned to face the two of them in the backseat. "You." She pointed her finger at him. "Stay."

Then, she turned to Rose.

"You," she said to Rose. "Come with me. I have just enough time to deal with you before I need to pick up your sister."

Andy noticed Rose glance back at him before slinking out of the squeaky vinyl seat. He gave her a sympathetic look through the window as she shut the door.

Mrs. Nolan was giving her hell as they stood in the drive. He felt bad for Rose. It wasn't her fault. That dickhead Devon and his boys were always ganging up on her. Then again, Rose was pretty easy to rile up. Still, she was a girl and that was just wrong.

Andy cringed a little deeper as Detective Nolan turned around in the front bench seat to face him.

Oh boy. He hated when he talked to him with his gun in that sling thing, and Andy saw him put it back in there as soon as they left the school. Rose's stepdad was intimidating enough without the gun. He wore his usual dress pants and casual shoes, button-down shirt and badge attached to his belt. He was a mountain of a man and he loved Rose deeply, which meant he wouldn't be one of those stepdads who shrugged and turned away any time his wife's daughter got into trouble. Everyone knew he thought of Rose as his own and would take the time to come up with just punishment, meaning she might very well be grounded for the whole damned summer.

"Did you see it happen?" Detective Nolan asked bluntly.

Lucky for Andy, *he* hadn't been caught. Rose would never squeal, and the gang would be too embarrassed about getting licked by a shrimpy girl. With Andy's aunt working at the school, getting caught would have been very ugly for him. Still, he trusted the detective and owed Rose. So, faithfully, he confessed. The skin on the back of his neck prickled before he spoke.

"Yes, sir, Detective Nolan. I saw it."

"Don't give me that *Detective Nolan* crap, Andy. I want to know what happened."

"She's tried all that conflict resolution stuff. They pick on her. You should check the left side of her ribs. I bet she's got old and new bruises from the times they nail her as they pass in the hall. She'll never tell anyone and kill me if she finds out I told you." He looked pleadingly at the big man. "They call her a dyke, Mr. Nolan...Dave."

His eyes darted to Andy's. "What? Why?"

Grabbing the seat next to his knees, Andy took one deep

9

breath and decided he probably should have left that part out. "She doesn't wear that stuff in her hair and the sandals like the other girls. She likes to shoot hoops at recess instead of standing around and whispering."

Mr. Nolan turned and looked toward Mrs. Nolan and Rose, then shook his head and muttered, "Age ten is too old for girls to wear Wrangler jeans and t-shirts and prejudices are already forming?" He turned back but didn't make eye contact. "Does she know what it means?"

"No, sir. I don't think she does." The fun was over. Andy looked out the window and watched his best friend already working off her crime by picking up sticks under their enormous weeping willow.

He watched as Rose turned to him and mouthed the word "chicken" just before they heard a scream so heart wrenching neither of them would ever forget.

CHAPTER 2

Fear wrapped around her feet and shot up to her heart. Rose stood perfectly still as sounds came from her mother she'd never heard before. Screaming, sobbing, choking. Her eyes darted from the house to Dave and back again.

He bolted out of the sedan and up the drive.

Her mother came running out of the house. Tripping down the concrete steps, she caught herself with her hands on her knees. She stood like that, bent over, before she vomited on the sidewalk. Her mom waved a hand behind her, pointing toward the front door.

Dave pointed his finger at Rose as he ran past. "Get in the car and stay there." She obeyed, but not before she noticed him draw his gun.

She sat in the backseat, windows up, side-by-side with Andy. Although her skin was chilled, beads of sweat formed along her hairline as they sat speechless with their noses against the glass of the side window. She could feel her thigh shake against Andy's leg and welcomed his warmth. She waited with him for what felt like hours.

Although visibly shaking, her mom tore back into the house. She left the front door wide open. Rose couldn't see anything inside.

Her stepdad brought her mom back out under his arm and

held onto her while she kicked and screamed. As he spoke into the walkie hooked to his shoulder, he hauled her to the car, opened the passenger door and gingerly placed her in the front seat. "Stay here for a few minutes. Amanda, look at me. I need to check the house. Stay with the kids."

The silence terrified Rose. She looked down and saw her hand was linked with Andy's. It was shaking as her mother's had done.

"Mom," Rose whispered in a voice so hardly audible she could barely hear it herself.

Rain drizzled on black umbrellas. The manicured grass wasn't yet soggy, but Andy could feel drips blowing on his pants. Air lingered cool and thick as they stood in silence, listening to more words spoken about his best friend's great-granddad. Didn't they already do that at the funeral home? Scanning the array of flowers and bushes, he thought of his parents' graves. It was tradition they brought fresh flowers each year to recognize their birthdays and wedding anniversary—never on the date they died in the plane crash.

The image of Clifford Piper in the dark wooden casket was unsettling. They had him in a crisp, white shirt, buttoned up to his neck with a black bow tie. He never wore that stuff. His face seemed alive, as if he was simply sleeping. But, his hands looked like a mannequin's.

Andy's family was there, of course, to share in the grief and offer support—his uncle, Nathan, who raised him and his brother after the death of their parents; his wife, Brie; and their three kids, who were like siblings to Andy rather than cousins. He felt oddly fortunate at that moment, and then guilty when he turned to look at Rose. She was so sad.

Although she never tanned, Rose looked paler than usual. Her fair skin might get a few freckles in the summer, but she would hit him in the shoulder if he ever teased her about it. He couldn't ever remember seeing her in a dress before or even with her hair down. The blondish-red waves made her look even more like her mom. He decided she looked pretty.

He thought he could see tears on her full cheeks, but her head drooped, covering much of her profile with the locks of large curls. He knew how much she hated crying, and it strangled his heart. Without thinking, he used a finger to tuck the waves behind her ear and over her shoulder. He watched as the tears fell down her face in sync with the rain that dripped from the tips of her umbrella. As her shoulders quit twitching, he noticed her breathing slowed.

Her eyelids dropped slowly.

Staring at her, he thought of five years before, when they stood next to each other like this. Only then, it was he who cried as they watched his aunt's house burn after Brie and Andy's brother barely made it out alive. He remembered how Rose reached out, took his hand and held on for what seemed like days as they stood among the chaos.

He didn't care how stupid it was; he stuck out his hand, twined their fingers together between umbrellas and let the rain fall on their joined hands. She didn't look at him, but the way she crushed his fingers, he guessed he did the right thing.

Andy appreciated Rose's relentless nagging to both their sets of folks about the camping trip they'd been promised. She lay next to him on a blanket as he watched the sky explode with sparks from the small campfire. They looked like baby orange stars floating irregularly up to meet their billions of bright, white cousins stuck high in the still sky.

He sat up on the blanket. He felt the hard dirt beneath him, thinking it was a shame it took death for their folks to finally keep their promise. Inhaling deeply, he took in the smell of dirt, trees and campfire. The site was compact and at this time of evening flirting with darkness.

Towering sycamores and red oaks swayed in the breeze as if to inspect the strangers below who were invading their turf. The strangers included all of Andy and Rose's families. Busy campsite. His tent looked like a hotel next to his best friend's small tent for four. His had two areas inside that were separated by zippered material and fit all seven of them. His uncle was the only father he could remember. He turned out to be a solid dad. Andy was thankful, yet wished he could remember them like his brother could. Duncan was only two years older, but Nathan said he could remember their parents because of his talent for art. He had a gift for drawing faces and remembering those kinds of details.

The bond between Andy and his uncle could only compete

with that of his connection with Nathan's wife. Brie's warmth and acute ability to read people saved both Andy and Duncan when they moved to Northridge with Nathan. Their uncle had given up everything, Andy remembered, as he watched him help his twin boys throw sticks at the fire. His young cousins jumped each time flames caught the dry twigs with small explosions of color and heat. He was thankful Nathan had moved him and Duncan to Northridge, near their grandparents, for help with raising them. After a time, he and Duncan came to think of Nathan and Brie as their parents and addressed them as such. Andy sighed and smiled.

He and Rose's little sisters used sticky fingers to maneuver marshmallows on wooden pokers before propping them over the fire, sometimes *in* the fire. Carefully, they centered chocolate squares on graham crackers as his aunt and brother sat on plastic folding chairs with their heads together, looking at Duncan's sketch pad.

On the opposite side of the campsite, he noticed Rose's mom as she sat on a blanket of her own, looking as white as a ghost. Dark rings dug beneath her usually bright eyes. She was sitting on the ground, leaning back against Mr. Nolan's legs. They sat in silence as he rubbed her neck and shoulders.

As the sky darkened further, Andy lay back with Rose, watching as more stars awakened between the soaring trees. They listened to the happy sound of neighboring families through the rustle of leaves.

"A puppy," Rose blurted out. Lying in her usual ponytail, jeans and sneakers, her full cheeks were rosy from the chill of the evening.

Andy recognized her wish on the first star she saw. "You've been trying to get your mom to get you a puppy since you were seven."

"First star I see tonight. I can wish it, can't I? Falling star." She slugged him in the arm.

"You can't slug bug a fallen star. Double backs."

"Chicken. And don't you tell me what I can't do." She crossed her arms and glanced at him through the corner of her eyes. "Thanks, by the way."

"For what?"

"Helping me get through great-granddad's funeral." She turned her head to face him, brows scrunched closely together. She leaned closer and whispered, "If you laugh, I'll kick your ass."

He shrugged. "I won't. You're welcome."

Rose looked at him and thought about that rainy day. Something she didn't quite recognize stirred inside her heart.

The evening was what it promised to be, cool and damp. A propane stove cooked sloppy joes and macaroni and cheese. Her mom had spent weeks and months, before Rose was born, in third world countries working with FEMA and the Red Cross at disaster sites. The propane stove would have been a luxury then. Her mom said using it was cheating but had no problem wolfing down two sandwiches and a small mountain of mac-n-cheese.

The smell of the outdoors mixed with the aroma of dinner and campfire turned out to be therapy for everyone. She listened as the parents planned a next-day hike through the trails, followed by throwing Frisbees and baseballs, then a trip to the small Seneca Park Zoo in Rochester.

Great-granddad would have been pleased, she knew.

Rose's younger sister stood in line with Andy's cousins. Each stuck the toes of their shoes through the spaces in the chain-link fence surrounding a polar bear exhibit, straining to get a better look. They giggled in chorus as the pair of large, white beasts took turns diving at a metal barrel in their pond.

The adults stood next to the Galapagos Tortoises, turning every so often to check on everyone while taking in the gentle nature of the enormous creatures. Rose thought about how each gravitated toward the animal that best fit their mood.

As the only teenager in the group, Duncan was leaning on one foot with a shoulder up against the fence of the polar bear habitat. Rose recognized it as a too-cool-for-the-zoo stance. She watched as Andy slithered up to him and sensed he was about to bait his stuffy brother.

"They swim as well as you do, Dunc." Andy strutted, nodding his head toward the polar bears that looked deceivingly clumsy as they floundered in the water. When Duncan went to shove at the side of his head, Andy quickly ducked and slipped out of reach. Duncan must not have been too cool to resist chasing Andy; they dodged spectators and earned sneers from the nearly missed adults.

She knew the real reason they were on this trip. Her great-granddad had been killed. An attempted burglary gone wrong, the police had said. The only father figure her mom had ever known was dead.

Andy's uncle had helped Dave change the locks and install an alarm system. That helped. Mr. Reed was always good with that kind of thing. Rose saw him give Mrs. Reed's butt a couple of pats when he thought no one was looking. It was kind of sweet.

Dave and her mom stood in the sunlight. He rested his large hand on the small of her mom's back. Rose watched as she closed her eyes and let the side of her head drop to his chest. Rose realized at that moment Dave had kept her within arm's reach since the day her grandfather was killed—was murdered.

Rose did love the zoo. Animals were simple. They knew how to love, how to protect their families. She was in her own kind of habitat here, which was likely another part of why they made the trip. She'd worked her mom mercilessly about getting a pet, but so far had to settle with an occasional frog or temporary turtle she could catch from the creek. They caught a birds of prey show, and she made no attempt to leash her excitement.

Andy sat next to her and rubbed his arm where she had hit him with the back of her hand over and over again.

She was on the edge of her seat. Literally.

"Sit down or they're gonna kick us out of here," he said.

"My wish," she responded. The zookeeper gave a command, and a red-tailed hawk spread his wings, lifted gracefully from her gloved hand and flew to a nearby oak tree.

Andy kept rubbing his arm. "What?" he asked as the woman recited facts that were of more interest to a group of younger children while she used hand signals to cue the bird. Genius. It swooped back down, gliding low over the heads of the ducking spectators and landed gracefully on the zookeeper's outstretched arm. Gladly, it gobbled down the treat its handler offered.

Rose clapped neurotically. "That's my wish; what I want to do. To be."

"You want to be a bird lady?"

She elbowed him in the ribs. "That and I want a hundred puppies."

The zookeeper lifted her arm to signal the bird to expand its nearly three-foot wings.

16

"Well, I'm going to build. My uncle says I can live with him in the summers in the city when I get older, and he's going to show me how he builds buildings."

Rose turned her head, almost in slow motion, and faced him. Her eyes drifted from one side of him to the other before focusing on his face. After a few unsettling moments, she turned back toward the show, but couldn't find it in her to watch any longer.

CHAPTER 3

Eight Years Later....

The plane ride was short and had given Andy time to gear up for a weekend away. His freshman year at Purdue U. College was a blast, but he could definitely use a weekend filled with a bigger bedroom, decent food and neighbors that didn't crank their bass until three in the morning. Before he had to buckle down for finals, he wanted to see his best friend and give his latest Mustang a test drive. Duncan was right when he said it was ready to go and purring like a cat, although Duncan didn't like people to know he could work on cars. His brother preferred to keep his sophisticated, right-brained artist image as fine-tuned as his engines.

Andy cranked The Boss and thought of the look on Rose's face when he showed up. She was terrible at keeping in touch, but so was he. He knew her well enough to know she rarely had down time. Working part time for the landscaping business their parents shared left just enough time for her to volunteer at the zoo, while applying for every scholarship she could get her hands on. He would have to pull her away from it all, even if it meant over his shoulder.

Rose hefted a load of brick edgers around to the back of the spec house. Her mom sat on her heels with her boney knees resting on a pad. She was working on securing landscaping fabric and steadied her hands as she worked the spikes into the black cloth.

The air was chilled but not enough to keep beads of sweat from dripping under Rose's sweatshirt and down her back. As she hauled and stacked, she thought of the black belt test she had the next morning and felt the butterflies in her stomach return. Her small size would make the boards difficult to break. She'd learned to use the momentum of her ninety-five pounds for just that purpose, but still. For whatever reason, this was important to her mom, and Rose rationalized that if she'd gone this far, she might as well finish and go for the black.

At the sound of Jimi Hendrix roaring over an ostentatious rumble from the engine of a sports car, she sprinted for the front of the construction site. She smiled wildly as she ran. If he knew her reaction to the sound of his approach, Andy would never let her live it down. He parked at the curb and got out.

"You came!" She skidded to a stop, then awkwardly hugged him. His shoulders felt bigger, if that were possible, even though his cheeks were thinner and covered with a layer of stubble. When did he get stubble? Andy looked different. He'd buzzed his caramel brown hair, losing the waves. Pulling back, she noticed that through the sharpened features, his eyes were comfortably just as she remembered. The soft brown carried a lifetime of shared memories, erasing the months apart.

He pulled her toward him, effortlessly lifting her off her feet and into a bear hug.

A rush of electricity flowed through her.

"Of course I did. Haven't missed a promotion yet, have I?" he said.

"I...thought college boys went to Florida for spring break."

He slid her down and stepped back. "They do. But this one is watching his best friend become a bitching black belt. As if you ever needed a belt to make you scary. And Regionals are this weekend. I'll hit the game and see Candi cheer her last time."

While digging one hand into the pocket of her jeans, she bit the already short nails on the other. "I may puke."

Andy sighed. "Are you going start on that already?"

"No, of course not." Grow up, Rose, she chided herself. It's none of your business who he dates.

He had on his time-honored faded blue jeans and scuffed boots with a long sleeved, classy brown collared shirt. So Andy. Expensive sunglasses rested backward on his head. She wondered if her heart would ever beat normally when they were together.

She wore sneakers and a sweatshirt.

"I'm just glad you're here," she said to him. "I feel better already. Come around and say hello to mom. She'll want to see you, too."

As they sauntered toward the back, Andy took her hand and tucked it through his arm. He set his on top. It felt rough and warm.

She glanced behind them. "New car?" she asked.

A smile as big as Texas spread across his face. "New for me," he all but hummed. "Like it?"

"Sure." She shrugged. "Your cars all sound the same. I thought college students were also starving."

"It's used and that's not cheap, either." He nodded over toward her F-150. "You're not even in college yet. Why don't you come with me to the game?" His eyes narrowed and he dipped his face closer to her. "Have you been to a single one since I left?"

"I don't have to go. I'm not sleeping with any of the cheerleaders."

Andy stopped walking and blinked rapidly.

"Fast forward past the girl-on-girl fantasy, pal." She smacked his shoulder with the back of her hand. "And why would I go when you're not playing? I don't even like basketball."

Andy shook his head, then rolled his eyes dramatically before answering. "You're a senior. It's Regionals."

"She doesn't want me there." Slowly, she lifted her eyes to him.

"She doesn't care," he said. It sounded sort of like a question. "Come on. Be a team player."

She took a deep breath through her nose and blew it out, letting her cheeks expand. "What day? What time?"

"You're a senior," he repeated as he shook his head again. "You should to know this."

"Andy," she pointed out playfully, "I thought you would have figured out by now not to tell me what I'm supposed to know."

She grinned at the thought of the first time he told her what she was *supposed* to know. At five years old, she had been stacking his toy Duplos in a single stick. He thought it was wrong, of course, and tried to show her what she was supposed to do with them. Her grin turned into a full smile as she remembered closed-fisting him in the nose, and the bloody mess that followed.

Amanda watched as Rose waited in the front room for the sound of Andy's Mustang. "Is that what you're wearing?" she tried to ask gently.

Rose was biting her nails, then looked at her wristwatch for the third time. "I refuse to wear that phony girly crap."

She tapped the top of her daughter's head. It was wrapped in a bandana.

Sighing, Rose yanked it off and pulled out the rubber band. Gathering the mass of dark strawberry blond around the side of her neck, she started braiding. Rose glared at Amanda like only her Rose could do. "Not a word."

Amanda made the motion of zipping her lips and walked back into their conservative kitchen. She heard the rumble of the car, the car door and then the bell.

She could hear murmurs, some laughter. Then, they came in to say good-bye. Amanda turned, trying not to look anxious, and spotted the small bouquet of flowers. White daisies. "Oh, Andy." She dipped her head. "You're a smooth one."

"Only the best for my favorite detective's wife. I'll have Rose home on time."

Amanda touched his arm before reaching for the cabinet that held the vases.

When she heard the door shut, she paused before clipping the stems of the flowers. Letting out a contented sigh for her daughter, she decided to choose a cigarette from her purse instead of the valium she'd been thinking about all afternoon.

As they drove with the top down and Zeppelin jamming from the speakers, Rose sensed Andy's gaze turn momentarily.

"This is new," he said as he flicked her braid.

Even though it was a platonic gesture, she was acutely aware where his hand had brushed her shoulder. Sighing, she warned him. "If you laugh—"

"Yeah, yeah. You'll kick my ass. When the hell did it get so long?"

"It's always been this long. I just don't wear it down. Is it too long?" She couldn't believe she'd just asked that.

Teeth gleaming, he smiled at her. "No, no. Just saying."

By the time they reached the parking lot, she'd forgotten about any leftover tension. Andy told her of the apartment he was getting for his sophomore year. She spoke of her work at the zoo and about the landscaping business their parents co-owned. They slipped into their easy way, and it felt right as rain.

She convinced herself high school politics were just that, high school politics. She would much rather spend time with Andy, fishing in the lake that overflowed into Black Creek, but if he could endure her dozens of martial arts promotions, she would do this for him.

She thought about how this must be awkward for him, too. The college kid coming to see his high school cheerleader girlfriend. Then, she thought of how Candi would feel about it. Ugh. Hot, college boy coming to watch her shake her boobs. Great, she thought sarcastically, as she recognized that she'd just thought of her best friend as hot. He was, though. Not that she was supposed to know. He had the strength of a linebacker, but he was fast and could handle a basketball. That's what everyone said.

The bleachers were just as she remembered—spectators crammed shoulder to shoulder with the aroma of popcorn wafting around them. She vowed not to use the bathroom since getting to her seat was a conspicuous venture that involved walking horizontally along the middle of the aluminum bleachers in order to reach any of the staggered access stairs. She had to admit the energy and unity stirred by the cheering crowd could be considered somewhat contagious. Maybe.

She forced herself to be pleasant and gestured to Andy's folks. It wasn't uncommon for them to come to the high school games. After so many years of working at the elementary school, many of the players once had Andy's aunt as their first-grade teacher. They exchanged polite nods of greeting before they sat to watch.

She had to lean into Andy and yell if she wanted him to hear her over the crowd. He smelled like a mixture of new car and guy soap. When her head cleared, she asked, "How come you never went out for college ball?"

"Too short. Quick only goes so far." He shrugged and picked a piece of popcorn from her hair. "Are you sure about NYU?"

"It has a good school of biology and it's in-state. So, that'll help with tuition. I've been really lucky with academic scholarships, but they don't all carry over all four years. I've got it mapped out but I'm trying to have options in case I hit a road block. If I work as a graduate assistant and do some research, I should be able to afford it. And...I'm rambling."

"I like it when you ramble. I should do the boyfriend thing, though. Can I get you something?"

She shook her head.

The game was nearing tip-off. Andy made his way down the side stairs to the edge of the gym floor. He hadn't anticipated feeling so out of place.

Nothing had changed, really. His old teammates were there, of course, and his coach. It was good to see them. But high school seemed long ago and, well, forgotten. Forgotten, at least, until he came within ear shot of Candi.

She was arguing with the girl who cheered next to her.

He reached the bottom of the stairs and walked in front of the bleachers.

"Look, Candi dear." Andy was sure the blonde was speaking up to make sure he heard. "He brought his *other* girlfriend."

Crushing the handles of her poms, Candi flipped her hair before turning to glare at her. She stood confidently with her long legs and thick brown hair tied with a large bow on the top of her head. He could tell she leashed her anger and hoped it wasn't only for his sake.

"Just kidding, dear," her friend chided. "Can you believe that girl? Her and her Chuck Taylors? And oh lookie, she gave up the doo-rag for a Little House on the Prairie braid. I can almost tell she's a girl."

Not-so-subtly, Candi dipped her head, adjusted her cleavage and then turned to him, acting like he couldn't have possibly heard.

She ran toward him like she hadn't just seen him earlier that afternoon. Didn't even bother to pull him aside before grabbing the collar of his shirt and pressing her mouth to his, along with the rest of her curves. Her tongue nearly reached his throat before he could take her by the shoulders and nudge her away.

"What the fuck?" she said. Candi looked around. "Everyone's watching us."

"Exactly," he answered, more than a little pissed off. Trying not to make any more of a scene, he patted her on the shoulder as he noticed her gaze slither up in Rose's direction. He couldn't help but follow her glare and watched as a tall blond dude slithered into the seat next to Rose. His seat. Andy stood and stared at them, feeling a sharp pang of something he decided must be overprotectiveness.

First, Rose had her typical look of, "Excuse me?" Then, it changed to recognition.

The whistle blew. He heard Candi's voice. He knew she would have to get back to the squad, but he couldn't peel his eyes away from Rose long enough to find out what she was saying.

With the game starting, he walked out of the way of the spectators and toward concessions just as Rose turned to face the blond straight on. Could she not see what the guy was up to? How could she fall for the frigging handshake? Andy needed to help her, warn her. Shaking his head, he looked at the floor as he walked. Lightly stained wooden slats, he said to himself. Pay attention to the wooden slats on the floor.

She had been talking, he thought as he ordered a popcorn and two bottles of water. She hardly ever talked to anyone. She had been smiling and talking.

So, what's the big deal? She'll be eighteen soon. She can't talk to a guy? When he came back out to the gym, the dude was still there. Not for long, though. Andy stopped on the stairs just as both of them turned to him. Andy sighed heavily as the feelings he assumed were overprotective anger turned to guilt. Blond boy got up and side-stepped over the row of knees to the opposite side of bleachers.

Andy returned and sat without speaking. He handed Rose one of the bottles of water.

"Problem?" she asked.

"Huh? Nope." Folding his hands, he rested them on top of his head.

"Candi looks mad. I'm sorry if you're fighting."

He felt her lean on him. She smelled like peaches.

"Beginning of the first quarter. We're winning," she yelled in his ear. Damn it, that was funny. Sure it was loud, but he wasn't deaf. He couldn't help but smile.

"You're trying to distract me." He lifted an eyebrow as he looked down at her. "It's working." Taking a deep breath, he confessed, "I'm gonna have to give her a ride home." He tried his best pleading look.

"Not." Rose lifted her hands in self-defense, palms facing outward. "I'll catch a ride with your folks."

"You sure?"

"Of course." She patted his thigh three times, then tucked her hands deep underneath her arms.

The game was a good one. Close. He gave her a play-by-play. They cheered at the great shots from their team and the air balls from the opposing team. They spoke of summer plans and fell right back into their groove of give and take. He was glad he brought her. Rose made everything easier.

Offering her one last shot at a ride home, Rose shook her head. "Two words. No and way. See you tomorrow." She rose to her toes, kissed him on the cheek and walked away with those quick, efficient steps she used when trying to look independent. Cute.

There were no signs separating student parking from adults, but there were rules. Everyone knew the rules. Rose headed toward the lot meant for the adults to hook up with his folks, and he waited at the exit on the student side, dangling his keys in his hand.

He felt better and came to grips with his overreaction. That's all it was. Rose would surely start dating in college. She's smart, and she's a black belt now.

He stood up on the concrete stoop next to the door so Candi could spot him more easily through the crowd. Except, it made it easier for him to see through the crowd.

His eyes zeroed in. His heart sped to double time and he went instantly back to anger. Rose was talking to the same dude who moved in on her at the game. That's right, buzz off, he thought as Rose waved her hand dismissively in front of him. The guy glanced behind him and nodded his friends off.

A handful of the cheerleaders broke through the door at that time, cheering the win. Candi led the group.

Andy balled his fingers into tight fists as the boy put his hands on Rose's shoulders and turned her around. She laughed and hit the palm of her hand to her head as he led her toward the student parking lot.

Candi took hold of one of Andy's arms. Her cold fingers brought his focus to her.

"Hey, hun. Are you driving the Mustang?"

What else he have to drive, he thought.

Another one of the girls took his other arm and they pulled him along toward his car.

Amanda stood in her warm yellow kitchen nervously spooning rich batter into a rectangular pan. Determined to be a supportive mother, she kept busy and away from her purse.

"What's all this?" A hand ran up her back.

"You wouldn't understand," she answered lightly, turning her head into Dave's arm. She was all hormones when he did that. She couldn't possibly concentrate on measuring and hormones at the same time.

"Try me." He leaned forward over the smell of chocolaty batter.

"Rose is growing up."

"She goes to New York University in a few months. Are you just figuring that out now?" Dave tilted his head back playfully.

"Did you notice how she was before she went to the game tonight?"

"With Andy," he said flatly.

"Okay. Point taken. It's just that she hasn't been to a school function since he graduated. She feels out of place, which is the reason for making the worry-about-our-daughter brownies." She set down her bowl and spatula and turned to wrap her arms around him, sinking her face into his chest.

He pulled her away gently, enough to look at her. Running his thumbs along the dark circles she knew were under her eyes, Dave sighed. "You need some rest. Why don't you let me wait up for her?"

"Don't start, please. I love you." Working up a smile, she lifted to her toes and gave him a soft, lingering kiss before smacking his butt and turning back to her baking.

She hadn't as much as lifted the bowl to scrape the remaining mix into the pan before she heard car doors. She and Dave looked to each other with puzzled expressions.

"No rumble from the Mustang," Dave said.

They stepped out onto the small, concrete porch even though she knew they ought not to.

In the dark, Rose dug her keys out of her front pocket. She barely noticed Tyler lose his footing, then catch himself as he looked toward the house.

He stepped close to her. "Is that your stepdad? Did you forget to tell me that you had a giant for a stepdad?"

Dave showed no teeth as he squinted and smiled at them. "You're home. Who's your friend?"

On the porch? Rose cringed. Are you kidding? "Dad, Mom, this is Tyler. Andy had drama. I was going to catch a ride with his folks, but Tyler offered." Uncomfortable silence. More uncomfortable silence. "We have math together. You know how I hate calculus. He's going to help me out sometime."

Even though Tyler remained speechless, she judged that Dave was satisfied. Without, fortunately, demanding a strip search, he and her mom went back inside. They left the porch light on.

As soon as the door clicked shut, she let out a relieved breath, blowing loose strands of her hair from her face.

Tyler took her hand, without linking fingers, and walked her up the steps.

"See you at school, then?" She smiled awkwardly at him. She'd never had a boy on her doorstep before. Pathetic. Andy didn't count.

She shut the door as he left and smelled chocolate. "Oh, great," she mumbled. Knowing her mom only baked brownies when something was up, Rose asked, "Problem?" Then, she dropped her unused house key on the kitchen counter.

"No, no. How was the game?" Her mom looked through the fridge for nothing.

"We won the game. Andy and Candi are fighting. I have a date for prom." Rose looked forward to their reaction. She wasn't disappointed.

Her mom turned her head quickly with eyes opened wide before leaning back against the kitchen counter and folding her arms. "Smart guy."

Rose shrugged and smiled.

Dave made vows to do a background check and that strip search before the dance, kissed them one at a time on their foreheads and slinked upstairs.

Biting her nails, Rose rolled out a summary of the evening. "It's the weirdest thing. I'm just sitting there, and we were talking about studying together sometime. Then, he was telling his buddies to get lost. Then, he was asking me to prom. I said, 'Yes.' Go figure. And you know what? I'm excited. I hate those kinds of things. I'm even looking forward to the dress."

CHAPTER 4

Andy walked painfully slow through the Seneca Zoo with Candi on his arm. Groups of crocuses willed the cold away as they bloomed among the leftover winter brown.

"I tried to tell you to wear comfortable shoes." He nodded toward her ice-pick boots.

Candi tilted her head and batted her eyelashes. "Why? They're not at all uncomfortable."

Spotting Rose in the petting zoo, the corners of his mouth lifted. She stood on sandy gravel with a broom in one hand and a long-handled dust pan in the other. He could see her scan the area with a motherly eye. The female goat must be pregnant. Very pregnant. The males looked for something to eat. A pot belly pig had found a patch of sunlight as a couple of young girls scratched his belly into oblivion.

He noticed Rose's brows press together as she watched two junior volunteers who were more interested in each other than in scooping goat poop. She rolled her eyes and walked over to give them what looked like a short lecture before they got back to work.

He glanced around at the other exhibits as he approached the gated area, remembering when she was a junior staffer and doing little more than scooping poop. Now she was the supervisor and, being a good example, scooped some droppings along with the juniors. The pregnant goat tasted the shirt of one of the little girls. The kid squealed in delight as Rose shooed the hungry, waddling female over to her feed.

By the time he reached her, Rose was sharing what must have been animal facts with the mesmerized girls. This would be her last summer here. The slam of the door as he entered the enclosure caused her to turn her eyes to him. He loved the way she lit up when she saw him.

"Happy birthday." He gave her an a-frame hug, leaving one arm behind his back.

"Andy! Now my birthday is complete. You shouldn't have come all the way up here."

"It was cool enough that Candi wanted to come." He nodded his head toward the outside of the fence toward her.

"Sure she did." Rose looked down with an impish grin.

He gave her a playful push on her shoulder. "Don't start."

"I just don't think anyone who wants to be called *Candi* would want to visit a zoo. I feel sorry for her. That's all."

"No you don't." He raised one side of his mouth. "I brought you a present." He pulled the arm from around his back that held a small package.

"You shouldn't have." She took it from him without hesitating. "I didn't get you anything for your birthday."

"Yes, you did," he whispered. "You got me out of going to that damned couples soup thing."

"Tastefully Simple party," she corrected.

"Open it."

The set of male goats wandered over when they heard the rip of paper. Rose glanced around Andy's shoulder toward the junior staffers, then turned her glance to Candi, who was dramatically rolling her eyes and pacing impatiently in her heels.

"Come on in, Candi," Rose practically sang as she tore the papers. "They won't bite."

Candi didn't answer, just made a junior high-type sarcastic look at Rose and went back to pacing.

Excitement bubbling through her, Rose peeked at the exposed corner of the gift. "Stationary. You got me stationary. With birds of prey! How did you ever find this? It's perfect." She looked up at him. Surprised at the proximity, she blinked several times before noticing he wasn't smiling this time but was looking intently in her eyes.

"Uncle Chase agreed to let me come and stay with him this summer. Sort of an internship. He's working on a resort and conference center in the city. Write me this time."

An instant sting burned her eyes. She dropped her head and tried to focus on the gift. She couldn't explain her degree of disappointment to him and wished he'd have told her over the phone or given her some kind of warning so she had time to gather her response. "Of course I will." She made herself look up and grin.

"Andrew, dear?" Candi called.

Andy lifted his head in polite recognition.

"I'm getting cold. Can we run along now?" Candi asked as sweet as apple pie.

"Yes, Andrew dear," Rose mocked. "You must be running along now." She adjusted the bandana that covered her mass of untamable hair and tucked her gift into her apron pocket. "And thank you. You're the best."

"I might not be the *best*. Wait 'til you get home."

A wrinkle formed between her eyes, then she turned to analyze his expression. "Tell me."

"No way." He lifted one brow and smirked as he walked away.

"You can't drop that on me and then leave."

He turned with just enough time to wink. "Watch me."

Eighteen years old with birds of prey stationary, a twenty dollar tip from the insistent father of the two curious girls and driving home from her favorite job. Okay, well her favorite *volunteer* job, but in her shiny pickup anyway. Keeping the windows down despite the chill in the air, she smelled spring. Fresh, wet and floral.

If she looked at the big picture, Andy's decision to spend the summer away was just as natural as her leaving for NYU in the fall. Wouldn't she have made the same choice if an opportunity like that had been presented to her? Then why did it cut so deeply?

Curiosity made her foot a little heavier. *Wait 'til you get home.* That was just playing dirty.

The combination of Andy's news and her coming of age must have turned on a philosophical tune for her. And what was she coming of age to anyway? The right to buy cigarettes? Vote?

Rent porn? Right. Still, she couldn't help but look at her neighborhood in a different light on her way home.

She drove past Andy's towering home. The mass of trees attempted miserably to conceal it from view. Her heart softened as next her tires bumped over the short Black Creek bridge. It held years of memories over and around it. Her house was on the next street with its elderly weeping willow and lifelong feeling of family and warmth.

Before this place, she and her mother spent the first few years of Rose's life on the road, traveling from country to country and managing disaster sites, first for FEMA and then the Red Cross. Rose had no memories of those days. She only had stories from around the dinner table and a few fleeting words from the Spanish language she once spoke fluently.

Except, this time when she walked through the worn front door, there was no warmth. Both Dave and her sister were out. Her mom stood in the kitchen visibly shaken with a bright red ring around her upper arm and one at the side of her throat.

Rose dropped her pack and hurried to her, trying to stay calm. "Are you okay? What happened? Are you all right?"

"Yes, of course. Happy birthday, honey. We have presents. Oh, we should wait for Dave and Jessica." She was speaking too fast. Her mom darted her eyes back and forth between the front and back doors.

Rose stood in front of her, hands dangling at her sides. "Your arm."

"Oh that." Her mom waved her hand in the air. "Someone grabbed me at the shelter today. Are you hungry?" Picking up a long-armed grill lighter, her mom turned toward the deck.

"You went to the shelter on a Saturday?" Rose felt the wrinkle between her brows return.

"Sure. I was called in. I'm making your favorite dinner."

"Stop." Rose reached for her arm. "Stop talking about my birthday."

Her mom took one, long breath. "You're absolutely right. I am shook up about it, but I want this to be a nice day for you. Let me let this be a nice day for you."

"Okay. All right." Rose didn't move. "Does dad know?"

Looking away, her mom answered, "No. No, I'll tell him tonight. I'll just go change my shirt so we don't have to deal with it in the middle of birthday bratwursts and corn on the cob."

Rose followed her up the stairs.

She walked in her room, deep in thought. Reaching behind, she absently pulled the string to loosen her zoo apron. As she took the contents from the pockets, the wrinkles in her forehead softened at the feel of the twenty-dollar tip. The endless questions from the quizzical girls ran through her mind as she lifted the lid to her money box. When she tossed in the bill, the wrinkles instantly returned. She leaned down for a closer look.

At that moment, her mom came back wearing a three-quarter-length sleeved blouse and asked if she had any extra eighteen-year-old dinner requests before she got started with the brats.

Rose stood with her zoo apron dangling loosely from her neck, staring intently into her money box. She estimated the amount with her eyes.

"Oh, honey, I misplaced my credit card. I borrowed some for your birthday presents. I'll pay you back on Monday when the bank opens, all right?" Her mom turned in a half circle and gestured with her arm. "How do you like your room?"

Rose looked around, noticing she must have cleaned it for her. "It's very nice. Thank you." Eight hundred dollars, Rose thought. She spent eight hundred dollars on birthday presents?

Dinner was ready and the table set when Dave and Jessica returned. Rose considered him one of her best friends. His towering presence wasn't only physical. He was the stability of their home. Her mom was clearly the love of his life. He stayed faithfully by her through her...issues. Jessica was their only biological daughter. Nothing like her mom or Rose, she was girly girl to the core.

Together they ate, sang and told embarrassing remember-when-you stories. Rose thought about how much she would miss her family, yet she was ready to move on to the next stage of her life. It felt natural.

Her gifts seemed to carry a prom-theme: earrings with a necklace to match, and gift certificates for a hair salon and one for one of those nail places. She tried to imagine feeding the snakes at the zoo with long, red nails and smiled.

"Best for last," Dave said as he headed for the garage. When he came back, he carried a lidded cardboard box. Inside, the contents scraped and whined.

"No. You. Didn't." Rose took off and quickly, but gingerly, grabbed the package. "Holy cow!" She set it down on the floor, muttering, "Please, please, please." As soon as she let go of the lid, a charcoal Labrador puppy jumped over the edge and fell on its face. Rose squealed, rolled over on her back on the Berber carpet and let the puppy drown her with kisses.

Amanda could hardly believe the night was a success. Weariness enveloped her and was mixed with an intense desire to walk upstairs and go right to bed. "Brie is expecting you whenever you're ready," she said to Rose. "And since he's going to end up my responsibility when you're away, she says we do puppy school together. The box of supplies she told me to have ready is in the car. Happy birthday, sweetie." She let out a breath as she leaned back against her chair.

The sight of her family playing on the floor with the puppy made her feel almost normal, like a regular family. She couldn't help it and let her lids drop, if only for a moment. Her arm throbbed, but it was nothing compared to her nerves...and her head and...her heart. The afternoon was a close call. She had no idea how to make it stop and still keep Rose safe...hidden. The dog would help. Brie would help her train it as a guard dog. She clasped her hands under the table to keep from trembling. It seemed only Dave had suspicions as to why she finally gave in to the idea of a pet four months before Rose left for college. So far, he kept his questions to himself.

CHAPTER 5

Andy sighed as he listened to Candi go on about her dislike of his music, the latest high school girl she hated and that she would be going with him when he ordered his tux to make sure the tie matched her dress...exactly. He forced a smile and followed her out his front door, fingers clasped and setting on top of his head. A thin, gray cloud cover promised rain, mimicking his mood.

As Candi made her way to her bright orange bug, he spotted Rose walking up his long drive with a bouncing, black fur ball tangling a leash around her ankles. He felt the first gut-laugh he'd had in a long time erupt from low in his belly as he sat back on his haunches like a catcher behind the plate.

The puppy spotted him—a new person who was down near his level. Taking a running leap, he broke free of Rose's grasp. She threw her arms up, and Andy hoped the little guy didn't get distracted before he reached him.

"Come on, boy. You're a beaut!" He held his arms out in front of him and kept bellowing as the pup seemed to run faster than his legs. He stumbled, rolled and caught his footing, rushing toward Andy without missing a beat.

Andy looked up in time to catch a glimpse of Rose's large, round eyes as they warmed to the sight of him. He would never get tired of it. The dog ran into Andy head on, twisting back and forth and rubbing his snout all over him. His ears felt like rose petals. Andy wondered how all puppies had the same scent. Like, well, puppy.

Rose walked up the drive toward them, passing Candi, who looked like she'd seen a mouse.

"Nice, doggie. Stay away, now." Candi edged closer to her car.

"Oh, honestly, Candi. It's a six-week-old puppy. Are you even female?"

Candi seemed to have no problem tethering her fears enough for a catchy comeback. "Look who's talking?"

Surprised that Rose would so randomly take a stab at Candi, Andy defended her. "She *was* here first."

"I didn't come here to see you anyway," Rose said.

Her comment hurt deeper than he would have liked. He watched as Rose blushed and, in a rare moment, dropped her chin.

"Your mom inside?"

He jutted his thumb over his shoulder toward the front door.

Rose and her new Lab walked into Brie's kitchen.

Andy's aunt brought her folded hands to her lips. "So, this is him. Happy birthday. You'll be such a great puppy mom." Brie ooh'ed and ah'ed as she rubbed his ears and head. "Let me call in Goldie and Macey from the back. They need some young blood to liven them up. Have you named him, yet?" Brie asked as she opened her kitchen window and let out two short whistles.

"I'm thinking maybe Charcoal."

The golden retriever and the yellow lab-mix came casually through the animal flap in the mudroom door and into the kitchen. Hackles rose when the seasoned dogs noticed the furry intruder. The puppy squirmed mercilessly in Rose's arms at the sight of the new four-legged friends.

"Release," Brie told her dogs and they walked to Rose, sniffing at the scratching, nipping bundle of caffeine.

"Can I let him down?" Rose pleaded.

"Yes. Yes. The old folks will keep him corralled. He's got good color. Wet nose, healthy shine to his coat. You must have passed the drama in the drive."

Rose bit her nails at the sudden subject change. "Um, yes. Drama's a good word for it."

"I don't know why any woman would name their child Candi."

"I know! I said the same thing. I have to tell you, though, that her name is really Candice. Mature, intelligent name. She prefers *Candi*." Rose watched Macey nudge the puppy when he tried to edge away from the group. "She had a sort of reaction to the pup." She closed her eyes. "I said something snippy and..." Confessional.

Brie turned wide eyes on Rose.

Rose tilted her head from side to side, nodding, and said, "Yeah, Andy's not too happy about it. I don't know what got into me."

"Ugh. He has such terrible taste in girlfriends. I'd hoped college would change that. And if you tell him I said any of this, I'll have to kill you."

At that, Rose let out a hoot of laughter and dropped to play with the dogs. Without warning, the puppy lifted his leg to Mr. Reed's custom cherry cabinets. Andy's uncle had made them, along with just about every other wooden piece in their house. Rose threw her hands on the sides of her head.

Brie clapped three times loudly. Startled, the pup lowered his leg and looked up as Brie hastily, yet gently, hauled him out back.

Rose followed. She forgot all about the doggie door and pushed open the people door for the older dogs.

Brie praised the pup when his paws touched the grass. "You'll want to focus on positive reinforcement. Occasionally, dogs need to be told *no* but for these first few days, he's learning to trust and love you. Some call it the honeymoon period." The puppy rolled in the grass, chewing on his leash. "Make sure he sleeps in his crate. He might not like it at first. You can sleep next to him for the first few nights if you prefer."

Goldie and Macey wandered out and picked up their sniffing where they'd left off before the evening interruption.

"I've called in a favor to a friend and the little guy can start puppy kindergarten as soon as this Tuesday. The further you go with classes, the better. Until then, you'll want to work with him at least three times a day on three things."

It always amazed Rose how Brie could plop down and cross her legs like a kid. Charcoal sat next to her in the cold grass and cocked his head. "Carefully, but firmly, flip him over and cradle him on your lap like this." Andy's aunt turned the black beach ball with legs around onto his back. His legs kicked madly and his head jerked in circles. "Be gentle and give him lots of praise, especially when he stills." Brie scratched his ears. "Good, boy. You're just a good boy, aren't you?"

"Dogs want to be the alpha. That's natural, but the sooner you help him learn he's not, the better. Lying on his back is a sign of submission and it doesn't hurt, although he's faking it well." She turned to rub noses with the calming puppy. "You're a smart guy."

Andy watched as he leaned on the jamb of the back door. Rose looked happy. His aunt wasn't just a first-grade teacher, she and Rose's mom co-owned their own landscaping and design business, and Brie was a pro at working with dogs.

He felt a mix of frustration with his girlfriend, rejection from his best friend, interest in what Brie was explaining, and entertainment from the bundle of C4. He turned his head, watching from the corner of his eyes while Brie instructed Rose in front of a backdrop of winter brown grasses and plants.

"When he quiets, rotate each of his toenails just a bit like this," Brie started, and the pup went back to thrashing. After he calmed, she praised and continued, "This will help him become accustomed to being handled and for when you need to clip his nails and such." Brie released him. The puppy spotted Andy and took off, struggling when the leash became tight.

His aunt walked over and handed the leash to him. "Finally, potty training. He's not too young. At puppy kindergarten, he will start to learn basic skills such as sit and stay. Until then, try not to over-train. He's juvenile and he can burn out. Take him out at least every hour, when he eats, and before and after bed. Bring him to the place you'll want him to go or else you'll have land mines all over your mom's yard." Brie took a deep breath. "He's perfect. Congratulations. I'll leave you two alone." She wasn't referring to Rose and her puppy.

He cut right the chase. "Why did you do that?" Andy frowned, but it was hard to be mad when being licked frantically.

"I'm...sorry about that. I just don't know what you see in her. Okay, dumb comment, but how can you stand it? She's horrible. She's not your first *Candi*, either." Rose crossed her arms, lifting her hand to place her chin on her palm and her knuckles over her mouth.

He was just as surprised at her bluntness. And hated that she was right. So, he decided to just say it. "You're right."

"Of course I'm...what?"

"Don't rub it in."

"I hate to see you unhappy. You know, I haven't seen you really smile for a very long time. Well, until this little guy." The dog looked like a boneless, black balloon with fur. He was limber and on his back in puppy heaven as they both rubbed his belly.

"I can't dump her two weeks before prom."

"I could. But you're too nice."

Her hand felt warm as she laid it on his.

"Mom, are you sure about this?" Just days before the dance, Rose stood in front of tri-mirrors with her toes and bony knees locked together. "You were right. I shouldn't have put this off."

The dress was skin colored, except not her skin color. Hers was alabaster. The dress was more of a nude. It wasn't one of those flared, Cinderella-type dresses. Sequined fabric hugged from the halter strap around her neck to just above her knees.

"I'm too skinny. I have no boobs." She turned and looked at the back of the dress that was open to low on her hips. "There's so much skin."

"You have long, muscular arms and legs, and our next stop is the boutique to buy you a padded bra. Dave's not going to let you go low-cut anyway."

Rose sighed and turned to her. "Why do you always call him Dave when you speak to me? *He* doesn't do that."

Her mother's shoulders dropped. "You're right. He's never thought of you as anything except his daughter. Your father was a bad man, Rosemarie. I don't like to remember him. I'll work on it. This is your day. Let's have fun."

Rose put up with her mom's brush-offs one too many times. She spun on her. "Yet, you slept with him. He was a bad man and you slept with him anyway."

Her mom ran a hand through the top of her hair, then tucked one side behind her ear. "Yes. I was young. And now I have you." She stepped to her and kissed Rose on the cheek.

"I've never kissed a boy," Rose blurted out. "I'm eighteen years old and I've never been kissed."

Her mom nodded as if she'd known that. How did they know

these things?

"Teenage boys don't want to just kiss. I guess you'll need to know that."

Rose turned back to the mirror with hands firmly on her hips. "Okay. This is the one."

The shoes were outrageously expensive. Her mom said she wasn't going to be one of those girls who had to carry her painful shoes before they even arrived at the dance. She had rubber pads nailed to the bottoms to keep her from sliding, which added another quarter inch to the already three-inch heels. But they were comfortable, and Rose thought she was actually getting the hang of walking in them.

The birthday earrings were simple lines of beaded silver. The necklace wrapped loosely around her neck with a line matching the earrings dropping between her nonexistent breasts. She grabbed hold of her chest with both hands and sighed. Life wasn't fair.

Walking in the dark, Andy readjusted his tackle box, fishing poles and the plastic grocery sack that carried two tubs of earthworms and a bottle of sunscreen. Moonlight shone on the dark ripples creeping down Black Creek. He spotted a raccoon as he crossed the bridge. Startled, the animal hissed at him. Andy stomped his foot and glared; he was in no mood for it.

He wondered what the hell he was thinking when he'd first decided to date Candi. Okay, he conceded to what he'd been thinking, but almost two years? He told himself he would get through her dance, and then go over to her house first thing the next day to end it and all of the maintenance that came with her. Never again, he vowed. He would be more like his brother, Duncan. Casual relationships. No strings.

But first, he needed Rose.

She would calm him down and lighten his mood, help him feel normal again. He looked at his watch and winced. What were friends for if you couldn't count on them to be there? Even at this time of night. Or morning.

Rose slept soundly in her twin bed dreaming of her favorite spot at the zoo. In the small rain forest building, she allowed a newly emerged monarch butterfly to dry its wings on her apron while sharing facts about the insect to one of two visiting young boys. The other threw pebbles into the nearby wishing pond. The sound of the small rocks plunked as they hit the stone wall before dropping into the water.

Oh, crap. She woke and sat up straight. The noise came from outside, not in her head. Through grinning teeth, she bit the nails on one hand and ripped her blankets off with the other. As she hustled to her window, she realized it was still pitch black out.

Grabbing the flashlight she always kept on her windowsill for just this occasion, she lifted the window and found Andy with the beam. "I thought you didn't get home until tomorrow," she whispered loudly.

"It *is* tomorrow." He held up fishing poles and tackle box.

"It's not tomorrow until the sun comes up." She smiled wildly as she pulled on her jeans. This reaction she had to him had to stop eventually, she convinced herself. It was *not* healthy.

"I've got the worms. Get down here."

Quickly, she tied her hair in a bandana, cleaned herself up and slipped on some sneakers. Scribbling out a note for her parents, she left it on the kitchen table, then tiptoed out without waking the puppy.

Mom and Dad,

I'm across the street, fishing the lake with Andy. I promised Mrs. Melbourne a game of canasta but will be home in time for the hair thing. Can you handle Charcoal for the morning? His treats (bribery) are in the box on the shelf over his leash.

Love you,
Rose

CHAPTER 6

A sense of familiar relief crept through Andy as Rose bounced out her front door drowned in a thick, hooded and lined denim jacket.

"It's not even four o'clock. What are you doing here?" she asked.

"I've got fishing gear and night crawlers. What do you think I'm doing here?" He ground his teeth at his curt tone but stopped short of apologizing. Looking to her, he knew she understood, knew she wouldn't question him and that he was incredibly lucky to have her.

She looked at him through the corners of her eyes. "I grabbed a couple of chairs," is all she said.

He was right. Lucky.

The morning was crisp and as still as his mood. He appreciated that she sensed it as they fell into stride, meandering in silence. Birds were just beginning to roust in anticipation of the sunrise. There were no streetlights along Rose's cul-de-sac, but the moon was bright enough to light their way.

Together, they strolled around the end of the circle, past Lucy Melbourne's house. White paint gleamed in the light from the moon, emitting the look of a well-kept, feminine home. A pang spurred in his gut at the memory of Rose's lost great-grandfather. He wondered how Lucy was getting along without him and thought it was best that Lucy's faithful housemaid agreed to move in with her. The two of them somehow got along and filled some of the empty space death left in its wake.

Next door to Lucy was the house his aunt and Duncan narrowly escaped the night of the fire. When she married Nathan, Brie gave it and the insurance money to her sister, keeping it in the family and the neighborhood a busy place. As usual, they cut between their yards to get to the lake. He never tired of the look of it, no matter the season. Small but pristine, the lake sustained the animal life he knew Rose adored.

Outlines of homes and floating docks shimmered in the water like a mirror in a dimly lit room. They could hear the rhythmic trickle of the water as it ran over the spillway and flowed into Black Creek. Wildflowers lined the water, waiting for the sun to illuminate them.

"Do you want to talk about it?" Rose broke the silence.

"Not really." He stopped and watched the water. "I'm glad you're here."

"Sure thing. Is this okay?" She gestured to a spot near the spillway where the fish liked to gather.

They startled a great blue heron that squawked much like a pteranodon before taking off in the dark to a spot farther down the creek.

He answered Rose by pulling the straps of the folding chairs from her shoulder and setting them up in the grass.

They could see the outline of the back of his house from where they sat. It was there that they first met. She'd been five. His uncle bought the home when it was still a run-down farmhouse and Nathan still a single dad, trying to raise two nephews orphaned after the plane crash that killed Andy's parents.

Andy remembered it as an adventure, living out of a cooler and on mattresses for several months while Nathan worked to restore the house from the ground up. The memories almost made him smile. Almost. He thought of all that Nathan had done for him and his brother and felt contentment.

Time with Rose was as natural as breathing. They never felt the need to fill silence with shallow conversation. Both were simply comfortable in the presence of one another; they could often communicate with just a look or gesture. On the other hand, he knew he was brooding and that Rose wouldn't stand for it too much longer. The fish weren't biting, not that that was why they fished anyway. The light was just beginning to show when Rose leaned her pole against her folding chair and stood to stretch.

Her efforts at inconspicuous need a lot of work, he thought as he narrowed his eyes. She tried to look casual as she faked a yawn and wandered slowly along the floodplain that framed the creek bed.

"Don't even think about."

"I don't know what you're talking about," she stated matter-of-factly, looking over her shoulder.

"The water's still cold. You'll freeze your feet."

She shrugged, took off her sneakers and rolled up her jeans.

"You'll be sorry, Rosemarie."

She lifted her feet, one then the other, into the frigid, spring water. The light was up just enough to see bubbles erupting from the smooth surface. She reached in and came out holding the back of a defensive crawfish between its front and back legs, claws waving madly.

He smiled wide, stood and straddled his lounging chair, trying to look threatening. "Don't you dare. Get that damned thing away from me."

Holding the angry crawfish in front of her, Rose ran toward him, chasing him from his chair, calling him *chicken* all the way down the bank of the lake. He and Rose laughed so loud they scattered a large group of mallards.

Stopping, he tried dodging. Damn she was fast. Rose maneuvered the snapping creature, attaching it to the bottom of his jacket. It held on with one claw while Andy held up his arms away from it. With one hand, he pinched the crawfish between its legs, much like Rose had done. With the other, he hefted her over his shoulder and carried them as they both squirmed in his grasp. He plopped her playfully in her seat before tossing the guy back in the water.

Sticking her muddy feet out and away from her chair, she grinned at him. "You have my favorite smile," she said as she wiped off the black mud.

Her compliment made him feel more than he could put his finger on. He could never go wrong throwing rocks at Rose's window in the middle of the night.

The sun lifted in the sky too quickly—faster than either of them realized. They spoke of the past few weeks and their plans for the summer, avoiding any mention of prom or his summer in New York City.

When he noticed the height of the sun, he tossed Rose the bottle of sunscreen he knew she wouldn't have thought of. "I don't know how you've never been burnt to a crisp. It's already early May and you haven't even gotten any summer freckles yet."

"I keep sweat-proof SPF 50 in my pickup. I didn't think of it at four this morning." She took it from him. "And, thanks. I really shouldn't stay out too much longer. I promised Lucy a game of cards, and I have a hair appointment with my mom after lunch."

Dipping her chin to the side, Rose covered her mouth and muttered something. He heard the word, 'prom.' Andy felt a quick tightening at the back of his neck. "I thought you didn't like that girl stuff. Who is this Tyler, anyway?"

Oops.

Rose bolted to her feet, arms straight and locked at her sides with fists balled. "I *am* a girl, whether you think so or not, and he's in my calculus class. He gave me a ride home the night you left with Bimbo Barbie."

He could hear the anger bubble in her voice and still couldn't seem to stop himself. "Are you dating him?"

She started to walk in a circle. No, she stomped, and he heard some kind of a growl that sounded suspiciously like a pissed off girl.

"No. We talk in class. He flirts with me. That's right. Me. Because I am a girl." Her voice kept getting louder. "I refuse to graduate from high school without ever—"

Overturning the tackle box, he shot out of his chair before she could finish her sentence. His fishing pole went flying as he spun to face her. "Son of a bitch, you're going to have frigging sex with him?" He clasped his hands on his head and started pacing. "You've never...and you're going to—"

"Don't you even start with telling me what I'm not supposed to do. And I'm not having sex with him. It's none of your business. Damn it. Do we have to talk about this?"

The relief was overwhelming and...confusing...and

embarrassing. "Then what did you mean?" He couldn't help but ask. But then, realization came into focus, and he felt like an ass. "Oh." He stopped pacing and turned to look at her.

"If you laugh...I don't think I could take it. So don't."

Her eyes turned glossy with tears. He knew she wouldn't let them fall.

"And yes, damn it. I'm going to be kissed for the first damned time on my damned prom night on my damned porch." She grabbed her line and started reeling it in.

"Wait." He reached for her.

"No, really." Her shoulders dropped. She turned so that her back was to him. "I should be getting to Mrs. Melbourne's."

"Well, yes that, but Dunc's coming soon. He'll likely want your pole."

Duncan dried the morning dishes as his aunt washed with her gaze directed out the kitchen window at his brother and Rose. "There. She has him laughing again." Brie pointed.

"He's an idiot," he added in routine, brotherly fashion.

"No. Just young yet."

"Okay. How about blind?" he amended.

Brie tilted her head toward him. "I'll give you blind and add a pot, or maybe a kettle?"

"I choose to be involved with Candi-types because I don't have to be...involved."

"Something a mom always wants to hear," she added, laughing.

He shrugged and took the last dripping plate she held out for him. "Andy's looking for something entirely different." He dried, then placed the plate in the cupboard, wiping his hands on the damp towel. "Are you okay here? I think I'll go catch dinner." He kissed her on the top of her head and grabbed his boots and jacket.

He took his time making his way to them. He'd noticed their conversation had heated up and knew to stay away from an Andy/Rose spat. He was surprised one of them didn't end up flat on their back. His boots scraped along the bridge that stretched over Black Creek as he swaggered his way to them. The bridge was comfortably weathered with age. His uncle had made it so that he, Andy and their cousins could get back and forth from Brie's sister's home on the other side of the creek.

He stalled on the bridge, waiting for Andy and Rose to cycle through their tiff. The variety of his uncle's woodworking led him to ponder his talents as he walked. The different color schemes and materials he chose when painting a subject, bringing out their personality and style, or the feel and mood of a certain location. He had painted and drawn this lake and creek many times, and each piece varied according to the weather, time of year and mostly his mood. When Duncan decided peace had returned, he meandered the rest of the way to them.

They both turned to greet him.

"Hey, shrimp. Are you ready for college life?" He picked Rose up and gave her a bear hug as he swung her around. "You still weigh as much as a football." He easily maneuvered her under his arm. "You sort of feel like one, too."

Rose laughed out loud and demanded to be put down. "I still have a few weeks of high school stress before I look toward college, but yes, I'm ready." She dug her hands into the pockets of her jacket. "We could do lunch sometime."

"NYU's a big school. We'll have to make it a plan or else we may never see each other."

"It's a date then. I really need to get going."

"Could you use another player?" Andy rose from his chair.

"Did you learn how to play canasta at Purdue this year?"

Andy shook his head.

"Another time, then. I can't both play with Mrs. Melbourne and teach you. See you at the dance."

Duncan sat comfortably, eyeing his bobber. "So, have you rifled through any Purdue secure files or data, yet? *Fixed* anything?"

"Holy shit! You do that? Change your grades? I thought we said never anything that counts as cheating."

"Slow down, little brother. Now you're just hurting my feelings. No grade changes...but I haven't had any classes start before noon since freshman year. Traceless." He smiled over to Andy and noticed that he returned the look.

"All of my classes are on Tuesdays and Thursdays. I have frigging four-day weekends each and every blessed week. Traceless."

"Ha," Duncan responded in one, short syllable. "The memories. It's not as fun as tracing Swiss bank accounts."

"Mmm mmm." Andy shook his head. "The governor's emails topped the list. The things people put on the net."

Sitting up, Andy leaned forward and craned his head. "What the hell? Did you already get a friggin' bite?"

Duncan's bobber sunk.

"Someone needs to get us peasants something to eat tonight while you're out sampling calamari and ribeye." Duncan jerked his line and started turning the reel as he leaned over and looked in the catch bucket. "Is this all you've managed to snag all morning? When did you two get out here?"

"I'm not sure. Around four, I guess. I suck at fishing."

"That's not all you suck at."

"Fine. Great. You come out here to cheer me up?"

"Nope." Duncan stood up and grabbed the net, walking closer to the shore. "I came out here to catch dinner. Giving you shit is just a bonus." He placed his one-pounder in the bucket of cold water along with Andy's palm-sized blue gills before he reached for a new worm.

Andy caught his eye and tried to stare him down.

Duncan broke first and they both started laughing.

Andy interrupted, "All right then, Gandhi, tell me what else you think I suck at."

Duncan tossed out his line and sat back comfortably in Rose's chair. "You don't see what you have right in front of you."

Andy squinted at him. Duncan didn't look back, but nodded his head toward Lucy Melbourne's house, then crossed his feet at his ankles. Andy quickly loosened his expression and looked away, then back again.

He let the idea sink in for a good long while before bringing Andy back to Earth. "I might be returning early this year. I've got a few orders. My history teacher wants me to paint his daughter's wedding picture." Good subject change.

Andy raised his br⊂ re much money in that?"

Duncan lifted one side of his mouth. "Oh, yes."

CHAPTER 7

She didn't believe her mother when she'd said this would take all day. It did, and Rose couldn't help but sort of like it. "Call me Candi," she muttered as she sat fidgeting on her living room couch.

The hair dresser had been all right. She went against her recommendation of wearing her hair up in intricate braids and dripping curls. For once, she wanted it down. The trim was great and her hair was smoothed to almost straight. Quiet waves framed her face and lay over her shoulders, down to the middle of her back.

The best was the nail salon. Not that she would ever go along with some dark color or fake nails, but her mom joined her for that part. They para-somethinged and exfoli-somethinged and came out with toes and nails that matched the color of her dress. Subtle. She looked at her beige toes as they peeked out of her strappy heels. She could handle subtle.

Watching the clock, she thought of how she hadn't liked this feeling the last time. Maybe Tyler had played a joke asking her to prom. She'd seen that in a movie somewhere, hadn't she? It had been six weeks since he'd asked her to the dance. Sure, they talked on the phone and made arrangements, chatted at school, but he never came over to help with calculus like he said he would.

Then, she heard the car. Her folks must have, too, because

they sauntered out from the kitchen arm-in-arm. She popped up from the couch and held up a hand before they could reach the front door. When she opened it, the look on Tyler's face made everything worth it.

He wore a white tux. How cheesy, she thought. "Hi. I have a flower I'm supposed to give you," she said.

Her parents stood behind her, and she wondered if it would be okay to just reach over and shut his gaping mouth for him.

"The dance is over at midnight?" She knew Dave stood with his holster on purpose. "I expect my daughter to be home by twelve thirty."

My daughter. That made the embarrassing comment worth it.

Without taking his gaping eyes from her, Tyler nodded with a, "Yes, sir."

They pinned flowers and took pictures before heading to the restaurant. The awkward silence during the car ride was nothing compared to the feeling when they walked in and she spotted the other girls, all in fluffy dresses, each with braids and curls. Why hadn't she looked into this more? And how did she eat at a place like this?

Tyler was...attentive. He was patient and acted like a proud peacock, hanging onto her every move. Was this what dates did? Because she specifically remembered he said PDA was stupid.

She ordered what he did, which turned out to be really good, but she assumed really wrong. The other girls ordered chicken. Every one of them. Was there a manual on this? She ate crab legs and steak and didn't pass on the dessert. Sharing the cheesecake with Tyler must have counted for something. Not a single drop of anything got on her dress. She was so proud. As they made their way back to Tyler's car, she lifted her brows at the girls who walked along the sidewalk carrying their shoes.

She had to admit the hotel conference center was decorated nicely, but the balloon arch as they walked in was over the top. Tyler moved in behind her, placing his hands on her hips as a camera flashed. As he pressed against her, she was sure she had a holy-shit-is-that-what-I-think-it-is look on her face, because that's exactly what she was thinking. It reminded her of her mom's warning about boys not wanting just to kiss. Well, this one would have to deal.

Andy's face remained stone cold as he watched from the

moment Rose walked through the door. He noted she was completely clueless that almost all eyes turned to stare...girls included. And, yes, he also noted that Tyler took the photo-op as a chance to cop a feel. Rose glided in as absolutely, without a doubt, the classiest, most beautiful woman in the room.

He wasn't sure how he felt about it; he guessed mostly happy for her. Rose deserved it. Worried creases formed low on his forehead. The guys weren't looking at just her face. The creamy, skin of her face made-up to look like she wasn't made-up. Her hair fell like red silk around her bare shoulders.

Her legs looked long enough to reach her neck. Maybe it was the dress that hugged her so tight it shouldn't have been allowed. Maybe it was the heels. How the hell did she know how to walk in those shoes?

Water.

He decided he needed water and walked out to the hallway in search of a fountain. The current senior basketball center huddled with a group of his buddies. Good. A diversion. Time reminiscing with an old teammate would do the trick. Until Andy got closer and heard what he was saying.

"...fuckin' see Rose Piper, man? Fuck me sideways. I could wrap those legs—"

Andy grabbed him by the throat, then shoved him against the nearest wall. His head hit and bounced.

"Shit, dude. Sorry. I didn't know you two were—"

"We're not and neither are you." He didn't let go and instead looked around at the other guys, many of whom he remembered. Through a glaze of red, he realized his fingers were dug into the dude's throat. Releasing quickly, he turned to warn the others. "That goes for all of you."

A low stream of disgusted murmurs rumbled as they meandered toward the ballroom. "Bros before hos, man."

Andy couldn't find it in him to care. Not entirely sure how long he stood there, he got the drink after all while waiting for his hands to stop shaking and trying to figure out what to do. Until he admitted there was nothing *to* do.

A former point guard, also in the same take-your-old-high-school-girlfriend-to-prom rut came as a welcome discovery. They exchanged college stories while Andy watched Rose from the corner of his eye. Completely out of her element, Rose still beamed and...flowed. Her dance moves weren't half bad and finally she did take off the shoes.

Rose was right, he thought, he needed to cheer up. Oh, shit, Candi. He looked around. She wasn't dancing. Assuming she was off pouting, he walked into the hall and found her wrapped around a blond in a white tux. Ha. How perfect. How truthfully, frigging perfect. He felt his smile come back. The two of them went at it for a good amount of time before bothering to see if anyone was watching. Candi looked funny in her phony *oops* face. But when the guy turned and Andy saw it was Rose's date, he went back to seeing red.

Tyler looked to have about six inches on him, but Andy could take him, he knew. Using one hand, he fisted his pretty white jacket and reared back with the other. Candi took off faster than she'd moved on Tyler, who pretended to cover his face with one hand while using his other to throw a sucker punch to Andy's ribs.

Dumb ass little slow shit. He grabbed Tyler's fist before it reached him and squeezed hard enough to hear a pop. "You have two choices." Andy noticed his hand tremble where he grasped Tyler's jacket.

Tyler, too, darted his eyes down to the trembling fist. He must have had sense enough to stand down before he came out with broken fingers.

"You can leave now or I can kick your ass. I could really use option two right about now." He figured Tyler thought his anger came from the toss with Candi. Andy didn't care what the hell motivation he thought he had as long as Tyler was far away from Rose.

"Man, she told me—"

Andy let go of Tyler's hand, pulled and gave him one violent shake. "What's it gonna be? You're not getting laid by either of them."

Realization crossed Tyler's face regarding the source of Andy's temper. He started to grin, before looking into bulging, red eyes. "All right. All right, man." Tyler lifted his free hand in surrender.

"I'll take care of the girls. You. Leave. Now." Smart, Andy thought, as he watched him sprint for the front door. His nerves were fried. It felt as if it was three in the morning, and he wanted to leave, but not before he got Rose home.

Candi played a convincing broken heart and didn't take long to weep into the arms of the closest jock.

Andy found an empty table far away from the crowd and situated himself where he could keep an eye on his best friend. It wasn't long before Rose made her way to him.

Sitting in the folding chair next to him, she rested her chin in the palms of her hands. "I'm sorry."

"No need," he said.

"I won't say I told you so."

He tilted his head to her and lifted a corner of his mouth. "You just did. Looks like you're having an all right time."

"I was. The guys are getting tipsy. I think they have flasks in their pockets." She shrugged. "A little too touchy for me."

He doubted it was flasks she felt and made himself shake off the visual. Odd, he thought, talking to her as they always did, in such a different setting.

Rose guessed Andy knew all about the flasks as he didn't offer a response. She was glad she came, but honestly didn't think prom was quite cracked up to be all it was meant to be. Absentmindedly, she took one of Andy's hands in hers. It was thick, lined with veins and warm, very warm. He was twitching ever so slightly. That worried her. It made her think of how the fast-talking, Andy Reed wasn't talking at all. He didn't dance once that night and she hadn't seen him around anyone really.

She tiled her chin up and looked at him face to face. "So...you're not going to tell me, are you," she stated.

His eyes matched the color of his caramel hair. They looked at her now with something she didn't recognize. He offered no response to this statement either.

"You *are* the nicest person I know," she said.

He looked at their joined hands, then up to her eyes. "Tell you?"

"That my date made reservations for us upstairs tonight. Well...until both of our dates were swallowing each other's tongues in the hallway." Why didn't this bother her?

Andy closed his eyes and sighed heavily. "He should be glad I didn't know about the room."

"I can take care of myself," she barked more defensively than she meant to. "I'm a frigging black belt." She wondered if part of the reason Tyler's plans didn't bother her was because Andy was here.

Andy shook his head. "I like you better in your Chucks. Then, I don't have to worry about half the room wanting to bed you."

Holding onto her stomach, she bent over laughing. "Did you really just say, '*bed* me?'" She reared back. "Not screw me or take—"

"Stop!" He ran his hands over his face, then rested them clasped on top of his head. "I'll give you a ride. I don't mind waiting."

"I'm done here. It was fun. Really. But I'm *not* doing that." She thumbed over her shoulder at the group gyrating on the dance floor.

They rode with the top down in Andy's classic Mustang convertible. Rose held her hair around her shoulder. Her bare feet rested on his dash. "Dave will be relieved. Home just after eleven. You should have seen him when Tyler picked me up."

"I'd rather not talk about it."

"My dad likes you. What's your deal?"

"I'm not talking about your dad."

Interesting, she thought. Looking out into the black, she thought about how she truly did have a great day. Not the best day. She could think of better: catching her first fish big enough to fry with Duncan and Andy, rock climbing with Andy at Catskills, the week in Destin spent with the Reeds. She noticed a pattern and looked over at him.

He looked so different and yet the same. A five o'clock shadow, sharp planes along his jaw. And yet, he still had the same comfortable mannerisms. He rested a wrist on top of his steering wheel, nodding his head slightly to the beat of the music on the stereo. His neck was too thick for his tux shirt. He'd unbuttoned it at the top and let his tie dangle. She looked back out at the streetlight-lit yards and convinced herself to be content with her almost perfect day.

"That's your sad face," Andy commented.

"Not really." Discomfort filled her thoughts. Heat started at her neck and traveled over her cheeks. She looked out the window, wishing he'd put the top down and trying to conceal the blush erupting on her face.

At that Andy remembered what she had said about her

mission for the night. Well, shit. "How is Charcoal doing with heeling?" Distraction.

The red faded. Rose blew out a breath before answering. "Great. As long as there's not a rabbit nearby. Or a blowing leaf. Or as long as his tail doesn't come into view." They spoke of lost puppy teeth and chewed shoes.

Charcoal must have been sleeping. The porch light was off and the house was quiet as they strolled up the walk. He loved the way her lips twitched when she was nervous and thought about why they were at that moment. Reaching the door, he turned to face her, watching her mouth as she spoke. Without thinking it through, he moved toward her in one, small step and inhaled. He smelled peaches.

Lifting her sandwich-sized purse close to her face, Rose fumbled for her keys in the dark. "Thanks for watching out for me tonight, although I didn't need it. And for the ride, because I *did* need it." With keys in hand and shoes in the other, she looked up. Her blue eyes opened wide and blinked.

He set his hands on her shoulders. Soft and smooth. The twitching from her lips seemed to travel through her, making the firm muscles in her shoulders flex beneath his hands. "When did cute turn into beautiful?" he asked.

With lips pressed firmly together, the twitching changed to trembling.

"What the hell are you doing?" Rose all but squeaked.

His eyes traveled back down to her full lips. Decisions. "You're eighteen." He stepped forward again, close enough that he could feel the warmth radiating from her skin. "You're not going in without being kissed on your damned prom night, on your damned porch."

"Oh." She tightened her lips a bit more, then confessed, "I'm nervous."

"Yes," he answered in basic acknowledgement.

Grinding her teeth, her breath quaked before she threatened, "If you laugh, I swear—"

"You'll kick my ass; I know." When he was close enough to feel the cool breeze from her breath, he whispered, "Chicken." She closed her eyes and tilted her head. Inviting.

Accepting the invitation, he brushed his lips to hers. Testing. An odd mixture of curiosity and longing twined together as he waited for a discomfort that didn't come. Andy sunk into those familiar lips that felt as soft and full as they looked. Waves of heat flowed from where their mouths mingled and from where his hands rested gently on her shoulders. It encompassed him. He wondered what the hell he *was* doing and why oddly he didn't care.

She was just the right amount of firm, the right amount of moist. The feeling of her shoulders quaking beneath his hands reminded him not to take her in too quickly.

Moving together as if they'd done this always, he carefully parted her lips with his and gently dove in. She tasted like Rose. Wild, sassy...fire. She tasted like home. Easy...familiar. Dizzying. He breathed in her scent as their lips and tongues moved together. Something warm, yet sharp woke in his heart.

Careful not to startle her, he kept his hands on her shoulders as their heads tilted and their mouths melted into one another. The bare skin of her arms was as soft and as firm as her lips. Resisting the urge to run his hands down her bare back, he felt hers move to rest on his sides. He pulled closer. Her small, toned body fit along the length of his.

It was like a well-rehearsed dance. Noses and teeth weren't bumped unless they were meant to. He lost some resolve and ran his hands slowly over her shoulders, gliding them along her neck. He wasn't sure how long they stood there moving together on her damned porch. Or when they should come up for air.

First kiss. He forced himself to keep it simple. So many thoughts swirled in his head. Feelings, needs. So much made sense to him now.

Damn it. Now was definitely the time to pull back.

He opened his eyes with her face in his hands, then kissed her once more gently. She kept hers closed for a few more staggering moments before looking up at him.

Her face was different. Serious? Scared?

She blinked twice and shook her head.

The corners of her mouth lifted slightly as she raised her shoes and jingled the keys. Still breathing fast, she rolled her shoulders before looking back up at him. "Nicest person I know. Thanks, Andy." She turned the lock and stepped inside, before giving a small wave and shutting the door.

He smelled warm chocolate.

CHAPTER 8

"Did I hear the Mustang?" Nathan asked.

He meandered into their kitchen and opened the fridge. The solid cherry wood had darkened with the years. It covered the common vinyl door to blend with the look of the cabinets he'd made with his own hands. Brie's heart gave a little jump as he twisted the cap of a beer, then leaned against the wall. Gray had invaded his jet black hair and lines formed around his eyes. She thought he looked sexier. His bold, blue eyes were presently locked on her. Standing in bare feet, she wore a tank and cotton shorts with a short house coat while wiping her hands on a dish towel.

"Yes," he said.

She turned and thought about his statement. "He didn't look right."

Nathan meandered over to her and pressed his thumb between her brows, rubbing circles over the creases. "Candi?"

"He wasn't sad. Not mad." She shrugged. "Different. Well, it's awfully early for him to be home anyway. Something must have happened."

"Andy's a problem solver. He'll figure it out." Nathan craned his head to look at her backside in her shorts. "Counter looks comfortable."

"Nathan." She put her palm in the middle of his chest. "The

kids could come down."

"Sleeping." He set his beer and her on the counter and pulled her legs around him.

"Not Andy. Put me down." But she locked the tops of her feet behind him and trailed her hands up his arms.

"Shower?"

She bit her bottom lip. "We should conserve water and share." They kissed long and hard before chasing each other up the long, arched staircase.

Andy paced his room, hands resting on his head. He heard the shower turn on, looked at the time and rolled his eyes.

What the hell was *that?* He kept asking himself the same questions. How did this happen? What had he been thinking? He could still taste her. Feel her skin under his fingers. And what was that look in her eyes? He couldn't read the expression. He had an entire conversation with himself trying to justify going over there right then and throwing rocks at her window. Would she answer? *Nicest person I know* and then shut the door in his face?

He plopped down on top of his bed in his boxers, moving his linked fingers behind his head. He would have to study for finals and catch his afternoon plane on little rest, he realized, because sleep tonight was going to come very slow.

This was Rose, he reminded himself. But, he couldn't quit thinking of her hair, her eyes. He would just go over there in the morning and straighten everything out. He rolled over and eventually sleep found him. His dreams were of red silk and painted toes resting on his dash.

With coffee in hand, Andy thoughtfully paced the kitchen floor. After looking up at the clock for the ninth time, his aunt walked in.

She stopped and stared, then mumbled, "Hmm," while walking in front of him and pulling down a mug. "So, how was it?"

"Stupid." He looked back out the window. The sun was up and the lake looked like glass from the windless night. Every few seconds a bubble erupted from the depths and caused a ripple in the calm. That was all this was, he told himself. A ripple. He looked up at the clock again.

"Stupid?" Brie repeated. "Now you sound like your brother. What was stupid about it?"

"Huh? Oh, high school, I guess. Don't miss it. Candi took up with...with someone else." He let the mug warm his hands as he lifted it to his mouth.

Brie quickly placed hers on the counter. "That's awful. I'm so sorry."

He stopped mid-sip and looked over the rim at her. "You sure about that, Ma?"

"Well." Brie nodded crookedly in concession. "I've never really cared for her, but that doesn't mean I want to see you hurt."

"Relieved. Not hurt." He took another sip while looking up at the clock. Was it moving?

Brie walked over and stood next to him, shoulder to shoulder. Overtly with purpose, she looked up at it with him. "Going somewhere?"

"Hmm? Yeah. Gonna help Rose with the mutt."

"This early? On a Sunday morning?"

"Pup gets up early, sure." He set his mug down on the granite counter with more force than he'd intended and strode to get his jacket from the coatrack. Distracted, he left without saying good-bye.

He could hear them in there. So, what was the big deal? It was not too early. He'd come over a hundred times this early. Much earlier two nights ago.

Rose stirred generic brownie mix with eggs and water. "Holy crap, I'm my mother," she said out loud as she nervously mixed the ingredients with a fork. "And what are you looking at?"

Charcoal sat up straight and tilted his head back and forth watching her.

"It was just a nice minute between friends. He was being thoughtful, like best friends do." She shook her head. Best friends don't kiss. Not like *that*. She ran her hands over her face. What had she done? He started it, she reminded herself, then sighed as her shoulders dropped. It didn't matter who started it. She couldn't bear to lose him.

She gave up on the brownie mix and slid along a base cabinet down to the floor next to the dog. Charcoal turned a few circles of excitement that she'd come down to his level, and then flipped on his back for a belly rub. She scratched as she tried to breathe. "I'm not his type," she spoke to the dog, closed her eyes and rested her head back against the cabinet. "I just need some time to get my composure back. We'll be back to normal soon enough."

The knock on the door was quiet, but Charcoal wasn't. A direct contrast stood between his fierce bark and his clumsy run to the door. She followed him, thinking he was so funny she almost felt better. When she looked through the peephole, her legs nearly gave out. Plunking her forehead on the door, she groaned. "This isn't time enough." More time, she needed more time. Hanging onto the knob, she took a deep breath and opened it before turning back for the kitchen.

She heard Andy greet the puppy. That was a good sign, she decided. Normal.

He came into the kitchen but stopped at the entrance, leaning along the farthest wall. Not a good sign. Goose bumps formed on her arms and neck. It was always so easy to read him before. Now, she had nothing.

"Didn't your mom make brownies last night?"

Pausing for a moment, she continued to spray the pan. "How did you know about...?" She shook her head. "They went out for breakfast. Charcoal woke everyone up early."

"Okay," he said slowly and stood looking at her. She heard him actually grunt but was too scared to make eye contact. Instead, she sprayed the stuff for the third time.

"What was that last night?"

"What was what?" She answered his question with a question in a fast, knee-jerk reaction.

"You know what."

Reaching for the bowl, she saw her hands were shaking as she dumped in the batter.

"There was prom. There was dancing. There was you being very kind to step in for Tyler on my porch. Thanks by the way." Clumsily, she placed the pan in the oven that was set for five-fifty.

"Why won't you look at me?"

She shut the oven door and set both hands on the counter, elbows locked. Standing for a long moment, her hair fell over her shoulders, safely concealing her face. It was at that moment she realized if she answered him truthfully, they would never come back from this. And by this time, she didn't have the resolve to make the safer decision.

"Because my legs will give out if I do." She closed her eyes as they began to fill, never remembering feeling so scared. She willed back the tears from falling.

She felt his presence as Andy stepped to her. He tucked her hair behind an ear, leaving her face exposed and a trail of electrically charged warmth along her cheek, over her ear and to the tender skin at the side of her neck. His fingers traced her jawline. She wasn't sure if she was breathing.

He took her arm from the counter by her wrist. She could feel her pulse beat beneath his thumb. Turning her to face him, he wrapped the fingers from his other hand around the back of her neck, under her hair.

"I see," he said. It sounded like more of a discovery than a statement. Now, she could read him. Yes, the look in his familiar caramel eyes was easy to read. Her pulse bolted; her breath quickened. But every piece of fear left her and was replaced with a solid punch of anticipation.

"You've held me up enough times; let me take a turn," he whispered.

This wasn't the cautious or gentle Andy from the night before. He was urgent, eager. Grabbing the sides of her face with his rough hands, he fused their mouths together. But he kept his word. When her legs staggered, he held her up using his weight without as much as a hitch in the kiss.

A beehive erupted in her heart and shot outward to every inch of her body. His tongue, his lips...his hands. It was more than anything she could have imagined and more than she was ready for. Her reaction to him, this time, surprised both of them. Weak legs or not, she wrapped one arm around his neck and the other up the back of his shirt, grasping at muscled flesh, pulling their bodies closer together. Feelings that were new to her sprang to life as the weight of him pressed against her.

She was perfect and he was drowning. Their bodies fit like staggered bricks on a building, their mouths like well-oiled gears that moved and worked in absolute sync. Small hums came deep from Rose's throat. Unbelievable. Andy tightened his grip on her neck and wrapped his other arm around her narrow waist to the small of her back. They sunk into each other with sounds of excitement and discovery until they realized Charcoal was half mad from being left out of the play.

Andy found it hard to kiss and smile at the same time. With the dog on hind legs, shoving his wet nose between their bodies, Andy broke free, both of them gasping for air.

"Mmm." Without opening her eyes to him, Rose reached a hand down to scratch Charcoal's head.

Andy placed both hands on the sides of her face and brushed his thumbs along her jaw.

When she opened her eyes, he saw the same look he had seen the night before. Only this time, he understood. Everything. He understood.

Charcoal pushed off them and raced for the front door. Rose sighed. "Newspaper...or family home from breakfast."

He kept hold of her face. "Let's drive to Rochester. Lunch. No, that would still be breakfast. You could use to be a spectator at your zoo for once."

"You have finals."

"I can study on the plane. Come with me."

A smile erupted. She nodded as they realized Charcoal wasn't barking at the paperboy. They were still twined together in the kitchen but quickly released as the door opened.

"Brownies again?" Jessica asked as she headed toward the kitchen. "What is it with this family and brown...oh, sorry, Andy. I didn't know you were here," she said as she entered. "Are you trying to fast-fry the brownies?"

"Oh crap." Rose reached around him and adjusted the temperature of the oven. She smelled amazing. It was disconcerting to hear her out of breath and working to appear uninterested. "Mom," she called out toward the front door. "Andy and I are going to get something to eat and hit the zoo for a while. Do you need anything while we're out?"

"No, I can't think of anything. You two have fun now."

Rose looked to him. "Ten minutes?" she mouthed.

He nodded and said good-bye to Charcoal and the Nolans before walking home. Cutting over the creek, he passed the guesthouse his uncle was working on—the guesthouse he'd promised to help with that weekend. Nathan would take a rain check. He would understand. What would he say to make Nathan understand?

Shaking his head clear, Andy walked toward the back door. Brie was already in the yard sprinkling something in the landscaping beds.

He figured he'd better stop and say something. His aunt had a knack for looking through people. "Hey, Ma. I'm going to Rochester with Rose. I'll be back in time to make my flight. Tell dad I'll make up for the lost help on the guesthouse, will you?"

Her eyes loosened, one brow lifted and she smiled. "Will you need a ride to the airport, then?"

"I thought you said you were taking me?" He paused for a minute, thinking about his plans. "Can I let you know when I get back?"

"Of course. You have awfully dark rings under your eyes. Be careful driving."

He took the deck stairs two at a time.

"It's about time," Brie mumbled as he passed.

Although the cloudless sky offered promises of warmth, the cool morning air kept Andy from putting the top down as they drove. He handed Rose a tube of sunblock as he placed one of her feet onto his lap. The Eighty-Nine North was quiet at this time on a Sunday morning. Mountains stood in the distance, just then, allowing the sun to peek above them.

"You're my best friend." Rose rotated her body to him as he drove.

"Yes."

"I want to keep it that way."

"Are you having second thoughts?" he asked.

"No. Our friendship is important is all I'm saying."

"This is right. I know you know this is right." He unlaced her shoe and took it off as well as her sock.

He could see her focus on him while coating herself with the SPF fifty. "Are you going to tell me what you're doing?"

He finished with her other shoe, took her feet, one at a time, and set them on his dash. "There. No, wait." He reached back and took out the tie from her hair.

Rose took his hand. "What's gotten into you?"

"That." He pointed to her bare feet. "Your hair and those feet on my dash kept me up half the night."

"Oh," she sounded honestly startled. "In that case, I'll take out

63

the braid myself."

He drove with one hand and with the other he ran the backs of his fingers possessively down her cheek. Rose closed her eyes and rested her head on the seat next to his arm. Her lips were sealed and the corners lifted.

He felt as if a light had been turned on—one that burned away a fog. Now that he could see, there was a desperate craving for more. More of this. More of her. It ate at him already. He wanted to dive in and explore this side of her. Of them. I *am* an idiot, he decided, and he hated that his brother saw it before he did.

Rose.

Real, determined, natural, sensible, selfless Rose. Soft, toned, sexy Rose. He shook his head clear. There was no way he was going there. Forcing himself to remember that she had her first kiss less than twelve hours ago, he pulled his fingers away from her face and instead slid them down to link with hers.

CHAPTER 9

Amanda tried to relax on her couch as the puppy snoozed next to her. Her feet were bare and crossed at the ankles as they rested on Dave's lap. Their stomachs were full of pancakes and their minds full of graduation plans.

"It's nice Rose and Andy have stayed such good friends even after his move to college. I wonder what will happen when she takes her turn to move on," she said.

Dave sat with one arm draped across the back of the couch and the other rubbing the ball of her foot. "Hopefully she'll get some new friends. Some *girl*friends."

She sighed in agreement. "Yes. Yes, you're right."

"When are we going to tell her?"

Reflexively, she pulled her feet from his lap and sat up.

"I don't mean to upset you."

"I know, I know." She closed her eyes and ran her hands over her face, through her hair. Dave was an innocent in all of this. The battle in her head between protecting her daughter and being honest with her husband was making her insane. Literally. "I'm okay, really." She forced herself to smile at him. She knew it didn't reach her eyes.

"No one expects you to ever be okay with it, but Rose is grown now. You wanted to tell her long before this." He reached and pulled her into him.

Dave was a smart man. He had become complacent to her consistent drop in weight and increase in nerves, but she knew he wasn't blind. Over time, he seemed to find a balance between worry, obsession and the fact that he simply wasn't her father.

After years of failing to find the man who'd raped her and fix whatever he could in her life, Dave seemed to come to the point where he accepted that she was a grown woman and merely offered her the love and support any woman would ask for...and space when she'd needed it. Discussing the origins of Rose's conception always caused a spike in those nerves.

She wanted desperately to tell him why. Let him take over and take care of her, take care of it. But, she was afraid. And she was careful. Her family came first.

Family photos were stored in closed albums and off of mantles and walls. She gave Rose's father just enough money to keep him at bay whenever he decided to show up. The man had no idea he had a daughter, and she would do whatever it took to keep it that way.

He murdered her grandfather. Behind closed lids, she forced back the tears. That bastard had his hand around her throat when he forced her to listen to the details of how he did it. She knew it was an attempt to control her, and it had worked.

All those years of defense classes were for nothing. Each time he showed up, it was like turning back the clock nineteen years when he forced his way into her Red Cross trailer. The smell of his sweaty body and stale tobacco breath blended with a feeling of helplessness and pain. She wondered if Dave ever suspected her motive behind pushing both of the girls through their defense classes. Rose appeased her, but Jessica still fought her with continuing.

Rose's birthday cut it too close. She knew he was due; he hadn't come lurking for over a year. Just enough time for someone to let their guard down, but not her. A thousand dollars every now and then was a small price to pay to keep him away.

She shivered. Dave responded by pulling her closer yet. He was the most loyal person she had ever known. He respected her when she didn't deserve it. Now, it was her turn to respect his peace. She would keep her secret, keep Rose safe and keep Dave from being dragged into her past or ending up like her grandfather.

"I know we need to tell her, but when is the right time? She's so happy right now. Seems more than excited about college. Do I send her off on her own with the knowledge of her violent beginning? With the fear of knowing first hand what's out there? What if she tries to look for him?"

"There's no trace of a Michael Rainer anywhere." He ran his fingers over the back of her hair. "She's grown, Amanda. She'll find out sooner or later. The longer you wait, the more it will hurt her."

Andy knew he was right. Rose as a guest looked different. Better. She wasn't rushed or looking like a mother watching over her kids, or trying to find something to work on. Still, she couldn't keep from acting as tour guide.

As they passed exhibits, she recited animal facts while he watched her face and reached down to take her hand. Thinking. Planning. Always planning. Start with a foundation. No. They already had that. It was solid with years of unwavering layers. They cut through the wallaby exhibit. Similar interests, same sense of humor. And the lips. How had he never noticed the lips? He ached to stop her and kiss her, but settled for lifting their joined hands and brushing the back of his along her cheek. She kept right on talking about a female that carried a joey, although when he touched her face, her blink lasted longer than natural.

Together, they took a seat on one of the benches around the outdoor stage, waiting for the morning's presentation. The split, treated logs were comfortable and reminded Andy of his uncle's bridge over Black Creek. While waiting for the zookeeper, they made pacts and plans for the summer, much like they always had. Only now they had impatience, excitement and...anticipation. They agreed to keep their relationship private. No one would question if they spent time together or offer any lectures if they decided to take off for a weekend—or every weekend.

Rose said they hit the jackpot when the senior zookeeper and her assistant brought out one of their two bald eagles. Two young brothers looked intimidated by the almost three-foot-tall bird. The boys seemed torn between cowering and curiosity. Rose assured Andy the bird wouldn't disappoint.

Draping his arm across her backrest, he resisted the urge to touch her. He tilted his body enough to give the impression of watching the presenter while actually watching Rose with his renewed sight. He never really felt the same obsession with animals and conservation that she had, but did have great interest in the way Rose ignited each time the subject came up.

Since Rose would already know anything the zookeeper had to say, he suspected she was thinking of the day she would be the one with the gloved hand speaking to spectators. Although she preferred the animals, Rose always had a way with the visitors as well.

Winking at her, the presenter explained to the small crowd that the two eagles were both from Alaska and both permanently injured and left flightless. A gunshot maimed the first, the other a car accident. The birds' zoo enclosure was without a roof and sometimes attracted an occasional wild bald eagle that would hang around for days at a time. The permanently wounded birds were able to hop along in their complicated enclosure and could even hover for a few seconds at a time.

As she spoke, the zookeeper lifted her gloved hand and the bird spread her wings their full eight feet, hovered above her, then set back down and enjoyed a hunk of meat as a reward.

Rose leaned closer to him. "They're named Frick and Frack. This is Frack, the female."

"How can you tell?" Andy asked.

"The female is bigger. The crease of her beak flows back underneath her eyelids, and she has a tiny dark feather on her head. There. See it? That's the female."

"Your wish."

"Hmm?" She turned her eyes to him and stopped. Inhaled deeply.

He watched her blink to clear her mind and couldn't understand how he had never seen her in this light before. She was absolutely beautiful. Not artificially. Real. "Is this still your wish?"

"Oh, I'm not sure. I want to work with animals. That end of biology. I'll see where the four years takes me before I narrow down my doctorate options."

He turned a piece of her hair.

"Eagles are not pets," the presenter continued. "I need to be careful around her. Even though I'm the handler and the one with the food, she'll fight me for it. Starting as eaglets all the way through to fledging, they nip at their parents when food is brought to them. Their instincts are not only to hunt, but to steal."

The brothers, as expected, decided on curiosity over fear and were the first to raise their hands at the question/answer portion of the presentation. "What do they eat?"

"In the wild, bald eagles prefer mostly fish but will also hunt waterfowl, gulls and turtles. They will, however, scavenge and eat animal carcasses like road-killed deer."

The boys responded appropriately with an "Ewww" in tandem. "They live by water?" asked the older of the two.

"Smart question. Bald eagles are found mostly in the Great Lakes region, Chesapeake Bay and Florida but can be found as far north as Alaska and Canada. They are not found on any other continent and, yes, they almost exclusively live near water."

"Alaska?" the younger brother spoke up. "How do they sit on eggs in Alaska?"

The zookeeper looked to the boy. "Intuitive. Nice. They don't mind the cold. Their feathers are well adapted for it. A mother eagle can lay her eggs on solid snow. Unlike other species, both the male and female take turns caring for the young, including sitting on the eggs. It's called brooding and, as many species do, eagles have special feathers that keep eggs warm in extreme temperatures." She switched the heavy bird from one arm to the other.

After the question and answer portion of the show, the presenter finished with a final, dramatic show of wing span. She gave Rose a nod before taking the bird back to her exhibit.

Lunchtime neared, so they made their last stop at the small water tank. The pool held two sea lions and a seal. The seal rested lazily on a protruding rock in the middle of the tank as the sea lions swam in bored circles around him. Rose had the same look on her face as when she chased him down the edge of the lake with the snapping crawfish. Suspicious, he followed her lead and stood on the concrete ledge in order to get a better look at the circling animals. Leaning over, she waved at the sea lions, and then ducked.

With lightning speed, the smaller sea lion sprinted out of the pool and splashed a tailfin full of water, drenching him from head to waist. Rose laughed mercilessly as he grabbed her, tossing her over his shoulder. With her like that, he walked back to the car, soaking her as she squirmed and squealed along the way.

Walking around to the passenger door, he slid her down slowly, leaving little room between him and metal.

"PDA." Rose trembled. "Parking lot PDA."

"PD what?" He touched his lips to just under her ear.

He felt her arms slide along his sides to his back.

"Parking lot public display of affection," she answered and quivered against him.

Reluctantly, he glanced around and noticed a family of four walking out the zoo's exit doors. "Mmm. True. Carried away."

Charcoal sat, looking broken hearted as Rose went through her list of things to bring in her head. "How do you know?" she asked him. She could tell that *he* could tell she was getting ready to leave. "All right. One more time through. Then, I have to go."

She wanted to get to the terminal early. Actually, she arrived everywhere early but this was different. After the short, barely twenty-four-hour fling with her lifelong best friend, they had spent the week with few and far between phone calls while Andy studied for and took his finals. Now it was time to see, in person, if they would pick up where they left off or if the week had cleared the air and they would go back to where they had been since they were kids.

Charcoal ran in happy circles when he saw her put a few small treats in her pocket. He looked as if he had two different bodies. The front of him was painfully still, and he tried desperately to focus. The back was like a caffeinated belly dancer. He heeled, almost, on their way to the front. She remembered to use gentle reminders followed by an occasional treat for an extra reward.

Rolling him on his back, she praised the pup when he lay still. She lifted his eyelids and pulled at his lips as they learned to do in puppy kindergarten so that he would be comfortable when handled at the vet's. As he gobbled his treats, Rose sat in the grass. She remembered to place her hands close to his mouth so he wouldn't feel threatened with people near his food.

Next, sitting practice. She lifted her fingers above his head and pulled back on his collar while adding an oral command. After verbal praise, she gave Charcoal a hand signal combined with the word "stay." She kept him on his leash. He was nowhere near ready to go without. After just over a month, they could make it about ten feet from each other with success. It was slow, but he was getting better all the time.

"You are the best dog, aren't you?" she told him when he came at her command.

Scratching his ears and rubbing cheeks with him, she finished a solid fifteen minutes of training before giving the command to get in his crate. "Don't look at me like that. I can't take you with me." She gave him a chew toy to help him pass the time.

CHAPTER 10

Flying over the Midwest, Andy reviewed the changes he'd made in the plans for his summer. Much like his computer aided drafting design class, he backed up, made some alterations and created an even better design. He used caution and planned to check the design frequently. Rose may be smart and sexy but she was also young and naïve.

They'd had the comfortable parts of a relationship for years. That foundation so many couples lacked. The trust. Falling into that dance of give and take and working it unconsciously. Now, they had fire. Dancing with the flames was easier when you knew you had steel underneath to hold you up.

He spotted her in the terminal almost instantly, biting her nails with wide eyes. She wore jeans, pleasantly on the tight side, light blue Chucks and a matching blue blouse. Very Rose. With one exception. She wore her hair in silky, loose waves that framed her face and hung over her shoulders. He suspected she did that to get to him. Smart girl. He was speechless, which rarely happened to Andrew Reed. It was easy to tell when she found him; her eyes softened and she sealed her lips together like she always did. Amazing. He winked as he inched along in the middle of the line exiting the boarding ramp.

When he cleared the line of passengers, she ran toward him much like she did when he'd visited her at the construction site in early spring. Only this time, she threw her arms around him and showered his face with kisses.

He grabbed her hands as he found her lips, kissing her hard before bothering with words. As he pulled away, he moved his face to her hair and inhaled.

"Are you smelling my hair?"

"Shh."

She sighed and he could feel her cheeks on his as they expanded into a smile.

He pulled her face away and looked in one eye, then the other and back again.

"Better?" she asked.

"Mmm. Hello." He kissed her again.

Rose tried to take one of his carry-ons, but he laughed.

"How are your biceps?"

She scrunched her brows. "Fine, I guess."

"That's good because I have a lot more downstairs."

It wasn't an exaggeration. Expertly, he piled smaller luggage on top of the bigger pieces, then draped the rest on both of their shoulders.

"You all right under there?"

"Yep. Black belt."

Pulling off the Three-Ninety South at a small town for breakfast, they found a cozy, hole-in-the-wall diner and sat on opposite sides of a cracked Formica table framed in metal. The place boasted seating for a total of about fifteen on worn chairs with lined vinyl and had the best French toast they'd ever tasted.

Rose speared a small square of the amazing toast and dunked it in syrup as Andy leaned back in his seat.

Cautiously, he turned his head and looked at her through the corners of his eyes. "I found a job in town for the summer."

She stopped the forkful of dripping French toast at her lips for a staggering minute.

"I'll be working for a general contractor. I start Monday morning, no break there, but—"

"Are you crazy?" Her fork dropped to her plate. "Are you stupid? What the hell are you thinking?"

"Okay." He set his fork down carefully. "Not the reaction I expected."

Heat started at the base of her neck and quickly ran over her cheeks. "You've been pining for a summer with your uncle, Chase, since you were eleven. This is your dream. Call him back!" She practically bounced out of her chair.

Andy grabbed her arm. "Calm the hell down. I know what I'm doing. This is good. Listen for minute. If you don't stop waving your arm, they're gonna kick us out of here."

She sighed, pulled her hand from him and crossed her arms.

"Greenberg Contractors. Chase knows the owner. He builds houses, buildings, subdivisions. I'll be the miscellaneous man. I should be able to get experience with all the different stages of building, and why am I explaining myself to you? I thought you'd be happy."

Her breathing slowed and she closed her eyes. "Okay. I think. I'm sorry. I think. It just sounded like you were ready to throw away your future...I'm sorry," she repeated. She looked up at his face. "You're not leaving."

She realized she said it like she'd just had an epiphany. Her eyes burned and she dropped her face in her hands. She felt one rough finger under her chin. Lifting her head to look at him, she refused to let the tears spill over. He ran his thumb along her cheek and she looked deep into the caramel of his eyes. They sat at the small, square table in the little town restaurant and had a complete conversation without speaking a word.

It felt like a noose had been released from around her throat. Her heart. Her mind went into overdrive at the possibilities as her breathing returned to accelerated. Didn't her mother say it was the *boys* that didn't want to just kiss?

"You're blushing." He craned his head forward. "I'm not sure I've ever seen you flushed."

She felt her cheeks burn even hotter and turned her eyes to her food.

Andy spent the last days of May in the sun, working with his hands on everything from grading yards to helping pour foundations, framing houses and fixing leaky exterior doors and windows. Each aspect was fascinating, like solving a complex puzzle in orderly stages. Whenever Greenberg became backed up or someone called in sick, Andy stepped in.

He was low man on the totem pole everywhere he went, but

he was building connections while making sure to leave an impression with builders and subcontractors all over central upstate New York. Life made so much more sense when he worked with his hands. And this time, it made more sense to him than he could ever remember...putting in a hard day's work and spending evenings with his best friend.

They made sure to try and spend at least some time together each night, although it didn't always work that way. Both their plates were full, as they generally were. It was just more irritating than it used to be. He quizzed her on her finals or worked with the pup if she had a job for his mom or volunteered at the zoo. If nothing else, they would catch a few minutes by the lake after nightfall.

Normally, they brought Charcoal with them and even let him off his leash if he allowed Goldie and Macey to saunter along. Tonight they lay, just the two of them, looking at the millions of stars freely illuminated without the lights of bigger cities. Rose was on her back using his arm as a pillow. The night was warm and dry and smelled of grass and fresh, drizzling water. They talked while he lay on his side, his hand resting on her stomach.

Interrupting, he poked at her belly and looked down. "You have washboard abs."

She laughed and looked up to him. "Isn't that something a girl says to a guy?"

"Probably."

She lifted her shirt and raised her shoulders up enough to flex her six-pack. She mentioned something about the contrast in color between their skin, but he left coherent thought behind the minute she'd pulled up her shirt.

Quickly, he pulled it back down and reluctantly willed himself to casually change the subject. "Graduation this weekend?" She shifted up on her elbow and eyed him suspiciously. "Subject change. Don't argue." Tricky, since he had, exactly, considered arguing. "Regardless, it's this weekend, and you have a speech to write."

"Written. So much for subject change. You don't want to touch me."

He gestured his free hand between the two of them, illustrating that they were touching. Practically from head to toe.

She fell back and sighed. "You've touched girls before. I

suspect several girls and plenty of times."

"You don't understand—"

She pushed from the blanket to her knees and faced him, sitting back on her feet. "Don't tell me what I understand, Andrew Reed, and don't even start with what I want." She stuck a fingernail between her teeth, pulled it out, looked at it, then stuffed her hands deep in the pockets of her faded jeans. "I may have had my first kiss just a few weeks ago, as you feel you need to keep reminding me, but I'm not a little girl anymore and—"

"Okay," he interrupted and sat up fully, facing her, and rested his forearms on his propped knees. "Then, I'll tell you what I know and what I want. I know that I'm in love with you. I've been in love with you longer than I realized. And what I want is to do this—" He gestured his hands between the two of them again "—right."

Rose sat there on her heels with her hands limp in her front pockets. Shoulders forward, she remained motionless for the longest damned time. Opened her mouth once, then closed it again. "Oh." She lay back on the blanket and pulled him down with her, rolling to rest her head on his chest. "I guess you're forgiven then."

"So, I'm forgiven. I can be forgiven all the way to another cold shower tonight," he murmured.

He could feel her round cheeks on his chest as they curled into a smile.

"It's a big decision." He clasped his hands and used them for a pillow. "I won't make it for you."

"Do I have to throw myself at you?" she said with both sarcasm and sincerity in her voice.

"That's my point. You don't *have* to do anything. That's not why I'm here." He reached over and kissed her forehead. "Last final tomorrow."

Andy rode on the edge of a three-to-a-bench seat in a shiny, red company truck. The dickhead rookie between him and the crew leader was one of Greenberg's masonry subs. Understanding that contacts mattered, he worked to brush off the dude's laziness and instead made a mental note of it for the day he would need a mason. He wouldn't be choosing him. They drove through a new subdivision where Greenberg owned several lots.

He grinned as they passed two redheads standing behind a pickup full of plants and shrubs. While her mom loaded containers into a wheelbarrow, Rose spread sunblock on her legs. Huh. So, she did remember to do that on her own. Spying on her as a fly on a wall was highly satisfying, except he wasn't the only one who watched her.

"Mother fucker, dude. Did you see that chick's hands on those long legs?"

The crew leader made no attempt to teach the asshole appropriate behavior while on the job. It took Andy several minutes to realize they weren't actually *on* the job.

Instead, he focused on two thoughts: the loose bricks around the front window of the next construction site and the weekend rock climbing trip he and Rose would leave for the next day. They'd already taken a few short day trips but couldn't spare an entire weekend until after graduation. Since she didn't die from her valedictorian speech, he guessed they were a go.

Miguel Ramirez—alias Michael Rainer, alias Maarten Ricks, alias whoever he felt like being that day—stood on the square-foot lawn of a house deep in Chicago. He could see Wrigley Field down the long street between rows of vehicles that were parked bumper to bumper.

The building of the bitch he was waiting on had been broken up into four apartments. Nearly a year since their last *visit*. He could always use some extra cash. Didn't really need any since the last two hits, but her place was on his way as he headed west.

He looked like an ordinary man in a busy metropolitan area, taking a smoke break before bed. He knew bitch lived in 3B. Knew her very, very well. He took time to study his girlfriends, as he liked to think of them.

He had girlfriends scattered all across the great US of A. It wasn't hard to keep them in line. Space out the visits. Change appearance whenever necessary. Scan the building for new security. Don't leave any tangible evidence. Scare the fucking shit out them.

Without moving his head, he followed the oncoming car with his eyes while keeping out of sight, leaning against a tree. His face reddened when a man got out of the bitch's car and walked around to open her door. The time he'd spent scouting her, four nights waiting in the fucking wind, was more than he would tolerate.

Then, he thought of how productive slicing the wimp's throat might be. He could use that to keep her in line. It worked good all the other times. People were murdered in a city this size all the time. He could spray a few gang signs and let the cops run with it.

As he felt for his trusty knife at the base of his pant leg, wimp guided her to the door of the building. Watching, Miguel realized she was blowing him off. Ha! What a tease. A peck on the mouth? No fucking way. She deserved what she was going to get.

He finished his cigarette while wimp threw his head back and laughed at something she said. Not gonna work, dumbass. He could still kill the mother fucker, just for the feel of it. So easy. He took the short set of steps in one leap just as wimp turned. Miguel purposely knocked shoulders with him, apologized using perfect American English, pocketed his wallet, and snatched the door before it latched. Not bad, he thought. Not bad at all. He took the stairs two at a time in his soft-soled shoes while slipping on his gloves and catching up to her in the hallway.

She turned with the anticipation of a woman half expecting her date to have changed his mind about third date sex. He locked her arms to her sides and used his body to push her up against the door to her apartment. The feel of her body tighten, then shake made him instantly rock hard.

"Go ahead and scream." He dug his fingers into her arm. "No, no, no." He grabbed the pepper spray she held in her hand. "Not unless you want to try it, baby." He chucked it down the hall and pressed her head, face first against her apartment door, hopefully cutting the skin along her eye socket. "Open it. Then, turn off that nice security system you had installed."

He loosened as she dug in her pocket for her keys and loved the way her hands trembled. "I told you what happens when you change the rules, baby. I always know. Maybe if you have a good load of cash in there and if you ask real nice, I won't hurt you...too bad."

They decided on leaving Charcoal. Rose turned her head and

looked sideways at the puppy. "How does he know? Look at him. It's ridiculous."

Andy stopped loading ropes and equipment into her pickup to look at the pup. "Huh. He does know. We can take him."

"No." Not for what she had planned. She hadn't walked into the lingerie store and bought the skimpiest camisole and shorts set she could find just to have Charcoal in the way. And the drugstore. She wanted to hide her face just thinking about it.

"Hello? You there?" He gave her a friendly elbow jab and waved his hand in front of her face.

"Oh, crap." She left the drugstore bag in her room. "I'll just be a minute."

As she jogged up her porch steps, Andy called the dog over and gave him the command to lie.

Her mom must have heard her dart up the stairs, because she was waiting by the front door when she came back down.

"Remember to use your bug spray—"

"And sunblock." And condoms. "Got it. Love you."

CHAPTER 11

Together, Rose and Andy lounged next to the red coals of the campfire. Clouds thickened in the late hour, causing the stars to disappear in the deep gray. They ate hot dogs with the works and had an apple to compensate. The crickets were so noisy she and Andy could barely hear the bullfrogs from the river down the trail. Balmy evening air meant hot climbing the next day. She took off her shoes and socks and let her toes rest by the dwindling fire.

"Red?" She hadn't heard Andy's voice crack since the seventh grade.

"Hmm?" Noticing him gawking at her toes, she pressed her lips together. "Oh, yes...go on."

He went back to explaining about his summer job. "The contractors in the area are like a tight-knit clique of junior high girls. They won't let outsiders in and ambush them if they try." He kicked off his leather flip-flops and propped his feet next to hers. "I like it, though. Working as the low man, I've learned what the crew leaders and bosses do that pisses us off, or is just unproductive and stupid. I can use that when I have my own crew leaders and I'm the boss."

Only half listening, she took a deep breath, got up and stood in front of the fire.

"Have you decided when you'll give your two weeks no—" He sounded as if his tongue stuck to the roof of his mouth.

With determination, she pulled off her tee. Underneath, she wore the low-cut satin with shoelace-thin straps. The color matched her toes.

Andy sat frozen with his hands clasped tightly on the top of his head. The look on his face gave her more confidence. As she reached for the top button of her jean shorts, he jumped from his chair. "Wait. Damn it." Grabbing her by the wrists, he looked around. "We're outside. What're you thinking?"

She stepped close enough to brush against him. With one of the most honest and sincere looks she could muster, she looked up at him. "You *know* what I'm thinking."

Closing his eyes, Andy breathed deeply and stood for what seemed like eternity. "Yes. I know. And I don't have it in me to push you away again."

Sparks of anticipation traveled through every inch of her body before settling low in her stomach. Feelings so strong left her legs weak. She willed herself to stand strong.

Guiding her arms behind him, bringing her closer, Andy pressed their foreheads together. Painfully slow, his hands ran up the length of her arms and over her shoulders before resting on the sides of her neck. Softly, he whispered, "I've never done this...with anyone who's never done this."

"A first for both of us, then." Anxiously, she took his hand, pulling him toward their tent.

Inside, it was too small to stand. She sat on her heels, turned on the lantern and watched as he zipped them in.

When he turned, she stretched up on her knees to get back to the button on her jeans.

He took her hands away once more. "Let me."

As his thumbs rested on her wrists, he spoke low and deep. "Your pulse."

"I know. I can't help it."

"You're trying to kill me."

Need and anticipation raced through her. She felt her shorts loosen as he released her button. A reflexive, muffled purr escaped her throat. Rough hands slid into the sides of her shorts and over her hips.

They didn't need words. Hardly ever needed words. She leaned on one leg for him, then the other. He slipped her shorts over and tossed them aside before sitting back to look at her.

Was she supposed to feel exposed or embarrassed at the way his eyes traveled over her? All she felt was flattery at his awe. And need. And want. Her lips tightened.

"You're beautiful."

For the first time in her life, she felt beautiful.

Reaching over his head and behind him, Andy grabbed the back of his shirt.

"No way." She stopped his arms. "Me." Rising from her heels, she ran her hands under and up his shirt, exploring muscle and flesh as she took the cotton over his arms. She'd seen him shirtless before. Her entire life. This was powerfully different and something she would never forget.

Andy lifted off his feet to his knees. Copying the movements he'd made, she took off his khakis. They wrapped their arms around each other, touching skin to skin and thin bits of material that covered warming flesh. The heat and humidity of the summer night added a seductive tone to her plan. A biological tone, like the rush of the water they could hear from the river in the distance. This was nature in its most basic element, and she felt completely right. Surreal. She could feel Andy was ready for her, too, and had to restrain herself from rushing in and exploring.

The feel of her heartbeat slammed against Andy's chest. He'd never had love attached to sex before. With bodies pressed together, he took her face in his hands and gently dove in. Tongues meshed. Teeth grazed. Never in his life had he held such a woman. And she had been here all along. The intensity shook him, took him.

He wound one hand around her back, under the satin while the other slid between the two of them to cup the silk. Her legs wavered at his touch. Fascinating. Supporting her weight, he lowered her to the ground before inching one of the straps from her shoulder, kissing warm flesh along the way.

Her small, breathy sighs echoed in his ears—reactions that were as intoxicating as her body. He wanted to savor this, her. This was not a performance. It was two people discovering each other. He felt her hands, earnest, gripping, exploring. When he felt her reach around to find him, he grabbed her hand.

He shook his head, steadying his breath. "Not this time."

Although he felt the deflated drop in her chest, she seemed to recover and lifted her arms straight overhead, inviting him to slip off the silk. Following her lead, he trailed his hands up her waist, then raised the satin over head. Rolling on his side, he propped on an elbow and rested his head in his hand. Watching her as she watched him. She was fit. The six-pack was as sexy as ever.

No nerves. He could tell. She looked flattered. He felt drunk. He brought his mouth close to her ear. "I love you."

"Mmm," Rose all but hummed and seemed to melt in his hands.

Taking her, he circled lazily with his thumb. She jolted and her reaction had him fighting control that balanced on a thread. He willed himself not to rush, not to just take. He moved his hand from her and leaned in to replace it with his mouth. She arched and quaked, grabbing his shoulders and digging her fingers in.

Running his hand down her sides, he took off the tiny, matching red fabric, and discarded it somewhere with the scatter of the rest of their things. He pulled her close to him. She reached and this time he let her pull off the rest of his clothes. They lay next to each other, flesh to flesh, arms and legs twined. They fit. He knew they would.

He took her mouth with his, mixing lips and tongues together, long and deep. Their hearts beat madly with nothing between them. He dug his hands into her hair, trying to get closer, legs twisting, hands groping. He wanted to learn every part of her: the expectantly firm lines of lean muscle, the soft and the tender. It unraveled him. Her uncontrolled response to his hands was enough to make him lose himself. When he reached her, she instantly bolted and sat upright.

Analyzing her cautiously, he caught his breath.

"Andy." She turned toward him, gasping for air. "Something's...happening."

He controlled his breath enough to smile. "That's...supposed to happen."

"Oh." She fell back on the single pillow, looking at the top of the tent. "Okay," then turned to him, winded. "Hang on to me."

He touched his lips to her ear. "Always."

She knew it wasn't a declaration. Just one tiny word said in the heat of the moment. But that word combined with the feel of his warm body against hers, his lips, his hands—oh, his hands. They sent her into a place she didn't know existed. The intensity was terrifying and glorious. Awakening and explosive. She would have never wanted this to happen with anyone else.

He kept his word and hung onto her. It probably was a good thing they were far away from earshot of any other campsite. Shaking with aftershocks, she experienced a whole new desperation. "Can it be time now?"

His head fell to her shoulder and he nodded but put up a finger to signal for her to wait. With wide eyes, she watched.

When she spotted the wrapper, she instinctively asked, "Can I—"

"Not this time," he halfheartedly said again.

The contrast of skin color between them glowed in the lantern-lit night. Alabaster against bronze. She felt no fear, only need. The weight of him was safety. She was floating somewhere with Andy to keep her grounded.

Linking fingers with both hands, he stared intently at her. "I won't hurt you." But, it was he who squeezed fingers, exhaling completely when they joined. He watched with brows tight.

Understanding, she answered by lifting to him, pulling him in. She kept her eyes on his, not wanting to miss any part of this. She heard sounds come from him she didn't recognize.

He let go of her hands and moved to grasp her shoulders. Gently, they moved together. United.

He buried his face in her hair before releasing. Andy covered her until their breathing slowed and finally returned to normal. He rolled next to her, pulling her partially on top of him, skin to skin, damp and lifeless. "Mmm," Andy mumbled and kissed the top of her head.

She pressed her lips together and smiled without lifting her head from his chest. "Should I feel this worn out?"

Tucking her hair behind her ear, he didn't answer but whispered, "Amazing. Sleep now, my Rose."

Brie stood looking out the window of Andy's room. The nearly finished guesthouse stood at the edge of their property almost ready for her out-of-town family. She didn't feel right about them staying in hotels each visit. Duncan was there for the week to help with the trim. She could hear Nathan down the hall as he rolled James out of bed for morning swim practice, then headed for John's room next.

She had tons to do that day and was looking forward to every minute of it. Picking up the laundry basket she'd set down, she opened Andy's closet. He was terrible at getting his dirty clothes into his hamper. She stood as she decided whether or not it was worth nagging him about when she glanced at the shelf above his hanging clothes.

She knew it.

Setting the laundry basket down once more, she stood with her legs wide and her hands resting on the back of her hips, thumbs facing forward. She could see Nathan enter the doorway from her peripheral vision but she didn't stop staring at the shelf. A small smile started at the corner of her mouth.

He was leaning against the jamb of the door. "The way the light is angling from the window around you, I could stand here for quite a while watching you."

He pushed off and walked over, stood behind her and slid his arms around her waist. Resting his chin on top of her head, Nathan asked, "Anyone in there?"

She covered his hands with one of hers and used her other to point at the top shelf. "Andy's tent is here."

She felt him shrug. "Rose has a tent," he retorted.

"And his sleeping bag."

He lifted his chin and stepped back. "Whoa."

"Yeah, whoa."

"Why do I have to putty holes while the woman uses the nail gun?" Duncan grinned as Brie puttied and wiped the walnut custom trim Nathan scribed to fit snugly along the walls of the guesthouse. Although she pretended not to hear him, he could see her smiling widely.

Near them, Nathan set the angle on his miter saw, then meticulously measured and trimmed off an extra eighth inch from his last cut.

Turning a smirk at Duncan, Brie loaded her nail gun, then politely responded, "I expect you'll use this house any day now with a nice family of your own."

He stopped and lifted a brow. Holy shit. "Like that's going to happen." Dipping his finger in the jar for another wad of putty, he lifted a corner of his mouth. "I sure could have used it in high school, though. What are you going to do when the twins sneak girls in here during the middle of the night to smoke pot and have orgies?"

He covered his head with his arms as stain rags and gloves came at him in rapid fire. "All right, all right!" He gut laughed, but when he dared to look, he didn't see her.

"Mom?"

Brie was on the floor with her wrist pressed against her chest.

"Shit! Mom." Terrified, he ran and skidded down next to her. "Dad!"

Brie rolled on her side, grasping her chest, but still craned her head up at him. "Don't use that language in front of me," she said and worked out a clearly jesting grin. "Nothing's going to happen to me. Just a cramp. Hell, you'd think I was in my sixties rather than my forties."

Nathan was eyeing her carefully, asked her a few assessing questions, then held out his left hand to give her a lift up.

Brie stepped to Duncan and took both his hands in hers. "Duncan. I can have a cramp."

Recognizing his overreaction, he tunneled a hand through his hair. He felt jittery, like an idiot. "I'm going to get us something to drink. Are you thirsty?" He rotated his glance through half-opened lids from Nathan to Brie and back.

"I could use a long neck." Nathan looked to Brie.

"Sure." She picked up the discarded nail gun, checking to see if it needed reloading. "Make it two. Thanks."

Duncan headed for the front door leading to the main house as Nathan walked to her, taking the gun from her hand. "Next week," he heard him say.

Duncan glanced back and saw Brie rolling her eyes dramatically. "I'm due for a check-up anyway, *Dad*," she said and kissed him soundly on the mouth.

Mulch tucked easily around clusters of young hydrangeas and day lilies in the hot June sun. As much as Rose didn't want to admit it, she did like this job. The exterior crews on the spec house were finished. The sod was coming in a few days. The only guys working were the heating/cooling crew and the electricians. She worked alone. None of the landscaping work at this spot needed more than one person. Another bonus. Not that she didn't enjoy working with her mom. She was just more introverted than most. Much more so than Andy, she mused.

Thinking of the many ways they were different unsettled her momentarily as she tucked mulch closely around delicate stems and leaves. She wanted to work with animals and conservation. He wanted to work with buildings and bulldoze trees. She knew what she preferred but was uncertain about her future specifically. He had always known exactly what he wanted to do and be.

And, she hadn't told him she loved him. Why was that? she wondered. Trying not to look too deeply into it, she decided it was just never the right time. The night he declared his love to her? Cliché. While they were making love? She tightened her lips. No way.

Finally, she admitted to herself it was all a big cop out and gave in to the fact that she simply wasn't in the same playing field as Andrew Reed. Or in the same universe. He was Andy. Gorgeous, well spoken, well liked. Gorgeous.

Sitting back on her heels, she sighed as a red truck pulled into the drive. Speak of the devil.

Andy stepped out of the passenger side, followed by a man that didn't look much older than him. The man wore stained jeans and possibly hadn't washed his hair in days. From the driver side, a much older man stepped out. He was fit, clean cut, with a full head of snow-white hair. She recognized the older guy as one of the masonry subs Greenberg Construction kept exclusively. She had no idea if the relationship between her and Andy was hidden to more than just their families and decided to be safe and just nod in polite greeting, then kept working.

Relief flowed over her when Andy walked right up, winked and introduced her to the men he was with. Trying her hand at extrovert, she worked up a friendly greeting and a few short minutes of polite, empty conversation before getting back to her flowers.

Hoping she wasn't completely obvious, she watched Andy's muscles flex as he unloaded equipment. She tried to get her work done. He was a distraction—a nice distraction.

It didn't take much time before the scruffy one carelessly laid a corner of his scaffolding right on top of the newly planted hydrangea nearest the drive. As she stood with hackles rising, she had a moment to realize that the mason work had already been completed and to wonder what the hell they were even doing there. Her mom specifically waited until the brickwork and siding were finished so that rude, careless workers such as scruffy couldn't come along and trash their work.

She picked up the edge of the scaffolding and rotated it to the drive.

"Excuse me, little honey, but I put that there for a reason."

She thought he sounded like he was speaking to a kitten.

"You'll need to step back out of the way now," he continued.

Andy's eyes widened. The palm of his hand wanted to instinctively hit his forehead. Instead, he waited and let his eyes dart between Rose, who was turning all sorts of colors, to the rookie, who had already started to put the scaffolding back on the mulch and flowers.

Without hesitating, Rose lifted the end of the metal frame and pushed it, not too softly, into the rookie's stomach. "Call me little honey again and you'll eat this. Ruin one more piece of my work and you'll eat more than the scaffolding."

CHAPTER 12

The rookie sighed and closed his eyes as if mildly annoyed before walking around and reaching to take Rose's arm from the edge of the bars.

Andy dug out of the hole he had crawled into long enough to speak up before he reached them. "Dude, I wouldn't touch her if I—"

Andy nodded as he watched Rose, expectantly, forearm block the rookie's grip with that lightning speed of hers and grab hold of his wrist, twisting it enough to really piss him off.

"Why you little bitch." The rookie cradled his arm where she twisted. Wimp.

He knew she could take care of herself. Knew he should feel sorry for the dude just about then but he struggled not to join her. Didn't matter. The rookie was slow as hell. He twisted from her grip skillfully enough, but he was actually winding up to backhand her. She saw it coming so easily, she knocked his arm down and dug her knee into his nuts before he'd even shifted his weight into the swing.

Andy smiled wide as he turned to the crew leader and assessed what he would do about it.

The crew leader shook his head and didn't look too surprised or unnerved by the physical altercation. Instead, he called out to the rookie, "Get your skinny ass in the truck before I join the little lady." He walked and stood over him, then lifted him up by the arm, not so carefully.

The rookie held onto his balls as he limped to the bench seat of the truck.

She didn't look nearly as offended when the crew leader called her, 'little lady.'

"Listen, Rose," the crew leader addressed her. "It is Rose, right? We can patch the loose bricks right up and stay on the drive. We won't touch your work." He reached out a hand to shake. "Pretty flowers."

Brie stood in her bedroom, looking out her back window this time. The outline of a great blue heron showed in the dark. It perched on top of the watermelon-sized rocks that held the lake back from gushing over into the creek. Leaning against the side window trim, she waited.

Nathan came up behind her and wrapped his arms over and around her shoulders. "Feel better?"

She curled the tips of her fingers over his forearms. "Much. Thanks."

"Duncan's reaction..."

"Yes. I worry about him. Mother's privilege." She let her head drop back on his shoulder.

"Speaking of worry, did you ever find out more about the unused sleeping bag?"

Just as Nathan asked, she saw what she was waiting for and nodded her head toward the window. "See for yourself."

Nathan narrowed his eyes and stepped closer to the window as a bobbing light came from the direction of their house. "What the hell?"

"Wait, wait. Don't get too close...and...now."

A second light bobbed from across the creek, heading toward the bridge. Both led toward the guesthouse. Nathan laid his hand over his eyes. "I built that bridge. And the house."

"They're grown, Nathan. Are you going to go down there and ground him?" She took his hands, much like she'd done with Duncan earlier that day. "You might feel better that I found a missed condom wrapper on the floor when we were working the other day."

Nathan covered his ears. "Hear no evil."

She pulled him by his hands away from the window and to their bed.

When they were close enough they could see each other's faces, Rose watched as Andy turned off his flashlight and dropped it in the grass. He took the last several steps in two long strides, taking her face in his hands and kissing her deeply. The electricity hadn't faded or even come to be something she was used to. It intensified each time his urgent mouth took hers.

"There you are." He linked their fingers and pulled away, looking at her.

She wore her cut-off jean shorts, a summer tank and flip-flops.

"Mmm, hello." Turning, she pulled him inside. "Today was like old times."

He followed her and plopped on the wicker couch, propping his feet on the matching coffee table. Andy explained that the rest of the furniture was due later in the week...along with the air conditioning. "It's different with you as my girlfriend."

Girlfriend. How could she possibly be Andrew Reed's girlfriend? Distracted, she tried to keep up. "I hate bullies. They never grow up."

"We're not kids anymore. The dude's a jerk, but he's a full-grown jerk."

She sat down and faced him, watching his lips as he spoke. She pressed hers together. "I'm smart and I'm careful."

"You are smart." He set one of her feet, then the other onto his lap. "And hot-headed and not at all careful." He ran his thick hands up the length of her long and lanky legs, stopping only when he reached her hip. "And beautiful and sassy and I love every part of you."

At that, she pulled his shoulders down and slid under him. He lay on top of her while tucking her hair around her ear. He set his lips just underneath, then clicked off her flashlight.

Miniature flags stood in rows lining the fronts of the landscaping plots in the Reeds' lush backyard. A steady stream of relatives covering four generations came and went between the Reed home, their guesthouse and over the bridge to Brie's sister's home. Each bedroom, guest room and couch was claimed for the weekend.

The scene played out like a small town. With the scent of freshly cut grass and blooming lavender lofting around them, young parents chased their toddlers away from the creek. Parents of older children encouraged their kids to go in the creek. Grandparents manned the grill and organized a pick up game of baseball for all. The rest enjoyed time lounging in one of the many lawn chairs. Eight-foot folding tables were scattered along one side of the yard while the other side was covered with a maze of metal croquet hoops.

Andy sat with Rose inside the house at opposite ends of the double-leaf kitchen table among a small army of friends and family. Everyone reminisced, shared their most recent news and made plans for future get-togethers. Around them, a beehive of organized chaos worked to prepare food while supervising children.

Rose updated Brie on Charcoal's progress in his intermediate training class. "He knows the boundaries of the yard. Well, unless something small and furry is within eyesight."

Brie set her hand on top of Rose's, patting it twice. "Remember not to scold him when he returns. No matter how frustrated you are. Dogs are simple. If you scold them when they come home, they won't be so quick to come home."

Rose shook her head as she leaned around Brie, checking on Charcoal. He was on the deck with Macey and Goldie, who lay so still someone might think they had moved on to a better place if not for the rise and fall of their backs. Running around the two of them, the pup switched back and forth between sniffing his surroundings and nudging the two geezers. It was a gamble, she noticed. He would either break one down enough to play with him or earn a quick nip from experienced jaws.

"It is frustrating, but I'll keep at him. Sit and stay are all but mastered, again unless there is something furry to distract him, or his tail comes into view." Rose lit up a broad smile.

Andy noted the contrast of his home to her quiet house of four. Rose had the ability to seamlessly flip between settings. She wasn't the type that needed constant attention. But instead, fell into the antics of reunions, joining in on the practical jokes and chiding that seemed to be expected.

She caught his glance for a fraction of a second. Just long enough. She laughed with his aunt, tossing her head back in response to something he couldn't hear. He watched from his peripheral vision as she casually made her way out the front door, pausing to actively listen to whoever stopped her on the way. The blood drained from his head, but he worked to make small talk with passersby.

After an acceptable amount of time had passed, he pushed off from the table and slinked to the front door well aware of exactly where she would be waiting. He closed the door behind him as she pulled him to her, smashing mouths and twining limbs as closely as their upright, fully clothed bodies would allow.

When would this fade? After all the years, how could there be so much that was new? The little sounds she made when he touched her. They could always communicate with a look or a gesture. That grew along with the way they worked as a team in everything they did.

Then why was she suddenly pushing him away with both hands?

The look on her face made him sigh, long and heavy. "Hannah," he said.

Rose nodded half smiling, half sorrowful.

Squinting, he slowly pivoted to face his cousin.

Crossed arms, she looked smug with a hip cocked so far to the side she could have been double jointed. A cat with a canary. "You're making out with Rosemarie."

"Yes, I know that." Turning his head away from her slightly, he kept his eyes on hers. "How much?"

Hannah held out a hand, palm up. "Five bucks ought to do it."

He dipped his head and looked at her through his lashes as he dug in his pocket. He slapped the bill in her hand but didn't let go. "Swear to it." He felt a little pride in the canning of his younger cousin.

He and Rose watched until Hannah finished strutting around the side of the house toward the back.

"She had her arm wrenched behind her." Rose leaned a shoulder against the front of the house with one ankle crossing the other. "Likely had her fingers crossed."

"Do you care?" He walked up and placed his hands on her hips, closing the distance between them.

Rose shrugged. "It's handy."

"Annoying."

"Play it by ear?"

"Mmm." He covered her mouth with his and quickly forgot what they were talking about.

A small army formed. Sides were aligned, and arsenals of squirt guns and water balloons were chosen. Others picked up a last game of baseball out in the field behind the completed Reed guesthouse. Together, Rose and Andy taught a handful of the younger kids how to catch crawfish from the warm creek. When it was too dark to see the water any longer, they rinsed black mud from several sets of small toes.

"They liked getting their feet washed and dried nearly as much as squishing the mud between their toes." She let Andy collapse first in the hammock that stretched under the tall deck.

Crawling in next to him much like she'd done for years, she kept as much of a platonic distance between them as she could in a hammock. "True. It reminds me of when we were that age." She yawned quietly. "I feel like I haven't had a full night's sleep in weeks. Oh, yeah, I *haven't* had a full night's sleep in weeks."

Andy clasped his hands as a pillow behind his head.

Around them, parents covered snack food while the pyros from the group organized tubs of Black Cats and sparklers. Duncan was, as always, ringmaster of the larger fireworks.

Rocking in the hammock, she and Andy discussed their next weekend trip and decided on a change of pace to Binghamton rather than climbing at Catskills. She let out the air from her lungs. "Questions will come up if we run off to spend the weekend together there. It won't just be a climbing trip."

Her body tensed as Andy slipped an arm under her head and the other around her waist. "I'm pretty sure Brie already knows." He rotated her body, tucking her back close to him.

"Well, hell. I thought we were going to play it by ear."

Andy nipped her lobe and twined their legs. "Wake me up when Duncan is ready to start the boomers."

Shivering from the feel of Andy's teeth, she let her head lay limp on his arm. She snuggled against him, trying to ignore the dozens of pairs of eyes that would certainly be glued to them. Never had she dreamed this would happen. Andy. She'd been in love with him longer than she could remember. Had always expected they would be there for each other. As best friends.

Now, he was in love with her. With her. She would tell him. She would tell him of her feelings soon. And of her...idea.

The next few weeks felt like a well-oiled machine for Andy. Days building houses. Stolen evenings with his best friend and lover. Although part of him wanted to kick himself for missing the fact that she had been right under his nose all along. Another part, the more sensible part, knew any time before now would have been too soon.

It was a rare night when they would have more than just stolen moments on a blanket in front of the lake or at the guesthouse. Since the rain would have made either option uncomfortable, it worked out well that tonight was dinner out and the rest of the evening to spend together without being rushed or exhausted at a late hour.

But when he reached her house, she wasn't there. Neither was her mom or sister, or even the pup. It might not have been so unsettling, except her stepdad made it sound like he didn't know when she was coming back. Stepping away from the door, Dave silently invited him in. Holy shit, he was a big man. Getting a closer look, Andy added really pissed off to the description.

Dave said just two words, "Sit down."

A magnet seemed to pull Andy to the nearest chair. He sat upright, on the edge, trying hard to assess Dave's expression.

Towering, Dave slowly paced back and forth across the living room floor, fingers threaded through the belt loops on the back of his detective slacks.

Possibilities raced through Andy's head. "Is...Rose all right, sir?"

Dave stopped and looked him in the eyes. "Cut the sir shit." Then, leaned back against the middle shelf of their entertainment center.

Andy didn't know what to say. Claim ignorance? That would be sincere. He had no frigging clue what Dave was so mad about. Looking at his forever-intimidating gun holster, Andy decided on reverent silence. He watched Dave's eyes and movements carefully. Dave leaned over and pulled a short stack of papers from the shelf behind him.

His face reddened as he passed the pile to Andy. "What game are you playing, son?"

"Sir? ...I mean...Dave?" He took the papers but felt defensive at the accusation.

"Have you or have you not been sneaking around with my daughter?"

Sneaking around? What the hell? They were both legal adults, but...shit. Andy decided on the truth. This was Dave's daughter. "Well, yes, sort of, but it's not like that." Yes it is. "...it's new and confusing...I'm in with love her."

Dave shoved off from where he was propped and started back with the pacing, shoving his hands through the sides of his hair. "Have you thought about what this will do to her?"

Andy was definitely missing something. Sitting back in the chair, not just a little pissed off himself, he started leafing through the stack of papers. And his world crumbled beneath him.

CHAPTER 13

The first several papers were polite and articulate letters declining one NYU scholarship after another. The last was a class schedule for a junior college near Purdue University.

Her future, her dreams.

He dropped the papers in his lap, felt panic, confusion, and...betrayal. How could she keep this from him? They didn't keep anything from each other. Never had.

He crushed the papers in his fists as the palms of his hands dug in his eyes. Trying to make sense of this. Keeping his eyes closed, he dropped his hands listlessly onto his lap, letting the papers fall to the floor. Standing, he instinctively folded his hands on the top of his head. It was his turn to pace, to stutter. What was she thinking? He collapsed on the edge of the couch with his elbows on knees and face in his hands. Unconsciously, he rocked back and forth as he tried to think.

"You didn't know?" Dave sounded almost as shocked as Andy.

Andy's thoughts and feelings became a dense fog as fix-it mode took over. He sat up trying to shake his head clear. "I'll fix this. I can fix this. Let me talk to her. Where is she?"

"You really didn't know," Dave repeated.

"Of course I didn't know. Do you think I would let her do this?" He raised his voice. "Where is she?"

"We already tried talking to her. You know how she gets. *Don't tell me what I am supposed to do.* Ran out of the house slamming doors."

Hadn't she said those exact words to Andy a few shorts weeks before? Of course she didn't tell him. She'd already made up that damned stubborn mind of hers. That damned beautiful stubborn mind. This wasn't enough time. He'd just found her, found them.

"She made it sound like you were in it together. About being a grown woman. That she wasn't throwing away her future but following it."

"I'll fix it," Andy whispered and slowly let his lids drop.

Rain drizzled on her windshield. Rose decided to do what she always did. Swim instead of sink. It wasn't her fault her parents didn't agree with her. Life was more than following some beaten path. It was about following what you knew was right. Following your heart. You can't help who you love or when that love presents itself.

She wanted to be respectful to them. Realized that she'd ignored them as much as she did the wipers waving in front of her. She knew they were trying to do what they thought parents should do, but they simply didn't understand.

She wasn't throwing her life away. She was changing the direction. She could still work with animals. She'd mapped all this out. Veterinarian assistant, animal shelter supervisor. As she pulled back into her driveway, she decided to be fair, apologize to her parents and politely reiterate that she was old enough to make her own decisions about her future.

So, then why hadn't she told Andy about her plans, her...decisions? She sighed, admitting to herself a simple, basic fear. She hadn't even told him she was in love with him. He was just so...Andy. She would. Soon. No sinking.

When she walked into her home, it was eerily quiet. She found her mom and Dave sitting at the kitchen table. Not eating or speaking. Just sitting. The dog didn't even do more than beat his tail on the floor when she entered the room. Her sister was nowhere to be found. "Did Andy come by?" She tried for normal, but it came out as needy.

Her mom's bloodshot eyes turned to her. "Came and left."

Sweat began to form around the hairline behind her neck. Surely they wouldn't have told him about the letters. That was personal. "What did...you say to him?"

Dave answered, "I said you were gone."

Relief seeped partially back into her body. This she could handle. She could apologize for being late and make it up to him. Then why were her hands shaking?

"I'm sorry for getting carried away, raising my voice to you. He loves me. We want to be together."

Jittery, her mom responded, "We've said our piece. Now, you need to make your own decisions, your own mistakes."

"Andy is not a..." No, she wasn't starting that all over again. She placed one hand on top of her mom's, one on her stepfather's, then finished, "Thank you for always being there. I love you." As she left the silence of her kitchen, Rose thought of how warm Dave's hand felt. Her mother's cool and clammy.

Deciding to walk to Andy's, she took the time to soundly stuff the argument with her folks securely in her subconscious, right next to her reluctance to tell Andy her feelings and plans.

When she saw the Mustang in his drive, she felt reassured. She'd decided on dressy boots for the night. Not spiky heeled, but enough of a boost that she didn't look like a shrimp. A cream-colored, buttoned-down blouse lay just over her snug, light brown pants. Knowing she would still look out of place next to him, at least she would look prettier than when in her Chuck Taylors.

He came out before she reached the door without as much as a hello. All right, she thought. Opening the car door for her, he asked if she had a place in mind for dinner.

She shook her head as he shut the door and was sure he couldn't have seen her response. Driving awhile in silence, she felt uneasiness creep between them. It was the first time in her life she could remember silence with Andy as uncomfortable. "I'm sorry for being late. Where would you like to go?"

"Azulo's."

She looked intently into his face as he drove but could get nothing from his expression. Why wasn't he talking? Why wasn't she talking? Knots began to form in the back of her shoulders.

She didn't feel hungry anymore. She assumed he didn't either as they sat in the Italian restaurant with him mostly moving his food around on his plate.

He asked her how her day went and what her schedule was like for the next week. Hell, she could have been out to dinner with one of her teachers. The uneasiness changed to a cold that made her skin crawl.

The evening continued much the same all the way to her front porch. "Would you like to meet later tonight?" As they stood together, she played with one of the buttons on his shirt to make sure he didn't misunderstand.

"Maybe tomorrow." He looked in her eyes for an unsettling length of time.

"Okay." She shuddered as if she was cold in the hot, humid night. "Um...talk to you tomorrow then." She reached in her purse for her keys, thinking how unbearably different this was from their first embrace on her porch.

Taking them in her hand, she looked up to say goodnight. He took the sides of her face. Kissed her urgently. It wasn't sweet. He didn't touch her, other than her face. Just kissed her long and hard.

A cold chill crept down her spine like life was being pulled from it. He parted as she gasped, nearly losing her balance, mixing the uneasiness and cold into a solid fear.

Rose bounced out of bed at the sight of the buckets of early morning rain down her window. Feeling like she could smell it through the walls, she smiled and reached down to scratch Charcoal's belly. This much rain meant no landscaping today and no Greenberg Construction. She would work with Charcoal for a while on the signal to lie from across a room. She might try heeling up stairs and around corners. Then, she would drive to Andy's and see if he was able to sleep off his horrific mood.

Casually, she went through her regular morning ritual, waiting for an appropriate time to call.

"Good morning, Brie." Rose tapped her fingers on her thigh as she held the phone. "Did I catch you at a bad time?"

"No, no. What can I do for you?"

Hmm. Formal. "Is Andy up and around?"

The pause was long enough to unsettle her.

"No...he left for the Greenberg central office, I believe he said."

"Oh." No offer to leave a message? She chided herself for being ridiculous. Andy loves her. How many times had he said it now? How many plans had they made? How many talks of the future? "Well, thank you. I'll try him later."

Don Greenberg was a middle-aged man with the beginnings of a pouch bulging over his belt. Average height and balding, he still held an air of confidence and efficiency Andy respected. He also knew everyone and everything about running a general contracting business. "Come on in, son. Tell me what ails you."

Nearing retirement, Don was easygoing and Andy recognized how much he enjoyed on-the-spot meetings. That would make this easier since the numbness had yet to subside. Andy was simply a machine going through the motions. "Things are going well on the job, honestly, thanks. I do think I might be able to save you near fifty grand, sir. Something I noticed on a site this week."

"I can always do with an extra fifty grand. Sit down, boy. Tell me your idea. I sure do admire a boy with ideas." Don leaned back in his reclining office chair behind his desk.

Andy unrolled a copy of well-worn blueprints. He explained that if the planned water lines, along a set of roughed-in city blocks in particular, were moved about eight feet north, it would save the surveyors and civil engineers time and cost in rerouting around a dozen full grown native trees. "You see here," Andy gestured to the prints. "Trees are scattered through this area." He pointed out a spot between a trio of penciled-in dots.

Don sat back and scratched his chin. "You know, this is really a job for the civils. Have you mentioned this to them?"

Andy copied his movements and also sat back in his chair. "Well, sir. Working under both the surveyors and the civils, I guess I could say that I've noticed they don't too much like to talk to one another. Since I'm with the surveyors, I wasn't sure that would be such a good idea."

Don closed his eyes in some kind of pleasant memory. "Ah. How times don't change. I appreciate the tip, Andy." He lifted from his chair and stuck out his hand in appreciation. "I'll get out there myself as soon as it's dry enough." Looking down his nose, Don added, "Is there anything else?"

Andy took his hand, held on too tightly, before realizing it and sitting back down. He knew what he had to say but couldn't seem to get his mouth to move with the weight that pressed down on his chest. After a full minute of grinding his teeth, he began.

Rose stood in the pitch black on the flat porch of the Reeds' guesthouse. Waiting. The cloud cover made the dark unsettling since she'd turned her flashlight off. She craved the feel of Andy's rough hands around hers. The sound of his voice when he told her he loved her. They would talk. She would make him. It was ridiculous how happy the far away bob of light made her feel.

She'd decided this would be the night she told him how she felt. It was probably the reason for his distance lately. Wouldn't she feel taken aback if she had said those words to him and he hadn't returned them in months? But he was Andrew Reed. She was just Rose. He was designer jeans and fainting good looks. She was bandanas and skin and bones.

When he came close enough that Rose could see his eyes, she sunk. No expression. No greeting. Just a kiss on the forehead.

The words stuck in her throat as she followed him to the back guestroom. He found the remote and sat alone in the wicker chair leaving the couch for her. After a moment, she lowered herself to the couch.

Thinking she might snap, she asked what she didn't want to know, "What's the matter with you?"

His eyes didn't leave the television. "Matter?"

She walked over and turned off the set and stood in front of it. "Yes. Matter."

The muscles in his jaw bulged before he took a breath and turned to meet her eyes. "I'm going to crash early tonight. Let's finish this tomorrow." As if she hadn't asked a question, he walked to her, gave her hand a squeeze and another kiss on top of her head. "See you then, all right? Same time?"

He didn't walk her home. She spent most of the night with her eyes open, curled in her sheets with both feet tucked under the weight of Charcoal.

The next day was her zoo shift. Andy's site was still muddy and inaccessible. She generally didn't mind working in the wet or even the rain. But, knowing that Andy had the day off made her feel left out of...of something. The feeling of panic and desperation took her over and made it impossible to think.

She spent the morning going through the motions of work, assisting the head zookeeper prepare bamboo leaves and formulated pellets for the red pandas and a mix of fruits for the tamarin monkeys. She walked silently along the concrete pathway from exhibit to exhibit, placing food trays in enclosures and dead chicks onto stands for the bald eagles and red-tailed hawks.

Numbness began to take her when she forced herself to remember that it was Andy who initiated their meeting that night.

During dinner, Charcoal sat on the carpet at the edge of the kitchen linoleum. She wished her mom would eat more. She was becoming so thin. She knew Dave worried and that they fought about it. They loved each other; she was sure of that. But she was feeling confused as to what love was supposed to look like. Feel like.

Jessica rambled on about her latest love interest. At the age of twelve, they lasted between three and four days. Rose looked around at her family and thought of how different it would be in just a few weeks when she moved out, when she moved to her future.

It was well past dark when she tiptoed out her back door, quickly walking down her cul-de-sac toward Black Creek. She cut between houses before turning on her flashlight. It was slightly overcast but not enough that she couldn't still see Andy waiting on the bridge for her. How sweet.

He stood in a light jacket, collared polo and worn jeans. Resting his forearms on the smooth rail, he looked toward the rippling lake.

She walked to him and reached for his hand. He turned to face her and placed his into his pockets. This time she could read his face. And it petrified her.

"Listen." He looked down to her. "We've been friends a long time."

Best friends and our entire lives, she corrected in her mind.

"I've decided to take off early."

The fear of understanding began to wrap around her feet and held them to the bridge beneath her.

"We've tried this dating thing. It's not working for me."

The fear crept higher, wrapping around her torso and strangling her lungs, her heart. She could feel her head slowly start to shake back and forth but words couldn't escape her choking throat.

Looking deep into the caramel of his eyes, she tried to see something. But what she saw confused her. A hole began to open in her heart. Gaping. More painful than anything she'd ever experienced. She didn't remember telling her lips to speak, just that they did. "I love you." She vaguely sensed a steady stream of tears that fell over her lids and down her cheeks.

There was no spark in his eyes from her declaration. No yearning. No regret. That was it? All this and then, *It's not working for me?* Andy's expression remained exactly as it was. Unreadable. He stood with his jaw flexing, eyelids half opened, staring at her as her knees began to buckle under her weight. There was no offer to hold her up this time.

Finally, he answered, "You're really just not my type."

And at that, she felt the wooden slats of the bridge hit her knees hard as she dropped. She welcomed the physical pain. The backs of her hands lay limp on her thighs as her shoulders shook madly.

"Don't write me this time," she heard him say as he meandered casually away from her.

To keep her head from exploding, she pressed her hands, fingers spread as hard as she could to around her ears, her face and let herself fall to her side onto the cool, damp boards. Somehow she sensed that she wailed loudly, but inside her head was a swirl of muffled noise. Curling into a ball, she lay listening to the sound of the water rush away beneath her, taking her heart along with it.

Amanda stood defensively against the counter in their kitchen, eyes bloodshot, hands shaking. "This is textbook eighteen-year-old," she barked. "You tell them what they can't do and they're going to do the opposite."

"Are we gonna wait until we wake up one day and find her gone? She's our responsibility. Damn it, Amanda. Think about it." Dave hit the palm of his hand on the kitchen wall near the phone.

"Nolans'." He ran a hand over his head and then stopped, grabbing the back of his neck. "Where? How long?"

Sloppily, Amanda grabbed his shirt.

"We'll go get her." He dropped his head. "Don't be, Andy. Take care of yourself."

"Mom. Dad." Duncan never walked into his aunt and uncle's bedroom this late at night.

They had been sleeping, but turned on the light in response to the awkwardness of his interruption.

"I heard something in the garage. Andy's car is gone. He's gone."

"He's nineteen, Duncan. He can leave the house if he wants to at..." Nathan looked toward the red digital numbers and looked back. "...one thirty. Shit." He swung his legs to the floor and sat up.

"I went to check. There are two fist-sized holes in the drywall. His room is empty. My wallet was open. He took my driver's license."

Both Nathan and Brie got out of bed. Pulling on a pair of pants, Nathan asked him what else he knew.

Duncan shook his head. "I looked in his room. It's ...well, clean. The dressers are cleared off. I think I know where he might have gone. I'm going to check around. Why don't you call over to the Nolans'? I'll call you if I find him."

Duncan did find him just where he'd suspected. Andy was at the dark end of the long wooden bar at Mikey's Pub and Grill, staring at the shot of whiskey in front of him.

He walked toward his little brother cautiously. Barely on his bar stool, Andy tossed back the shot and hesitated before setting the glass back down on the scuffed counter.

The bartender efficiently took it and glanced up at Duncan, understanding they must be together. "Glad you're here. I was about to call him a cab. Just about closing time."

Andy must have had enough presence to figure out that the bartender was speaking about him. He turned his head groggily to see who was there. "F-f-fuck," he slurred when his eyes landed on Duncan. Then, he signaled for another shot.

"Enough, Andy. We're leaving."

"Fuck you." Andy missed his hand as he tried to set his chin on his palm.

He'd never seen his brother drunk. "It's closing time, Andy. I'm taking you home."

Duncan paid the bill and was relieved when Andy followed like a mindless puppy.

Hanging onto him, Duncan said one word in question, "Rose?"

Andy's eyelids slowly drooped closed and opened again. "Mind your own f-f-fucking business."

Carrying much of his weight, he led Andy toward his car. "We can come back and get the Mustang in the morning. Let's get you to bed."

Andy shook his head and held his hand out to stop himself, hitting only air. "Not going back. New York."

"You were going to drive to the city? Tonight? Drunk?" He pulled Andy reluctantly along.

"Didn't think that far." Andy stopped and held his stomach. "I'm not going back," he repeated before tossing up half the whiskey while bracing against the nearest tree.

He leaned Andy against the puke-free side of the oak, looking for some answers. "Okay. Talk."

Andy took three long breaths. "I'm gonna go stay with Chase. I've got all my sh-shit. Shit." He turned around and walked toward the Mustang. Duncan felt at least a little better when Andy waited by the passenger door.

Okay, Duncan thought. "Driving into the city tonight. No problem," he muttered sarcastically. "All right, Andy. All right. Let me call Nathan and Brie. You should have told them."

CHAPTER 14

Eight Years Later...

"This is Jenna Woith reporting for WCEL TV here at the Seneca Botanical Gardens where a pair of wild eaglets are about to be banded. A crowd of just over a hundred is waiting eagerly this morning as Dr. Rosemarie Piper climbs to where the nest lay twined in branches nearly ninety feet in the air. Jay, pan the tree, if you would, please."

The crowd stood in a semicircle behind a line of yellow caution tape secured by staggered saw horses. Behind them spread acres of thick green grass, trimmed to precision and framed with large clusters of coordinated color from hundreds of different flowering trees, bushes and perennials. Eager spectators ranged in age from the very young to the very old and nearly all held binoculars zoned in on Rose. The reporter spoke into a microphone that not only recorded for the station but amplified for the crowd. She was used to it. She wore a pair of loose-fitting carpenter pants, climbing shoes and a hard hat secured over her red bandana. Her slender, muscular legs held her easily between branches of the American Sycamore.

The bucket of the cherry picker reached only seventy feet into the warm, sunny sky. She created an organized maze of leads and safety lines so she could climb the rest of the way to the nest. Slowly, she loaded the first compliant eaglet into what would look like a common duffel bag to the cameraman below.

She noticed as the reporter rotated her stance and slightly faced Rose's assistant who stood next to her while Jenna still profiled the camera. "Next to me is Dr. Piper's assistant, Graciela Perez. Miss Perez, can you give us an idea of what we are about to see here?" Jenna craned her head up toward Rose and shivered.

As Rose began to use a simple pulley system to send down the first eaglet, she kept an eye on her favorite assistant. Grace stood in sandals and tight jeans that hugged her healthy hips. Her shiny, brown hair tied in a low ponytail, exposing her black eyes and the smooth, caramel color of her face.

Grace pulled her head back a bit. It made Rose smile. Grace never could get used to the microphones. They had been together since Rose was one of Grace's professor's TAs in grad school. Grace was more into parties than worrying about little things like a doctorate. Rose watched as she prepared herself to give this speech for the twelfth time this season. Grace took a deep breath and began explaining the first eaglet's descent, followed by descriptions of the myriad of measuring instruments that waited on a long, rectangular table in the center of the group of onlookers.

Andy faked patience like a pro. He schmoozed the oldest builder in central upstate New York into letting him in on some lots in the new Country Club Estates II subdivision. Knowing he owed Don Greenberg a beer for the contact, he reaffirmed his commitment of quality to the older builder he had on the other end of his cell and listened to the latest story about his grandchildren. Uncharacteristically, Andy was only half listening. Mostly, he was watching the WCEL broadcast.

The times he saw Rose were few and far between, each the same punch as the one before. A mixture of pride for her success and a stabbing pain at the sight of her choked him.

Hanging up the phone, he propped his feet on the walnut desk his uncle had made for him. The expansive top was stained dark, exposing the tight lines of grain. The sides were complicated without being ornate. It was the centerpiece of his office and portrayed an image of sturdiness and proficiency, which was exactly what Andy was going for. Nathan was a genius.

Lifting his arm, he tilted the remote so it could reach his office television to raise the volume. His secretary rang him twice through the intercom, then gave up and texted him. *If you keep ignoring me, I'll have to tell your mother.*

Since Delores only recently learned to text, he laughed and walked out to see what she wanted.

Completely gray, she had lines scattering from eyes that could light up any room. She'd worked part time for him for going on three years. They'd grown as a team, and together built Reed Builders from the ground up.

He hardly made it out of his office before she began, "You've got an eleven o'clock with the excavator at the Fox Hills business strip. Jonathon wants his summer job back this year. Here are your phone messages, and you need me here more than part time."

"Push the eleven back a half hour. I'll call John myself, and why would I hire you full time when you do full-time work in a half day?" Although he could probably afford it now, she had bridge, her Silver Sneakers class and a standing hair appointment-thing every Thursday afternoon. He took the phone messages from her hand and winked.

"You keep up that flirting and I'll move myself to the front of that line of girls you have following you."

He shot her a toothy smile before heading back to his office, pulling a set of blue prints from his stack. He had just enough time to see about modifying the space over the garage on a lot in Country Club II. Unconsciously, he picked up the remote and pointed it behind him toward the television as he walked around his desk.

Her assistant held one of the eaglets on its back like a baby while Rose measured its beak, talons and tail feathers. She spoke into the microphone as she worked, moving around as if it weren't there. "The bald eagle has made a sizeable recovery thanks mostly to the Endangered Species Act. Although it's no longer on the Endangered Species list, it is still a highly protected animal. We're the ones who are partially responsible for the senseless death of these helpless creatures through environmental threats and loss of habitat. We're the ones who need to help protect them from those dangers now."

Pulling out a set of pliers, Rose took a silver band and gingerly wrapped it around the bird's enormous foot. "The eaglets each receive two bands. This first one..." She took the tool and firmly secured the ends together. "...is a rivet band issued by the US Fish and Wildlife Service." After checking that it fit comfortably, she picked up the second.

The eaglet flexed and grabbed with its talons. "He may be young, but his talons can effortlessly slice through skin." She waited patiently for it to calm. "The other band I have here is an auxiliary band. Notice the bright color and large numbers. The bird will be easily identified with binoculars using this band. Each habitat area has its own color. This bold blue means New York. You can help by supporting The Center for Conservation Biology, the National Foundation to Protect America's Eagles and, of course, the Birds of Prey Research and Action Center." She added the latter as a plug for the center she currently worked day in and day out.

Grace walked around passing out pamphlets regarding these centers and others as Rose worked the television reporter for a few more bites of advertising.

"There is a threat, right now, to one of the migratory wintering grounds of the highly threatened Whooping crane in western Florida. Developers have offered a local reservist an offer he apparently couldn't refuse. We'll be departing within the week to hold a protest." Gently, she placed one of the eaglets in an ordinary looking green plastic tub and then placed the tub on a scale while rattling off numbers to Grace.

Before it was time to haul the birds back up to their nest, Rose walked around and permitted the visitors a semi-closer look while allowing a question and answer session. Realizing how crucial donated funds were to the action center, she took her time answering questions while emphasizing conservation efforts.

The Northeast was fortunate to have a biologist who could not only band the eaglets but could do the climbing herself. Rose liked to do things on her own. But she was sensible enough to know she couldn't do everything alone. Hired an assistant, hadn't she? She just preferred doing things herself when at all possible. The interns were a different story. As an undergrad at NYU, she had been granted several prosperous internships in dozens of capacities. In return, she provided the same opportunities to promising interns whenever possible.

Methodically, her table, supplies and equipment were packed in the back of her truck. She climbed in, but before turning the ignition, rotated to Grace who sat in the backseat. "What the hell are you doing back there?"

Grace politely pointed a thumb out the passenger window, then rolled her eyes as she looked away. The door opened to a professor of ornithology who pulled himself up to the passenger seat by the hand grab attached to the ceiling.

"Hello, love." He leaned over and kissed Rose on the mouth. "Sorry to have missed your show."

She laid her hand on his cheek. "It's no big, but you know it's not a *show*." She turned away and looked out the front windshield, starting up the truck.

"No, of course it's not. I meant your presentation." He buckled his belt and waved off his ride. "I came to help you, darling."

Pulling the truck into gear, she looked at him. "I've got blogs to check, Oliver, a site to update, an intern to chew out, and avian chicken pox to scrape from an eaglet's beak. I'm not sure what you could help with, but you're welcome to come and hang out." She looked in the rearview mirror, knowing Grace would be looking back. Slyly, she squinted at her before accelerating.

The trip was one of their shorter ones. The Birds of Prey Research and Action Center was only an hour north of the botanical gardens. She and Grace generally had several hours behind the wheel to and from banding sites.

As she drove, the Whooping crane protest burned a hole in the back of her mind. She'd already used a half dozen of her media connections to line up a nice showing for the damned developer. Getting there was another story. How would she, in this lifetime, afford to fly both her and Grace to Florida and back?

The action center nestled comfortably in a valley between hills and along Seneca Lake. Large Shiloh pines filled the landscape. Behind the facility, a large field provided the perfect spot for presentations, fundraisers and activities for classroom field trips.

They pulled up on the gravel drive and parked in the farthest visitor's spot just as a group of small children walked out of the main building with their parents. The structure was efficient. Off the lobby was her office; the office of the owner and director, Biologist Dr. Paul Gray; and a break room for the interns and receptionist. To the back of the building was an enormous area with small habitats scattered around the perimeter. The center housed mostly animals that were in the process of rehabilitation. Many would be reintroduced back into the wild, yet some had been permanently injured and the center served as their home.

"Love...I, err, need to check my voice mail and I'd like to use your big screen to check my email. I'll come out and help in a few minutes?" Oliver gave her fingers a squeeze as he kissed her on the cheek before heading to her office.

Threateningly, Rose pointed a finger at Grace before she had a chance to chide Rose about Oliver shirking a hand at unpacking the gear. "I'm not looking for a pack mule. I can take care of myself. Let's get this stuff into the shed and go inside to see if we can find Mr. Bend-the-Rules." Using a dolly, they hauled the load into one of a dozen metal sheds, locked it up and headed across the side of the field to the back door.

When they entered the lobby, the suspect intern stood behind the reception counter at the computer. Tall, sandy brown hair curled over his ears and lay on his neck. She walked and stood opposite him.

Overtly, Grace pretended to blend in with the scenery.

Without greeting or warning, Rose spoke up, "Don't think just because you're a grad student it means you can make administrative decisions around here. I hired you, Wes, granted at shit for pay, because I think you have potential. If you use that potential to do the undergrads' work again, I'm going to kick your potential ass out of here. I'm the boss and when I tell the undergrads to do something, I want them to do it." Frustrated because he wouldn't look her in the eye, she dipped her head down to where his gaze pointed.

Wes turned to focus on the other side of her.

Silence. More silence.

Moving her head dramatically over to where his gaze wandered, she asked, "Well?"

"Well, Dr. Piper, they asked me if I would just close up for th...okay...yes...I see what you're saying and..."

"How can you see what I'm saying when you won't look at

me?"

Wes' chest expanded slowly, then he exhaled deeply. But instead of looking to her, he focused over her shoulder. She turned to see Grace was clearly holding back a smile.

"Oh, hell. Listen to me. If you're going to make it around here, you're going to need to know the difference between teamwork and being a doormat. You're a quick study with good ideas. Let the others learn for themselves. That's. Why. They're. Here," she said, poking at his chest with each word. She looked over at the clock on the wall. "And clock the hell out. It's past time for you to be here."

Wes did as he was told and walked toward the door in his baggy jeans and work polo. Grace stood in front of it with a wide smile and whispered, "She likes you, ya know." Then, opened the door for him.

Doing a double take at Grace and blushing, he looked at the floor and walked out to his car.

"Isn't he just the cutest thing?" Grace asked as they turned for Rose's office.

"If you say so, in that so-cute-I-can't-speak sort of way."

As she and Grace turned together, they both stopped short when they noticed Dr. Gray leaning against his doorjamb, arms crossed with a brow lifted high.

A thin-brimmed leather hat circled his head and well-worn work boots on his feet. "I was never that hard on you."

She smiled adoringly at him. "I never needed it."

"Point taken. How is Wart coming along?"

"Shall I give you a lecture on the problems associated with naming a wild animal?"

"You know the likelihood of her reintroduction into the wild is slim. She hasn't been with her parents for weeks now. How is the pox looking?"

She sighed at the thought of the bald eagle spending its life in captivity. "Much better. It doesn't look like there'll be permanent damage, and she eats just fine if I keep the wart...I mean the pox shaved." She shook her head. "Her wings are strong. She needs a bigger space to fly, as all the rehabs do."

Dr. Gray set his hand on her shoulder. "Do what you can, Rose. Then, let the rest go," he said and headed back into his office.

As she wandered to her office, she stopped at the sight of Oliver. Damn it, she'd forgotten he was there. Standing in the doorway, she realized he didn't notice her. She was going to spend the rest of her life with him. He was definitely maintenance free, she reminded herself. That was a plus. Cute in his professor sort of way. They certainly had a lot in common. She cleared her throat.

Looking up at her, then at his watch, Oliver blushed. "So sorry, dear. Did you finish already? I must have gotten caught up. What can I do to help?"

She walked to him and kissed him lightly. "You can get out of my chair."

She answered questions on her blog, put out a new post regarding a class for the public featuring Wart, or N3, as was the eagle's public name. Then, listened to her voice mail while checking her calendar for the following week. In between the daily chores of running the action center, she had an eaglet banding near Chesapeake Bay on Monday; field trips for third-through sixth-graders Tuesday; a new intern coming to apply for the summer position Wednesday; followed by a trip to see her mother and dropping off Charcoal—all between caring for the present occupants and any that would be brought to the center between now and then. She decided on Thursday and through the weekend, if necessary, for the Florida protest. She would rearrange those days for it. Damned developers. Dollar signs in their eyes and to hell with the wildlife.

She sent out a few tweets, posted on the action center social network page and pulled a few more strings with the media. She was hoping for a helicopter.

She was smart. She knew the deal was likely set and the developers probably cared about the protesters little more than they did the Whooping cranes. Her objective was aimed at the land reservists. She needed the next in line, anywhere along the east side of the country, to think twice before selling any locally owned land reserves to the highest bidder.

Andy meandered up the drive of his uncle's home, admiring the professional work Brie had done with the landscaping. He could kick himself for keeping his business and his personal life separate and not hiring her for his new construction sites. She was good. Really good. Late spring flowers bloomed in front of dying early spring color. Clusters of different shades of green were organized, yet weren't overbearing or overdone.

He took the first of two floral arrangements from the passenger seat of his Maserati. Climbing the porch stairs, he ran his hands along the smooth, square pillars. Andy stuck his face into the bouquet and smelled the mixture of freesia and daffodils, then opened the massive front door.

The voices of his aunt and Amanda came from the kitchen in the back of the house. He frowned down at the flowers. Turning, he traced his steps back to his car to get the second bouquet. He would have to make another stop at the florist and replace the bunch meant for the elderly Lucy Melbourne before he gave her a Mother's Day visit.

Walking through the front door, he raised his voice loud enough for the women to hear him from the kitchen. "Aren't you worried about who is walking in and out of your home unannounced?"

Reaching the kitchen, Brie and Amanda beamed at the sight of the flowers. Women, he thought. They can be so easy sometimes.

"You came announced all right. We heard your car from down the street. Between you and your dad, we could have a dealership right in the drive." Brie took the flowers from him. "They're lovely, Andy. Thank you so much."

Ensuring the second bouquet was safely held to the side, he pulled her into a tight hug. "Happy Mother's Day, Ma." Turning to Amanda, he held out the other. "And happy Mother's Day to you, Amanda."

She hit him playfully on the shoulder. "You know these weren't for me, but I'll take them anyway." She kissed him on the cheek, then followed his aunt to get a vase.

"Amanda was catching me up on the plans for Jessica's wedding. Have you mailed your RSVP?"

"RSV who? Jess knows I'm going. I ran into her last week."

Brie shook her head dramatically. "I'll check on the card, Amanda." She turned her gaze back to Andy. "Are you bringing a date?"

He looked at her from the corner of his eyes. "I can probably find one of those."

"I convinced Jessica to go ahead with an open bar," Amanda

interjected. "I'll be fine with it. It's been three years, six months and twelve days, but I understand why they get worried. So, you come, Andy. Bring a date and have yourself a nice time."

He realized she was completely sincere. She looked healthy, he thought. Strong. She had color in her cheeks and had put on weight, although it was hard to notice with the work apron she seemed to wear every time he saw her now.

The vast local reserve was dotted with large shallow bodies of water. Rose couldn't decide if they were large ponds or small lakes. Regardless, the low water was perfect for Whooping cranes as they searched for snails, crabs and snakes while wading on their stilt legs. It was not meant for a shopping mall and office strip.

Trees huddled in clusters, erupting from the light brown soil that framed the water's edge. Bulldozers stood empty in the dawn ready for the drivers to start their careless destruction. For crying out loud, the cranes were so close to her, she could see a pair through her binoculars. They towered at five feet tall and were solid white with a blood red patch on top of their heads.

The support of the public continually impressed her. Donations, time. It looked like a few hundred faithful followers were there, along with a half-dozen media vans. According to the response from the social networking site, people attending were from fourteen different states and from Mexico. She'd been worried she might have forked out the funds to fly herself and Grace down here just to find out the media had a different breaking story. Yet, here they were. In force. She squinted and smiled.

Grace handed her the bullhorn. Rose did her best to prepare the crowd for what would likely emerge and to fire them up with whatever statistic she thought would be the most inspiring.

Slowly rotating the bullhorn, she spoke earnestly, making introductions and carefully describing the lay of the land. As she spoke, she made sure to face in the general direction of the television cameras and radio microphones.

"Due to human hunting, the Whooping crane population dwindled to a mere twenty-two in the 1940s. The folks at Operation Migration have sweat blood and tears to raise crane chicks and act as their parents, guiding them behind their glider planes to locales very near here. It costs over a hundred grand per chick to pay for the feed, equipment and cost of flying them behind the trikes to their wintering sites."

She gestured with her hands, encouraging the crowd as they created a sea of disgusted mumbles. "The local reservist who owns this land decided money was more important than a species." The crowd erupted into shouts of jeers and boos. She nodded her head dramatically as she and Grace rotated, back to back, like a team.

"Brady Construction swooped down on this property with its shopping mall blueprints and truckloads of waiting asphalt without one glance at the magnificent creatures just to the west of us. And we are here to say, 'No!' Someone has to stand up for those that can't help themselves!" Dramatically, she sighed at the sight of dust from a line of the first heavy equipment operators reporting for work.

Signaling to the mob, they circled the dormant earth movers and sat.

The construction crew was forced to park far away from the lines of vehicles and walk through the crowd. She lifted the bullhorn back to her mouth. "We must remember that we are the civilized in this face-off. We are here to exercise our right to protest and must keep our hands and objects off the workers at all times."

Grace rotated her head and whispered in her ear, "Mood killer."

Rose elbowed her in the back of the ribs. Watching the crew head to their equipment, she was always surprised at the number of relatively small and skinny heavy equipment operators. She always expected big, burly men. Noticing the one on his cell phone, she decided he must be the foreman. Go ahead and make that call. She smirked.

The operators kept their distance, waiting like they were in a standoff. The protestors held their ground. It took less than an hour for a set of black SUVs to dust up the gravel road out to the reserve. As Mr. Brady found the same problem with parking as his employees, he pulled into a spot well away from the commotion and stepped out with his own bullhorn.

Show time. Rose grinned.

She heard the helicopter flying overhead but kept her eyes on

Brady. She wanted to give the flyby a good shot. Both she and the developer turned when it was clear the copter was making a landing. It was small. Looked like a two-seater. When that passenger stepped out with briefcase in hand, she felt her face redden and her clutched hands turned all sorts of colors of red. She knew that damned walk anywhere.

Andy.

CHAPTER 15

Andy avoided asking his uncle for much of anything. Nathan had given up enough, in Andy's opinion, when he took in him and Duncan as toddlers. But, he needed a plane and a pilot and had needed them fast. And, it wasn't for him, exactly. It was to help out an old family friend. Well, it would turn out to be for him once the economy picked up again. But for now, he was just making a wise investment. And helping Rose.

Her reaction was just what he'd expected. Pissed as hell and ready for battle. In this case, he wouldn't want her any other way. His reaction was what he was never prepared for—a choke hold on his heart that seared through him. Her low-heeled leather boots and khaki dress pants hid what he knew was underneath. Smart and dangerous. Her round cheeks and porcelain skin concealed the best friend he had lost. She'd cut her hair. Andy was used to it now, short and croppy, exposing the nape of her neck. The t-shirt she wore mostly covered a blouse that matched the blue of her eyes. He could read the large print even from the distance. *Craniac.* Shit. He let out a half-laugh.

As he walked toward Mr. Brady, he kept an eye on her. She recognized him, of course, but hesitated. Analyzing what the hell he was doing. Good. Let her wonder.

Nodding to her as if passing on a sidewalk in the old neighborhood, he saw her eyes widen with rage. He wanted the developer to see that he and Rose knew each other. He could use that. The look on Brady's face said, *young, dumb real estate agent with waste-of-time deal.* He could use that, too. He'd done his homework like any good businessman would do. Brady had been iffy on this deal from the get go. Andy knew he could get him and he had a sixth sense for that kind of thing.

Keeping Rose in his peripheral vision, he approached Brady with an outstretched arm. Using a firm grip, he shook with the developer. "Insane, isn't it? Damned tree-huggers. It's a bird deal this time, right?"

Brady nodded.

"Oh, sorry. Name's Reed, Andy Reed. See that pretty little lady with the bullhorn getting ready to make her way on over here?" He turned, then shook his head. "That would be one Dr. Rosemarie Piper. Nasty as they come."

Mr. Brady had to yell over the rumble of the crowd. "Listen, boy, I assume you've come all the way out here to..."

"You've got that right, Mr. Brady, sir. We builders have to stick together. We're not breaking any laws. If the good people of this country didn't want our services, we wouldn't be in business, now would we?" He crossed his arms and shifted his weight between his legs.

"I think it's only fair to let you know Dr. Piper and I have been in our share of scuffles. Look. There. She's making a plan with her assistant." He let out an exaggerated shiver.

Brady looked around at the crowd. "Free damned country all right."

"And sometimes that freedom comes back to bite us. I've got a list here of business owners and developers Dr. Piper there has placed on her hit list and it looks like you're the new addition. Like I said, nasty. She knows the law, sir. Works around it. Digs in until she wins. This is just a sample of her followers."

Brady frowned. "Get to the point, boy."

Andy pulled out the first contract he'd drawn up on out-of-date carbonless paper in triplicate. "This is my offer. It's nearly double what you paid. The rent from the mall's a gamble. We both know that." The next set of papers was full of graphs and stats. "These." He placed them in Brady's hand. "These are hundred-year rain reports, hurricane data. You can get rid of a weather gamble, tree huggers and a swamp, and make a profit in one swipe of your signature."

Brady scratched the back of his ear as he watched Rose start to make her way over to him. "Boy, I've got all these equipment operators out here. Your deal's tempting, no doubt..."

Andy pulled out the second contract he had prepared. He held up his empty hand, palm forward. "I get it. I get it. Let me add this to the deal so we can pay these fine men for their time and trouble." He forced back a smile at the look on Brady's face from the offer. "All you have to do is sign; let me take care of the mob and Queen Mob on her way over here, sir. You keep your good name in these parts. I'll take the fall."

He hadn't anticipated the sincere satisfaction from helping the...whatever the hell animal it was he was helping. He smiled, not only for the developer's handshake, but for the benefit of Rose who looked sexy as hell as she reached them.

The contract was already in review with Brady's lawyer and the check practically passing between them. He felt pretty damned smug. Smug until Rose gave him an earful.

"You selfish, money hungry, heartless son of a bitch." Her chin seemed to arrive three steps before the rest of her. Elbows locked, fists bundled. "You think all these people are going to just stand by here while you outbid a species into extinction just to fill your damned pockets?"

He could swear he heard her growl. It was a good thing he knew her like he did, because she spun around like lightning, aiming her heel right at the side of his head. Her foot came to a screeching halt in his hand. She nearly lost her balance, panting like she'd just run a marathon and juggling to stand on one leg.

From behind Rose, he spotted who he figured was her assistant with one hand on the side of her head and the other outstretched as if she could somehow stop what was going on from a hundred yards away.

The crowd silenced as he held Rose's foot near the side of his face. His smile dropped. He waited a beat. "I know that move," he said quietly to only her before releasing her leg. She looked more shocked at her outburst than he was. He turned from her and faced Brady who was clearly glad to be rid of the mess. The old man held Andy's copy of the signed contract out awkwardly.

"All rights to the property become mine." Andy knew you could say almost anything with a smile on your face. "Take your time getting the equipment moved. I'm in no hurry."

Without acknowledging Rose, he picked up Mr. Brady's bullhorn and headed closer to the crowd that was now standing and booing him. He lit his best killer smile and humbly raised his hands. "If I could have your attention, please. Just for a moment, please." He knew they could hear him. Knew that Rose was standing, full of herself, behind him. "If I don't buy this land, how long do you think you can hold back the bulldozers? If I don't buy this land, how long before someone else does?" He dipped his head slightly in humility as the crowd quieted. He could feel Rose's glare pierce holes in the back of his head. "The perimeter of this land will be sold in two-acre lots to buyers who are willing to pay substantially more per acre in order to preserve the territory and keep it a haven for the..." He looked to Rose as her mouth gaped open.

She shut her eyes in disgust and answered him with two words, "Whooping cranes."

"...haven for the Whooping cranes. The back of the lots will stop no closer to the habitats than can be reached with a powerful set of binoculars. As an incentive to preserve the land, the owners will have their names embossed on a special plaque under a solid marble carving of a life-size Whooping crane. I've already got over a half-dozen enthusiastic..." He looked back at Rose pleadingly.

With her eyes still half closed, she answered, "Craniacs."

"...half-dozen craniacs interested in building."

The crowd looked at Rose, at each other, then back at Rose before erupting in applause. He handed out copies of sample agreements as both a way to please the crowd and to get the word out to any potential buyers. I am good, he thought. However, the clock was ticking, the helicopter was paid by the hour and not part of his uncle's favor. He turned to give himself one last look at her before leaving. She stood a few feet away. Squinting. Arms crossed. Smirking? What the hell?

"You promised a life-sized carving of a Whooping crane? With room for engraving?"

"That's right. More incentive to look good and keep their promise to give the birds their protection." He smiled wide.

She smiled back. "How much are you making on this, Andy? Because you just promised to carve a bird that tops five feet tall out of solid marble. With room for engraving."

He leaned his head in, close to her ear as he neared her. "Two hundred-fifty grand."

He could sense her mouth drop, even as he walked past.

"Per lot." He winked at Grace and headed back for his helicopter.

Charcoal nuzzled his nose to Amanda's ear as she lay on her yoga mat working on stretches and strength training. "Go on now. Can't you see I'm busy?" She smiled and felt a bit of serenity. Rolling on her side, she propped up on her elbow and gave in to scratching his ears.

Looking around, she sighed. She would never get used to the quiet. Pulling herself up, she walked over to take a photo album from the entertainment center shelf. Crossing her legs on her couch, she gave the command for Charcoal to stand down and flipped through pages. She was grateful Jessica and Rose faithfully emailed her pictures.

From her AA classes she learned to accept the consequences of her actions and she felt peace from it. Jessica was right to move in with her dad. It took Amanda nearly five years after that to get herself clean. As she turned pages, she watched her girls grow before her eyes. Watched the love of her life age. Why was it that men look so incredibly better as they got older, she wondered.

When she reached the pages that displayed the public part of Rose's growing career, her heart sunk. Her girl was no longer hidden. In the spring through the summer months, Rose was often on the local stations. Banding those eagles she loved so much or working to raise money for the action center. Like mother like daughter, she thought. And that ruined everything.

She hugged her arms close. He would come. He always came. This time she would be ready.

Rose rode coach in the center section of an eleven-across seated plane. On one side of her sat a young woman downing small glasses of wine, and wondered how much she could spend on a two-hour flight. Although wine might be helpful right about now, Rose thought.

How could she have let him get to her like that? After all this time. And why the hell was he there? He could give a rat's ass about the Whooping cranes. Was it to mess with her head? She had to admit, as much as she didn't want any part of Andrew Reed, it wasn't in him to play games like that.

"You've been quiet ever since we got on the plane. What's up?" Grace sat on the other side of her, eating peanuts and sipping on her miniature can of soda.

Rose shook her head and forced a smile for her friend.

Grace wasn't finished. "The only thing missing was the white horse. The man came literally flying out of the sky to save the day for every-freaking-one. Oh, yeah, did I mention the incredibly hot, built, sexy man part?" Grace squinted at her and ate a peanut. "You know him."

Rose shook her head slightly. "Old friend of the family's."

"It was really genius, you have to admit. He's making a killing while saving a species. Everyone wins. If I were you, I'd be giving Mr. Hot, Built and Sexy a very personal, very lengthy thank you." Grace ran her tongue over her top lip.

"He's all yours." She glanced at Grace through the corner of her eyes. "You could bring him to the wedding." She leaned her seat back the half inch it allowed and closed her eyes.

"I've got a date for the wedding."

Rose rotated her head. "Who? When? Why didn't you tell me?"

Grace chewed on her straw. Shrugging, she answered, "Wes. I asked him just last week and I didn't tell you because of that look you're giving me right now. Don't be hard on him. I like him."

"Wesley McGee? Are you kidding? You're opposites. Complete opposites. Boisterous, confident Grace with insecure, boring Wes? How old is he anyway?"

"He's not boring. He's adorable. He's just scared to death of you." Grace pointed a finger at her. "And he's our age. Well, almost our age. What does that matter?"

Rose turned her head slightly but kept her eyes on Grace. "It doesn't." Leaning back against the seat, she added, "I scare him?" She closed her eyes and smiled.

Jessica Nolan and Pete Matthews weren't the first couple to marry under the oak arbor in his aunt and uncle's expansive backyard. Nathan and Brie had exchanged vows there themselves. Andy understood they didn't lend out their property to just anyone, but Jessica was practically another cousin.

Brie and Amanda were downright self-righteous about the lush green and multicolored landscaping plots dotting the corners of the property and scattered around the home. The two of them had pruned and weeded, edged and pampered every inch of the property to prepare for the day.

Andy sat with his date among the other guests in white, cloth-covered chairs lined in rows on the soft, thick grass. On cue, silence waved through the crowd when the young bride trailed behind her attendants to the end of the white runner. It led from the back of the house, through the middle of the lines of chairs, to a platform standing in front of the arbor covered in hundreds of deep, red roses. The only sound was that of the whispering music from the string quartet and the trickle of the waterfall that lay beneath the corner of the home he grew up in.

Rose stood as Jessica's maid of honor with his cousin, Hannah, as her bride's maid. They wore simple dresses. Strapless, tea-length satin in blue so bold it could compete only with the blood red of the complex bouquet resting in Jessica's hands. The dresses mimicked the bridal gown somewhat as they dipped into a revealing V along the tight-fitting front and back.

The bridal gown, however similar, stood alone. Intricate trails of shimmering pearls followed the natural lines of the dress and Jessica's hourglass shape. The skirt blossomed outward from her tiny waist with a modest train boasting the same complicated twists of pearls. Jessica's auburn hair stood elegantly at the crown of her head, woven and dripping with curls.

Andy politely worked to keep his face expressionless as he watched the ceremony, as he watched Rose. With her arms and shoulders exposed, he could tell, over the years, she'd put on weight. It looked good on her, too good. Her milky skin glowed against the bold color of the tight-fitting dress with her darkened strawberry blond hair smoothed and pinned with glittery stones. He'd never seen her like this and wished he never had. It had taken him enough time to accept he would never completely get over her. He had moved on. Business was better than planned and headed in the direction he'd always wanted. Life was fulfilling, even with the noose strangling his heart. But this—the look of her smile as her sister walked reverently down the aisle—wasn't going away anytime soon.

Reminding himself Rose was happy, he looked over the wedding party as the blue June sky dribbled with small tufts of clouds. He thought of how Rose was living her lifelong dreams to their fullest extent. Surely this was more than she could have expected by this stage of her life.

She despised him, he knew. Probably for the best. And she was always...engaged. He moved his gaze to Dave and Amanda.

Unlike many divorced parents, they stood next to each other after Dave kissed Jessica's forehead and gave her to the groom. Andy was sure they did this not only for their daughter, but for each other. Amanda was healthy again with full, chipmunk cheeks and bright color in her brown eyes. Yet, both she and Dave carried worn rings of dark beneath.

Even through whispers from adults saying she and Pete were too young to be married, Jessica floated on a cloud. Andy was definitely no judge for that. The ceremony went without a hitch.

The wedding crew seemed invisible. Impressed, Andy realized the groom's parents must have bucked tradition and paid for much of it. As soon as the receiving line ended, the wedding party gathered for pictures. White tapestries were pulled aside, exposing tables covered with appetizers and dotted with floral bouquets. Waiters in black ties carried flutes of champagne as the open bar readied for guests. Tables sat on large sheets of firm tiles that would change to a dance floor later in the evening.

He tucked his date's arm through his as he and his brother caught up from the last few months. Andy knew to maneuver conversation around Duncan's deployment in the Middle East. Living in Vegas, Duncan played the odds and made a killing painting the rich and famous. "Not saying you're not good, Duncan. I just think you're lucky as shit. Not at the cards. You've got that crazy memory. I'm talking the paintings. Sophia Cleau? She really had you paint her?"

Duncan lifted a brow. "She had me do more than paint her."

Andy shook his head dramatically. "Shit."

"Hot, built and sexy is here." Grace popped a canapé in her mouth. Her dress was a russet that accented the color of her bronze skin and showed just enough cleavage, Rose figured, to drive Wes crazy and still leave some for the imagination.

"I told you; he's all yours." She shrugged slightly, watching

Andy laugh with his brother from her peripheral vision.

"Tempting, but I have a date." Grace gestured to the snack table as Wes tipped over a bowl of dipped chocolates onto the white linen tablecloth. Grace pulled her along and headed for him. "I don't know what it is about him, but I could just eat him up."

"Still very confusing."

Rose noticed Andy and his date as they walked toward a table holding the shrimp and sushi samples.

Grace elbowed her playfully in the ribs. "It's the knight. Don't kick him in the face this time. He saved the cranes."

"I didn't...kick him the face." She wasn't sure what was more humiliating, striking out at him right after she told the crowd not to touch anyone, or missing. "And if you call him that one more time, I'll kick you in the face."

Grace laughed and threw her head back along with the rest of her flute, then headed for Wes.

Feeling petty, Rose made her way to Andy and rolled her eyes behind his back at the, of course, drop-dead gorgeous blonde that was with him. She put a hand on his shoulder to get his attention. Stupid move.

His face was tight as he turned to look at the hand on his jacket, then softened instantly when he followed it up to lock eyes with her. They stood there for just a moment. But, it was enough. And it hurt. Damn it, Rose. Sheer determination had her primly lifting her chin before she spoke, "Hello, Duncan, Andy. I...suppose I owe you gratitude. And...an apology."

One of the many waiters who carried flutes of champagne ventured close to them. She rarely drank but looked longingly at the sweet, calming bubbles. Andy took two and handed one to his date.

"Apology?"

So predictable.

Tucking loose strands of hair behind her ear, she played along. "For, you know. The other day, or week or whatever."

"No. I don't know." He took the glass and lifted it to his lips, obviously hiding a grin.

Taking the higher ground, she elaborated, "I apologize for misunderstanding your intentions in the purchase of the reserve land, and thank you for going out of your way to interfere, or intercede I should say."

Andy held out his flute. She forced herself to look at him, then absently took the champagne from his hand and tilted back a long drink.

"Anything else?" he added.

She looked at his date. Her eyes were darting between them. Rose took another drink. "And for trying to kick you in the face."

He placed his hand on her exposed shoulder and squeezed. "Try a new move next time." And walked away.

She sighed and closed her eyes. When she opened them again, she looked down at the empty flute in her hand. "Son of a bitch."

CHAPTER 16

Andy wasn't in the mood for dancing. He shouldn't have touched Rose, but her bare shoulder was right there. He looked down at his hand. What was he looking for? Was it going to show some sign of her skin? He rubbed his fingers together thinking of the silky feel, of the toned, soft muscle.

Discovering his date was the dancing type, it suited him that she spent the better part of the evening doing just that. Purposely, he caught up with his cousin, Hannah. She would soon return to college. He missed her sassy tomboy attitude. Of course, how else would she turn out growing up with four boys? He found James and Jonathon, too. In a few months, they would start their freshman years of college. Small talk with family was just the ticket. Yet, he didn't and couldn't let Rose out of his sight. He found himself maneuvering around friends and family as they reminisced in order to keep her in view.

He knew the minute she walked down and stood at the bridge over Black Creek. Looking around he found Otto? Otis? Hell if he could remember. Andy spotted him with his nose inches from his smart phone.

Though he knew better, Andy meandered toward the bridge.

Rose rested her forearms on the railing. She could tell someone was walking in her direction and knew it was him. He left ample space between them. Mimicked her stance.

"You marrying Owen, the teacher?" He gestured toward the reception crowd up the hill.

She felt sure it was obvious she came down here to be alone. She lifted her left hand and stuck out her ring finger.

"Okay." He sighed loud enough for her to hear. "You sure he's your type?" He turned, facing her with one arm still resting on the railing.

Fumes filled every inch of her body so similar to what she'd felt at the Florida reserve. Damn it, why did she let him do this to her? She wasn't like this anymore, she reminded herself. Shifting, she looked him full in the face. "His name is Oliver and he's a *professor* and an intellect and has the same interests I do. We've created the educational portion of the action center together and, and it's none of your damned business who I'm marrying and who's my type and what the hell are you doing down here?" She panted with anger and heartache and...heat. Her eyes dipped to his lips for just a fraction of a second. She forced her eyes back to his, keeping purposely expressionless.

"Does he know you press your lips together like that..." Andy motioned toward her mouth. "...when you're...you know?"

She could feel the warmth grow in her cheeks, the veins bulging at her temples. "What gives you the right? Who the hell do you think you are?" Yelling now, she gesturing wildly.

Andy took a step close enough to her to smell peaches. He stared down into the light blue of her eyes. "Does he know you burn in five seconds in the sun?"

Waving her arms madly, Rose yelled at him, "What does that matter?"

He couldn't stop himself. Why couldn't he stop himself? "Does he know you turn your pillow over to the cooler side a dozen times through the night?"

Her brows pulled together. He realized if she let the tears escape now, she would never forgive herself.

"You don't know anything," she said sounding defeated.

"I know what you look like when you're in love, and you don't love him."

"You don't get to say that." Her shoulders dropped, suddenly exhausted. "You lost the right to say that when you told me you didn't want me. I didn't know what I was doing. I was young and stupid in love."

He put his face inches from hers and lowered his voice. "You weren't the only one that didn't know what you were doing. Or young. Or stupid in love."

She lifted her beautiful eyes to him. They stood speaking without talking. And it wasn't good. She was angry, so angry. And...sad? Solemnly, she strolled around him and back to her sister's wedding reception. He watched her maneuver her strappy heels through the grass, then purposefully sat next to her fiancé, putting a hand through his arm.

After an extended morning of inspections and on-site meetings, Andy pulled into his parking lot. Sitting in the small area, he sipped a cup of cold Starbucks and frowned at his office manager's Prius. Working late again.

Taking a minute to catch his breath from the rapid-fire meetings, he looked at the etched sign mortared in the brick. Reed Builders. He personally oversaw each step of the construction of the building from excavation to trim. He thought the look was pretty damned perfect—clay-red brick with the occasional darker bricks to break up the color. It carried a look of professional quality without being over the top. Stones were soldiered, protruding around windows and the front door frame. The landscaping was simple, direct and done by his aunt and Amanda, of course. So, why was it so difficult to give a damn?

The sun blazed hot into the late June afternoon. He barely made it in the front door before Delores carefully began running over the day's messages, mail and tomorrow's appointments.

He put his hand over the planner she recited from. Waiting until she looked up over the rim of her reading glasses, he asked, "How was your day?"

She stopped and folded her hands. Lines pulled away from her eyes as she smiled at him. "Why it was fine, Andy. I'd ask how yours was, but I have a feeling it's not nearly over."

Nodding in consent, he took the stack of papers and winked at her before heading into his office. "Go home."

Finishing his review of appointments for the following day and his calendar for the next week, then month, he turned to the waiting stack of paperwork. Piles of blueprints for sites from a business strip mall and golfing range that he bought on the north side of Northridge waited as well as ones to the individual lots in a country club south of Rochester.

Flicking on the news, he picked up his coffee and scowled into the empty cup. He went to make a fresh pot and saw Rose on the screen. Turning up the volume, he measured and poured fresh grounds. He couldn't think of a single woman more beautiful. Rose in her familiar red bandana, work boots and blue jeans that hugged her long legs.

"Speaking with me today is Dr. Rosemarie Piper. Perched on her arm here is Gracie, an adolescent bald eagle who needs our help. Dr. Piper, tell us about Gracie." The reporter held her head away from the giant bird. It steadied itself often on Rose's gloved arm by pulling out its wings.

"Huh," Andy said aloud. The reporter was scared shitless. He assumed adolescent would mean small and that bald eagle meant white head and tail. This bird had neither.

Rose was in her comfortable groove, he could tell. "Gracie is the third of a clutch of three eaglets hatched in late April of this year. She came down with a case of avian pox that formed on the side of her beak right here." She pointed to the spot on the dark brown beak.

"A growth formed, causing her beak to curve, leaving her unable to feed. We had to, therefore, remove her from the nest, raise her in captivity, hand feed her, and regularly shave the pox. She's healthy now and the pox has cleared up other than the scar left on her beak."

He leaned back against his desk. Smooth, he thought. Professional.

"Unfortunately, Gracie was removed from her nest when she was very young, and we're not sure she'd recognize others of her species or whether or not she knows she's even a bird. Therefore, we'll work to train her as an education eagle."

Rose waved her free arm toward the small enclosure behind her. "As you can see, the enclosure we have at the center is small and was built, primarily, for flightless birds and minimal recuperation of the injured. We need a much larger and extensive area for Gracie to live her life with the freedom of active flight. The funding and manpower alone will cost tens of thousands. We're turning to the public for their help in making this possible."

He clicked off the TV and walked around to sit in his chair. As the smell of coffee filled his office, he thought of Florida. A half-dozen buyers had already committed and put down large down payments for the lots around the crane reserve. What a damned relief that was. He'd put up half his business for collateral to cover the loan on the deal. He knew he would get his money back. Maybe when the economy picked up again. He had no idea he would get it back so soon. Who would've thought tree huggers would be interested enough in some birds that they would fork up that much? Some of the buyers purchased their lots with no plans to build.

But that wasn't it, he thought, as he propped his feet up. The feeling left in his gut at helping out the damned cranes actually felt good. Very good. So good, in fact, he decided to repeat the gesture.

Known as a solid building company, Reed Builders' customers appreciated his thorough manner. His crews respected his knowledge, his personal attention to each project and his follow-up. As he gathered his piles and turned off the office lights, he considered adding "volunteer" to his description, then decided to go incognito.

"You're not supposed to be here. Go home, beautiful. I'm heading out to inspect the work the new excavators did on the country club lots and make a pit stop near Seneca Lake. I've got a stack of snail mail to be sent, and some priority blueprints to be scanned and entered into the data files. All this can be done... In. The. Morning." He set the stacks on the edge of her desk. "Is there anything I can get for you?"

"I can't work as your office manager if you don't keep me updated on your projects, Andrew Reed. Even the potential ones. What's at Seneca Lake?"

He scratched the side of his face. "A gorgeous redhead." Damn it, when did he shave last?

Rose stood around the side of the action center, where mostly storage buildings and sheds clustered. The air was clean and a brisk wind blew scents of pine needles and earth over her. She worked, stacking spare equipment out of sight along the sides of one of the sheds. The blogs still needed to be checked before she went home—Chesapeake Bay Reserve and North Carolina Action Center. The Florida reserve blog made mention of the hero, Andrew Reed, and how many lots had already been sold to single families who were digging ground far from the reserve side of their property. Knight in shining armor? Damn it.

As she worked, she quickly changed her train of thought, refusing to allow him into her head. She was smart, she was careful and she would stay away from the images of the way he looked at her at Jessica's wedding—the sexy faint lines that were beginning to spread from the corners of his eyes when he smiled his million-dollar smile; the familiar scent of him when he invaded her space on the Black Creek bridge; and the look of his mouth. Exasperated, she leaned against the nearby shed and looked around.

There would be room there for the ornery eagle to roam. She'd named her Gracie, much better than Wart. It was fitting. She had ideas for making the space more aesthetic for visitors and donors. She looked over at Gracie, who was tethered to her post and stabbing at the ratscicle she had given her. "Sorry, girl. We'll get you off that leash soon enough."

Grace walked up beside her, looking at the eagle, then at Rose. "Why did you name her Gracie? It confuses the hell out of everyone."

Rose grinned at the feisty bird. She knew if she came anywhere near her, Gracie would defend her rat dinner. "Because she's spirited and noisy and impatient."

"Damn straight. I'm taking off for the day."

Rose stacked spare equipment onto her four-wheeler. "Isn't tonight the big date with Mr. No Eye Contact?" She didn't look to her friend and colleague but knew the smirk she would have on her face.

"Oh, yes. Cute. As. Can. Be. See you bright and early." She turned and started walking back to the main building before yelling out over her shoulder, "Oh, yeah, and there's a donor in the lobby. Wants to donate the money for Gracie's aviary and build it himself."

"What the hell?" she said aloud, jumping to her feet. "How long has he been waiting?" She was a mess. Oh, well. She could use that as a pitch.

Quickly, she rushed to ride the loaded four-wheeler to a spot and park it for the night. Walking to the main building, she entered through the back. Quickly washing her hands, she dried them on her jeans as she entered the lobby area.

She dropped against the jamb of the doorway as soon as she spotted him. "What are you doing here?"

CHAPTER 17

"I saw your broadcast."

Andy watched as Rose rubbed clean hands over her dirty face. "What are you really here for?"

"Okay. I deserve that." He got up from a row of rustic chairs and walked toward her. "I guess it's my turn to apologize. You were right. Become Dr. Owen Witherspoon. I have no right to judge any decision you make. It's none of my business."

"It's Oliver and I will never understand why women feel the need to change their names."

"Right." He looked around at what she had helped build. "It's nice here. I've really, honestly just come to build an enclosure for a bird...eagle. Gracie, you called it? Isn't that the name of your assistant?"

"Grace." Rose sighed. "Put the animal first," she mumbled. "My assistant's name is Grace. The bald eagle is Gracie."

"Okay," he said slowly. "But that's just going to confuse the hell out of everyone."

Her eyes closed, and slowly shaking her head, she stood to the side of the doorway, motioning for him to pass. "Come on. I'll show you the spot."

They walked in silence through a large hall that housed smaller animals along the perimeter. He spotted a few opossums and at least one raccoon. Each enclosure led to a habitat area on the outside of the building. He thought the layout was genius. Efficient.

Electricity radiated overtly between the two of them, but he had no idea if it was positive or negative. So, he worked to ignore it.

"I've decided not to marry Oliver."

He paused only for a second before responding. "I'm...sorry to hear that."

"No, you're not, but you were right. Love's not everything, but I suppose you should have it before you marry someone."

"Stated as artfully as Hallmark." Fighting the urge to fist bump the air, he kept pace with her and, instead, chided, "Or, how about this one? Another fiancé bites the dust."

The muscles in her jaws flexed and she picked up her pace, walking with quick Rose-like steps.

The back was a myriad of organized sheds lining an open space clearly meant for presentations and workshops. Very efficient, he thought. It wasn't until they walked around the side of the building that he saw the bird.

Damn, it was big. Amazing. Giant talons on the ends of thick legs, their brown color matching its beak. Predatory eyes stared him down, head on. He felt instant respect, followed by sympathy at the sight of the size of the small enclosure. Yes, he thought. Rose or no Rose, he had a great desire to give this animal what freedom he could.

Waving her arms toward a line of trees some hundred yards away, Rose explained her ideas.

"How long have you been here?" Delores walked in Andy's office as he sat at his desk. Her keys were still in her hand. He watched suspiciously as she made her way to the coffeemaker. She let the keys slip into her purse, then placed her palm on the glass carafe. "If you keep going like this, you'll start making mistakes."

He kept working, but responded, "Thank you, but it's only temporary."

Delores brewed a fresh pot as he went through plans, outlines and contracts. He made neat piles of work for her to do for when he headed out to meet customers and check on crews. He planned on still having enough time to put in some hours at the action center enclosure.

They both looked up when they heard the outside door.

He hadn't realized his face was tight until he felt it relax. "Ma."

Brie carried a small basket covered with a red and white checked towel. The size of the lumps underneath it told him *muffins*. He got up to greet her, then stopped at the frown on her face.

Delores walked to stand with her shoulder to shoulder. His assistant crossed her arms before commenting, "I know, Brianna. I keep telling him. He looks just awful, doesn't he? Maybe you can talk some sense into him."

He hated when his aunt did that thing where he felt like she was looking right through him. Defensively, he spoke first, "I've just got a project. It'll be done within a month. I want to get it off my plate." He walked over, trying for casual and lifted the corner of the towel.

Brie smacked his hand and pulled the basket away. "I'm going to need a little more than that."

Sighing, he explained, "It's an enclosure for a diseased, well formerly diseased, eagle. She's incredible. Rose has her taking food from her hand, but she won't let anyone else near her. Scratch your eyes out if you give her the chance."

Brie's brows came together, then lifted as the muscles in her face softened.

"The senior biologists want to keep her as an education bird. Something about being in captivity while she healed from the disease and missing the period when she would learn to recognize other eagles or know that she is one of them."

Fisting a set of knuckles beneath her chin, Brie smiled.

"I think it's bullshit—"

"Language," Brie reminded him.

"Sorry."

"Go on."

"They should let her go." He carried on as he went back and closed some files on the corner of his desk. "Let her take the risk and see if she can do what she was meant to do."

"Hmm," Brie mumbled. "Déjà vu."

"The girl needs a place to fly. They've got her cooped up in a ridiculous enclosure. It's awful." He put his keys in his pocket and looked up, stopping at the sight of Brie and Delores.

"What?" he asked at their red-eyed expressions.

Brie smiled. "You have time for a cup of coffee and a muffin before you go to the center. You could call Duncan and have him go with you. His plane landed earlier today."

He hit his head with the palm of his hand. "Fourth of July. Right."

"You will make it to the Fourth," Brie said as a statement.

Yes, she was looking right through him. "Right. Right, of course. I might have to make the tail end, but I'll be there." He picked up a muffin.

Since Rose rarely carried a purse, she walked into the bar with her money in one back pocket, her ID in the other, her smart phone in a front pocket, and the Swiss Army knife she held as dear to her as any woman might a tube of lipstick in the other. She saw Duncan right away. His dark brown hair that waved to just over his shoulders was easy to spot, even from the back. She nodded to the bartender before kissing him on the cheek, then slid in the booth opposite him.

Pinned to the dark paneled wall were yellowing newspaper articles from years past, featuring Northridge's favorite pub and burger joint, Mikey's. She learned never to be surprised at how the place always felt the same. After months since her last visit, she still recognized old friends and the smell of a great grill.

She had forgotten, however, how much Duncan and Andy looked alike and seemed to be more so as they grew older. They were very different, though. Predictably, Duncan had on black Armani jeans and a charcoal-gray, button-down shirt with sleeves rolled up to three-quarter length. "Hello, Duncan. Welcome back. Here for the Fourth?"

He lifted his chin once in agreement. "And to look at some land. I've decided it's probably time for me to own some."

She jutted her head back. "You don't own a place? No condo anywhere? Apartment? What about Sophia whoever?"

He lifted a corner of his mouth. "That's history. And no, no *place.*"

She looked into the deep, dark brown of his eyes. No condolences were needed about the break up, she could see that. "History?"

"Yes. Her paintings are finished. I've moved out and on. Do

you care for something to drink while we finish the small talk?"

Sighing at his predictable abruptness, she smiled and nodded. He motioned to the waitress waiting at the end of the bar then leaned a hand toward Rose as she approached.

"Bud. Bottle, please."

"Bud Light?"

Rose shook her head. "Budweiser. Bottle. No glass. Thanks."

She looked down at the points of black flames peeking out from beneath Duncan's left sleeve. She tapped the tattoo, questioning.

He shrugged.

"What will your mother say?"

"Brie's not my mother."

"Bullshit." She smiled wide now.

"Well, now that we seem to be past the chitchat portion of our visit, I'll answer by saying that I believe I am past the age where I ask my *mother* for approval before giving myself a tattoo."

She felt her eyes grow large, then they must have changed to a look of *eew* because that was exactly what she was thinking. "You mean you did that to yourself?"

"I wouldn't trust anyone else with drawing on my body. It is permanent, you know?" he said sarcastically.

She winced. "So, what did you want to see me about?"

"Thank you for coming on such short notice. Brie mentioned that recently you and Andy have been spending time together."

Her wince turned to a purposefully flat stare. "She's wrong."

He lifted a brow. "Really?"

If this was why he'd asked her out here..."He's working for me...for the center. Donating some time and material, nothing more."

Duncan leaned back and rested an arm on the back of the booth. "Is that why your face has turned such an interesting shade?"

She began to get up, but he grabbed her arm. "I had no idea you still had such a temper. I apologize. Please. Sit down. I want to share something with you. Please."

She relaxed slightly as her beer arrived. Bud Light. Shit. She watched as he reached inside his discarded black leather jacket and pulled out a small roll of yellowed papers. He turned them to face her. Then, unfolded and pushed them across the table.

A hurricane of emotions blew through her as she looked down at the pile. There was no need to touch them. She knew what they were. "How did you get these?" She didn't look up to him.

"I found them eight years ago on the floor of Andy's old Mustang. Beautiful machine." Duncan took her hand gingerly now. "I picked him up from the end of this very bar. He'd been spilling tears into shots of whiskey. I drove him to the city that night and found these on the floor on my way back."

She sat speechless, thoughts racing. Images. Memories. She tried to piece it together. He was here? Drinking? Duncan drove him? The papers. The timeline that night. She shut her eyes as they began to burn. That night.

When she opened them, he was there. Andy stood in the same doorway she had entered. Years of stuffing these feelings, any feelings, under her metaphorical rug felt like a hornet's nest that had just been kicked. This was too much to take. To understand. She was over him, over this.

Duncan must have noticed the direction and context of her glare, because he patted the top of her hand, then picked up his coat. "I'll leave you two alone." Reciprocally, he kissed her on the cheek as he tossed some money on the table.

Andy flexed his jaws as panic set in. His eyes darted back and forth between the two of them. It was a familiar panic from years past and it crept back as if it had never been tucked neatly away. He walked slowly, trying to run possible scenarios through his head as to why Duncan had asked him there that night just to find him with her. With her. He walked cautiously to the booth and sat eagerly, working to assess Rose's face.

Spotting the papers, he wanted nothing more than to get his hands on his brother. The silence could have broken him in two.

Her arms were lying listless at her sides. He could see her chest rise and fall quickly as she looked at him through half-opened lids. She spoke just two words, "You knew."

CHAPTER 18

Andy looked into the ice blue and thought the color matched the tone. "Yes." He reached and brushed the backs of his fingers lightly down her arm.

She pulled back as if he'd burned her. "I know that move." Her voice was uncharacteristically and unsettling soft. "You knew and you didn't tell me."

"I couldn't."

"You couldn't?" Her voice cracked. "Or wouldn't?"

"Both, I suppose. I didn't want to hurt you. Don't want to hurt you."

"You told me you didn't want me anymore. No explanation, just left me there, but you didn't want to hurt me?" She spoke through her teeth now. "You broke my heart."

"Where would you be today if I hadn't? What would you be if I hadn't?"

"I can't do this again." She left her untouched beer and ran out the side door.

He threw his own bill on the table before going after her.

She rounded on him before he'd made it all the way out to the parking lot. "You didn't even talk to me. You just made that kind of decision without even talking to me?"

"You'd already made plenty of decisions without me. I didn't know what to do. What would have happened if I did it any other way?"

"And all these years?" She raised her voice now. "There was never a time when you could have said something? Anything?"

"You...you were happy. And you hated me. Hate me," he corrected. "And you were always...engaged."

Shoulders dropping, she nodded. Stuck her hands in her back pockets and looked him square in the eyes. "Andrew, I can't do this again. Finish the enclosure. It's what's best for the bird. Then, don't come around anymore. Love isn't everything. You taught me that."

He watched as she walked carefully to her pickup.

Andy wasted no time in finding Duncan. Knocking loudly on their uncle's guesthouse door, he concentrated on the rise and fall of his chest as he waited for him to answer the damned, frigging door. Duncan took his time on purpose, he knew. Rattling the locked knob, he filled his lungs, ready to give his brother an earful when the door opened. Duncan stood, squared on both feet. So Duncan. Andy jutted out a quick jab to his face. "Mind your own fucking business." It felt good. So, he went for another.

His brother made no attempt to block the first one, but apparently wasn't going to take another without a fight. He dodged and pushed him out to the grass and straight on his ass. Andy spun around like a cat falling from a rooftop, then sprung.

They charged each other like bulls, rolling in the thick grass, throwing punches and gut jabs. He had forgotten how tough Duncan could be when provoked and sucked air when he took one to his solar plexus. They broke free and stood, Andy with his hands on his knees waiting for an opening. Both panted as they stared.

Duncan dabbed the back of his hand to his mouth and looked down at blood. "Feel better?"

Andy lifted from his legs. "No, mother fucker. Stay out of my life." He started back toward his car, but his brother took his arm. Duncan kept his head back, like he was ready for a fist.

Andy looked down, then up to his eyes. "You really want to touch me right now?"

"Come on. I want to show you something."

Reluctantly, Andy allowed him in his Maserati. They rode in

silence as Andy let the fumes die down. The tussle actually helped. Some.

Trees started to thicken as they drove to just out of town. Duncan motioned for him to turn the car down a gravel road he would have missed. They drove slowly. "Not exactly a road for a sports car, bro."

"It's just at the top of the hill. If you drive any slower we might not get there before dawn."

The road simply stopped. Andy cut the engine.

The hill was the highest spot as far as the eye could see, but not by much, and the eye couldn't see all that far through the thicket of old-growth trees. The smell was a soothing mix of leaves—dead and alive—grass and earth.

Not really up for riddles, Andy followed him out of the car. "What are we doing here, Duncan?"

"I bought it."

"You bought what? There's nothing out here."

"I bought the land. Forty acres. There's a creek down that way, a clearing the other." He turned in a slow and meaningful circle. "I'm standing in the library I think."

Andy lowered his brows. "You're staying?"

Duncan shook his head. "No. I've got an order in L.A. waiting. Chloe Lace, but I can't keep staying in the guesthouse. I need a builder."

"Chloe Lace? You sure can pick 'em, man."

"They pick me, mostly. She's wants three. I believe she said four-by-eight for over her fireplace in her great room or something or other." Duncan carelessly waved his hand and turned.

Andy smiled now. "Four-by-eight *feet?*"

Duncan grinned back. "Mmm. So, what do you think? Will you do it?"

"Of course I'll do it. How much is she paying you?"

Lifting a brow, Duncan peered over his shoulder. "More than I'll be paying you."

Even over both the noise of Charcoal barking from inside and from the garage door closing, Amanda still heard the quiet press of soft shoes ducking underneath the large door before it lowered completely. She paused only for a second, then reached inside her apron. Even though she knew it was coming, the feeling of her head slamming against the steel door that led into her kitchen blackened her vision.

As Michael put his hand around her throat, he whispered in her ear from behind, "Miss me, baby?"

It was strange how the fear of him discovering Rose's existence almost completely erased her fear of him. She looked through eyes with purpose and vision. The smell of him churned her stomach, but she kept her resolve. "How long has it been, Michael?"

"Over a year, baby. Where is it?" He tightened his grip. She knew he would be able to judge just when to stop in order to give her enough air to answer.

She croaked, "No, I mean how many years have we done this now?"

He turned her, keeping his hand around her throat. He looked at her, from one eye to the other with only inches between their faces. "How the fuck would I know?" The tips of his fingers dug into her neck.

Her throat began to throb. "You dyed your hair black." She choked out. "And your eyes. Contacts?"

"No more questions. Where's my money?"

Closing her eyes, she braced for the blow, then asked slowly, "Your money?"

He hit her, closed fisted, in her right temple. The blow sent her along the top of her garage workspace, clearing off gardening tools and fertilizers. She landed on her stomach on the cold, concrete floor in front of her car.

She could feel her eye instantly swelling but made herself lift to her hands and knees.

Michael pulled her up using a handful of her hair. He dragged her back to the steel door as Charcoal scratched and barked madly on the other side. He pressed his forearm against her throat and reached toward his ankle.

She turned her face away from the feel of sharp metal pressing against her neck. Her eyes began to water from the pain, leaking from the corners of her eyes, stinging the swelling that was growing. "Is that the knife you used to kill my grandfather?"

He brushed the deep lines of wrinkles from his cheek against hers and whispered in her ear, "Oh, yes, it's a classic, and you're next if you don't come up with my money. You have thirty seconds."

She forced herself to turn into his stale cigarette breath and look in his lifeless eyes. She had plenty of experience with ways that would get him to talk. She reminded herself that he hadn't killed her in their sixteen years of doing this dance and that he needed her. She braced and croaked, "No."

His hand shook so hard, the blade made shallow cuts along her throat. Tiny red lines formed in the whites of his eyes. "Whore!" he screamed.

The door shook against her back as the dog threw himself into it.

Michael unbuttoned his pants with his free hand, pulled his zipper as she scrambled with her hands while trying not to move her neck. The dog barked behind her and Michael grunted in front of her. She yelled as loud as she could, "How many women? Where are they?"

He pinched, bruising her nipple through her apron. As she bellowed in pain he answered, "As many as I want. All over the country." He pulled at her shorts.

He was too close. She couldn't maneuver her arm with his body pushed up against hers. Pressing himself to her, she could feel he was hard. Panic began to creep back into her mind like an old recurring nightmare. She'd always kept him from going this far. But, she had never pushed him like this. Trembling, she worked her hand inside the pocket of her apron.

She refused to let any more tears fall and instead looked up at eyes that were half mad as he groped between her legs. "Then, here's for each of us all over the country, you fucking bastard." And through the fabric of her apron, she tasered him in the balls.

He fell into a heap with his pants around his ankles, convulsing rapidly.

She looked down with huge eyes at her shaking hands. Flying into automatic pilot, she ran around him on the floor, punched the garage door button and opened the back door for her dog. Charcoal snarled and bit, clamping on Michael's neck as he lay twitching on the floor.

"No, Charcoal. In the car!"

The door opened, and the Lab obeyed but continued to snarl

and bark through the window. She scrambled for her keys and noticed Michael fumbling to pull himself up. She started the engine, rammed the gear into reverse and sped out of her drive without looking back.

CHAPTER 19

Rose stood in the warm, late afternoon sun, preparing for her last presentation of the day. She aimed the base of Gracie's four-foot, wooden perch to the spot on the ground where the galvanized steel extension would sink into the premade hole. The scent of hot, dry July pines soothed her. She loved upstate New York.

Tucked nicely in her back pocket was her favorite pair of leather gloves. A spare pair for her assistant hung from a hook along the side of the podium that she never felt comfortable using.

A few spectators had already arrived and were browsing around the perimeter of the main building. If they were lucky, they would catch one of the smaller rehab animals sunning itself in the outer portion of their habitats.

An hour. She shook her head. There was just over an hour before she had to *be on*, as she thought of it. She wanted her alone time more than ever these days. She'd worked for years keeping her mind focused on the job. It meant less time to daydream, to think.

Unfortunately, the work was so second nature to her she couldn't completely block out ideas—ideas like Andy might have had a point. They had both been young, not just herself. He was stupid, she reminded herself, but so was she. Regardless, it took everything she had back then to turn away from the nightmares and from the endless despair, and pull herself together enough to make it to NYU. And she did it. Even with the few scholarships she never got back. And she was happy, damn it.

To hell with Duncan for butting in. If he didn't mind his own business so much of the time, the moments when he decided not to wouldn't be so potent. She should have known the moment he called that Duncan would have been up to no good. Or maybe it was some good. Shit. She shook her head quickly and noticed a middle-aged blond woman approaching. Trying to look busy, Rose used a mallet to secure the wooden perch into the hole.

"Hello. Dr. Piper? Hello?"

Rose smiled, but knew it didn't reach her eyes. "Good afternoon, ma'am. We have another sixty minutes before we start."

"Oh, yes. I just wanted to know if I could ask a few questions beforehand."

"Of course." It was for the animals, she chanted in her head. "What can I do for you?

Dave and his assistant worked separately for the day. Leg work, mostly. Tips on a man found shot near Seneca Falls had led to one dead end after another. Half the county seemed to have motive to shoot the poor bastard. The only positive he could come up with for the damned day was they were able to shorten their list of potential suspects. As he listened to his assistant's summary of solid alibis, he sat at his metal desk marking charts. He thought of how glorified his position tended to be when, in reality, it was mostly a lot of Ps—paperwork and pounding the pavement. The intercom buzzed and when he saw it was the lieutenant's extension, he held up a finger silencing his assistant.

"Detective Nolan."

"Tanner here, Dave. You alone?"

"Nick's here. What can I do for you, sir?"

Lieutenant Tanner paused, then continued, "Your ex is on the way up. Uh, pretty beaten up. Do you want me to stop her?"

Closing his eyes, Dave let his chin drop. Damnit. He thought she'd cleaned up for good this time. Damnit. "No, sir. I'll take care of it."

"Should I leave?" his assistant asked. "We can do this in the morning. I'd like to make a stop at a suspect's place on my way home. I missed him this morning. Maybe I can catch him at this time of night."

Dave said nothing, just nodded in succession.

He didn't stand up when Amanda walked in. She was obviously shook up. His gut reaction ranged from an intense need to pull her into his arms to a reddening anger that she'd let herself fall off the wagon.

She looked around at first without speaking. Her eyes paused at the framed picture of her on the corner of his desk. As if she was cold, she hugged her purse close to her chest and, without asking, sat in the wooden chair across from him.

"Look at you," he judged. "We agreed it was best if you didn't come here anymore." It pained him to see her like this. Always pained him that she chose this over him.

"Yes, Dave. Look at me. You know I'm not using. Look in my eyes."

She was right, he realized. Average-sized pupils, even though he could only see one of them. The other was completely swollen shut. Good color in her skin. He also noticed that the blow to her face was still bruising. The cuts on her neck were fresh. Although taken with concern, he remained guarded. "What happened?"

"Please let me get this out. Then, I'll leave and promise never to come back. I'm sorry to bother you at work. Sorry for...everything. I've lied to you. Kept things from you." She looked in his eyes, then her shoulders fell. "I'm not talking about the drugs. I was wrong to turn to that. I know that now. You know that I know that now. I lost everything and I'm tired, Dave. So tired." Her eyes dropped to her hands. "I lost you."

She straightened in her chair and took a deep, cleansing breath. "I didn't know what to do. He, he killed my grandfather, said he would do the same to you—"

"Who—"

"Please. Please, let me finish. He said he would come for you," she repeated. "So, I gave him what he wanted." Her eyes darted up to meet his. "Never that. No. I was lucky...able to keep him from that. The money, I just gave him money. He really prefers using his fists anyway." She leaned back in the chair and closed her eyes. "Rosemarie is on television now. It's only a matter of time before he sees her. Recognizes her. Comes for her."

Dave stood now. "Who? What are you talking about?"

"Michael. Although I'm not sure that's his real name. I can't keep her hidden anymore. He'll come for her." She placed a fist to her lips.

"Are you talking about Rainer? You know where he is?"

"No. He comes and goes. I'm so sorry. I didn't know what else to do. He has pictures. Of, of other girls he's hurt, other people he's killed...murdered. I gave him the money. I didn't spend it on drugs. No, that's wrong. I spent some on drugs. A...lot on drugs. But it mostly went to keep him away. All he has to do is see her and he'll know. She has his eyes, Dave. The timing. He'll know. He's evil."

Her eyes glistened as she took a tape recorder from the second pocket of her apron and set it on his desk. "I don't expect you to believe me. Or forgive me. But please listen to this. It's as much as I could get out of him—that I could get for you. Find him, Dave. Protect our daughter. I can't do it on my own anymore." She got up and turned for the door. Stopping, she closed her eyes and whispered almost inaudibly, "I love you."

Rose spoke about the Birds of Prey Action and Research Center, the latest east coast conservation efforts and, of course, about Gracie. She was uncharacteristically worn. Days with too much to think about and nights with even more. She wanted Andy to hurry and finish with the project. Or, was it that she wanted to drag it out?

He knew. His reasons for not telling her made sense. Too much sense now, which obviously meant she wasn't thinking clearly.

Grace stood next to her in her usual painted-on jeans with her own set of thick, leather gloves as she was being groomed as a handler herself. Rose demonstrated how to hold the bird away from her face and angle her arm so that when she stretched her wings for balance, they wouldn't tangle with the handler's head. Try as they might, so far Gracie wouldn't let anyone touch her except Rose. The wooden perch would have to suffice once again for this portion of the presentation.

The middle-aged woman raised her hand and asked, "If it's a

bald eagle, why doesn't it have a white head and tail?"

Weary, Rose wanted desperately for some time to herself. How many times had she answered that question? A vacation would do the trick. Somewhere she could lie on a hammock and be alone. Working to sound sincere, she lifted her chin. "Bald eagles don't get their white plumage until between the age of four and five when they become sexually mature." Juvenile giggles rumbled through the crowd. She was relieved when a young man asked a halfway intelligent question.

"Why do you tether her?"

She looked toward the back and tried her warmest smile. "Area biologists recently held a virtual meeting to discuss that very predicament. The decision was that, due to the human intervention mentioned, Gracie here missed the stages of upbringing when she would learn to recognize those of her species and, in fact, learn that she herself is an eagle. Therefore, in order to best ensure her survival, she'll be trained as an education bird and spend her life in captivity. Since her aviary isn't finished yet, each time she is outdoors, we tether her."

The young man leaned his head to the side before he nodded, then asked, "Did all of the biologists agree?"

She chewed on the side of her cheek. "Biologists rarely all agree."

Murmurs of laughter, once again, waved among the small crowd.

"How did you—" He leaned farther before a hand appeared on his shoulder and nudged him aside.

In the vacated spot, Andy stepped into view.

Andy.

Was here.

Of course he was here. He must have been working on the aviary, the young man an employee of his. She noted the absence of the thousand-watt smile for the crowd or even a wink for her. Solemn and hard as stone, he spoke loudly and finished his employee's sentence. "How did you vote?"

No part of her body moved as she played back the former questions evidently coached by him.

The fog that had clouded her weary mind for weeks parted as if burned away by the sun. She looked to his ever-so-sincere caramel eyes. And she understood why he would ask a question he already knew the answer to.

Amanda sat alone at her kitchen table, staring over her cold dinner with a frozen bag of peas on her eye. She thought about cleaning up the mess in the garage. Other than the shambles left from where she flew along the top of the work cabinet, no sign of Michael's presence remained. Then, she realized Dave would likely send someone out to inspect the scene. Of course, he would. She just wasn't thinking clearly yet. There would be no prints. Michael was far too thorough.

Charcoal stayed close to her feet. Her faithful watchdog. And ears and nose dog. She refused to be afraid in her own home. Dave had evidence and a voice print now. He knew to look across state lines. He would find him. He had to.

Sitting at the kitchen table in the quiet, she wondered how her life became like this. The kitchen still had the same soothing yellow paint and the same small, square table, but she was alone. Charcoal growled low, sending her on alert. She'd set the alarm. The power hadn't been cut. The knock at the door made her jump anyway, tossing her chair.

Charcoal took off for the door, barking cautiously.

She knew she was likely just jittery from her day. As she walked to the door, she felt a relief in the fact that, even after her horrific day, she knew she would not turn to chemicals to get her through. Reaching for the handle, she gave the grumbling dog the command to, 'lay.'

Rose's croppy red hair framed her alabaster face, setting off the intense blue of her eyes.

Andy could see that beautiful mind of hers racing. Making connections. He realized he was looking at the most incredible woman he would ever know in this lifetime. The conversation that took place between them was silent and powerful and long enough the crowd parted on the brittle grass to see who she was looking at.

Her eyes began to fill as she answered, "I voted to let her go."

Baiting her further, he asked, "Why is that?"

Rose closed her eyes, allowing the first tear to spill before nodding with sentiment. "It would have been a risk," she said before opening her eyes. "I love this animal. I didn't want to let her go." Pressing her lips together, she kept her eyes on his. "She might have failed. Starved or been hurt, but I voted to give her the chance to live. To become what she was born to be."

Tears flowed freely then and, as if watching a tennis match, the crowd moved their gaze back to him.

Charcoal sniffed the base of the door, then lay without protest. Amanda patted his head before looking through the spy-hole.

Dave.

Her forehead dropped against the wood. He came to look at the scene himself. Of course. He would do that. How long had it been since he'd been at the house? Instead of allowing her mind to continue down that path, she stood tall and opened the door for him.

The look on his face frightened her. She'd never seen him look so worn. The color had drained from his face and was a direct contrast to the red in his swollen eyes. Her brows pulled together. "What is it? Are you all right? The girls?" She lifted a hand to him, then let it fall to her side.

He collapsed to his knees in front of her. Wrapped his arms around her waist and pulled her into him, clinging as he pressed his face against her.

The years of walls she had meticulously built and guarded turned to instant dust and crumbled at his feet. She stood with her arms still at her side, squeezing her eyelids tightly. Slowly, she wound her arms around him, burying her face in his neck. In his hair. In his smell. She'd never forgotten one part of the dizzying scent of leather and metal and of the only love of her life. Tremors radiated from his body to hers as this large man shuddered in front of her.

Forbidden tears flowed freely down her face, stinging the cuts on her bad eye. Pent up longing for the feel of his warmth, for the loving safety of his arms made her legs wobble, then completely give out. She had been so sure she'd never feel this again.

His large arms took her in as she collapsed. He picked her up. He kicked the door shut behind them as he carried her into the living room. Gathering her, he sat and cradled her silently in the middle of the couch—their couch.

For the first time in her life, she curled in a ball and forgot about everything in her life, letting the tears fall—buckets of them. Sobbing as he rocked her, he stroked her hair and whispered in her ear. She blessedly didn't think, only felt. Tears soaked his shirt, leaving smears the color of pink blood.

CHAPTER 20

Andy walked a few steps through the parted crowd, then stopped. Why did this feel like his last possible chance with...with her? Because it was. She knew everything now. Understood everything. That he could see on her face. What he couldn't see was her answer, her choice. It had been so long, too long? Patience and honesty was all he had left.

"I never wanted to let you go." He waited where he stood. "You're the best thing that ever happened to me. I left my heart with you on that bridge. I left my best friend. Come home, Rosemarie."

One hand covered her quivering lips, the other she used for speed as Rose ran toward him. A lifetime of memories sped through him as he watched her familiar jog: eating crawfish at his uncle's house, breaking the board at her black belt promotion, her valedictorian speech, her on TV, the feel of her under him, and the look on her face the night on the bridge.

The crowd erupted into applause as she reached him, smashing her mouth to his. Ignoring the crowd, lips and tongues danced like they'd never missed a beat. Like riding a bike. He laced his fingers through her hair, lifting her from her feet with his other hand. After all this time, how could she taste the same? Like home. How could she smell the same? The peaches. He could feel her tears on his face as she wrapped both legs around him and hung on. It was a meeting of mouths, of minds and of hearts.

When he let go, he slid her down, taking hold of the sides of her face, then pulled back to look at her. And found everything he'd been missing.

The crowd silenced, and still neither he nor Rose looked around. Instead, he reached down and scooped her up beneath her legs. She held onto his neck, pressing her cheek to his shoulder and hanging on tightly in his arms.

She left Grace with the eagle. He left his worker with his SUV. They walked in silence away from the crowd without so much as a wave good-bye.

Reaching her truck, he kissed her forehead and hung on a few more lingering minutes.

He slid her back to the ground between the truck and himself. When was the last time he saw tears on that beautiful face? Looking at her with hands cupping her cheeks, he used his thumbs to wipe them away.

Her mouth trembled as she spoke, "PDA." She let out a half-laugh before pulling him in for a smooth, drawn-out kiss.

He leaned back and smiled wide. "Mmm. True," and opened the truck door. "Come with me."

In his large ski boat, Andy and Rose slowly trolled along the coast of Seneca Lake. Rose snuggled tightly in front of him as he drove. His heart wild, his mind void of thought, the only feeling was of Rose tucked in front of him. She rested her head against his shoulder, closing her eyes as the warm wind blew through her hair much like the new path their lives were headed. Trees whisked by at a steady pace. Rose tilted her face into him, eyes closed. She had never even asked where they were going.

The sun lowered in the sky, causing lines of stratus clouds to appear orange and pink. The fresh smell of the water mixed with the aroma from the Tulip Poplar into a cocktail of atmosphere.

With one hand on the steering wheel, one on the accelerator, he rested his cheek to hers. She fit just as perfectly as she always had, nestled in the driver's seat with him.

He felt her head turn before she spoke over the noise of the boat and the wind. "Is this yours?"

"For the next week or two. Here." He reached in his glove box and handed her a pair of sunglasses.

Smiling, she put them on and rested her head against his shoulder again.

He found the cove he was looking for. He dropped the anchor while she waited on one of the padded seats at the front of the boat.

He gently pulled her forward, slipping in behind her much like he had at the wheel of the boat. He felt like it had been a lifetime since he held her like this. He pressed his lips just under her ear. Linking fingers with her, he whispered, "I feel whole."

Every inch of her content, Rose smiled and sighed. "Why only a week or two?"

"Hmm?" He tucked his face in her neck and chilled her when he smelled.

"Why will you have this boat for only another week or two?"

"That's when I'll unload her and the car."

She pivoted to look at him. "You're getting rid of the Maserati?"

He shook with bits of laughter. "Man toys." He pulled her back to him and ran his lips along to her collarbone.

Closing her eyes in delirium, she focused. "Unloading?"

He tugged slightly on the shoulder of her shirt, trailing his mouth down her freshly exposed skin. "I need the money for a down payment on a house."

She shivered, sat up and this time turned to face him head on. "I can't think straight when you're doing that."

"We've had enough thinking to last us a very long time. Can we just be for now? We're about to lose the daylight. You need to decide if you're all right with camping here for the night."

Her insides woke, tightened, curled, and then everything traveled low in her stomach. "First explain."

"Simple." He stuck his hand in a bag on the floor of the boat, pulling out two granola bars and trail mix and handed her some. "Dinner of champions, cheers." He sat on the seat across from her. "I can't marry you without a decent place for you to live and we're not staying in either of our apartments."

She tried fiercely not to smile. "Don't I get a say?"

"House or apartment? Sure."

"No. Marriage." The smile took her over.

He looked around, took a deep breath in, then blew it out, letting his cheeks expand. "Nope. Nope. You don't." He set aside the bag and stood, linked their fingers and pulled her up. "You will never get away from me again."

Floodgates of emotion spilled around her. "I'm not hungry for food, Andy." She pulled his hands around her, then released to copy the movement around him. Her fingers still couldn't touch around his back. "I want to stay here for the night."

Their mouths joined in a swirl of tenderness and anticipation. He led his hand up her back, over her neck and laced his fingers in the crops of red. Clutching a handful, he carefully tilted her head back to sink into the kiss, parting her lips with his tongue. His hand on her lower back pressed her closely to him.

She pulled his tucked Henley loose and her hands inside and up his back. Age had not taken him. She could feel his heart beat rapidly, and it made her insane with need. Sexy purrs of desire hummed low in her throat.

"Down below," she said to him. "Take me down below."

Andy didn't let go of her, just as he didn't from the time she'd ran to him that afternoon. They twined and groped and twisted their way to below the deck of the boat.

The warm, humid air felt much like their first time, and she felt much the same yearning. Only this time he was a man and she was a woman.

Without letting go, he held onto her hands as he locked the hatch behind him.

Patiently, she let him look into her, straight into her. Having an idea of what was racing through his mind, she watched the expressions change as he looked at her with flatter, then warmth, then seduction. The warm turned to hot and she braced. He grabbed her face, thumbs on her cheeks with fingers wrapped over her ears and into her hair. The rough feel of his hands was as sexy and male as the scent of him—clean wood, earth and twilight.

Their mouths melted together, much like their bodies. He tilted her head farther, deepening the kiss. She would never live without this again and knew she would never have to. They dropped to the floor in a waterfall of need, toeing off shoes as they went.

Andy attempted to rotate her out from beneath him, but this was no longer an inquisitive, reserved Rose. She drove her hands down his back and over the muscle of his legs, then traveled around to the front of him. He choked from her assault on his resolve, making him crazy with frustration from all the damned material keeping him from her.

Impatiently, he tried to pull her shirt over her head. As it was too tight, she tried to help and fumbled with the first button. She barely had released it before he took her hands, grabbed at the line of buttons and muscled them apart. The sudden flash of creamy white skin shined in the light of the setting sun. He caught his breath and dropped his forehead to her chest. He could stay there, right there for a very long time.

With eyes closed, he hitched one of her legs up and over his shoulder as he leaned to her and trailed his tongue over the swell of flesh that lifted above her lace. His insides shook. She was warm and slight sounds whimpered from her. He trailed a hand down her neck, over the lace and down the silky skin of her waist.

Arching to him, she gasped, "Now." Sloppily, she tried to release her slacks.

He grabbed her wrists. "Me."

"Mmm." Her labored breathing was in direct contrast to the patient lift of her arms, inviting him to finish with her clothes. He followed her lead, trailing his tongue painfully slow as he went all the way to her feet. He traveled back up her legs, sending her over an unexpected and brutal crest. Her fingers dug into his shoulders.

She pulled him up, and with shaky hands she could hardly control, groped off his shirt. The feel of his body ripped a rush of memories through her. Nails scratched as she rotated, carelessly dragging off clothing, grasping to feel every part of him along the way. Trying to take him where he could take her. Everything around them was a cloudy blur, with tight circles of sensation wrapping them together. She felt her latch release and she spilled out into his hands. The only thing for them now was flesh, hot and moist.

"Now," she repeated breathy. "I need you now."

His demanding lips kissed her as rough hands trailed down her neck, teasing circles around her before moving his hands down and whispering, "More."

Her short nails held onto muscled flesh, this time at his back as she lifted to him and cried out. Desperate, she struggled through the aftershocks to roll over and straddle him. Taking his hands and linking fingers, she held on and lifted, taking him. Holding there, joined, she closed her eyes with drunkenness before she let her head fall back.

Lifting, they began to move. She watched his eyes turn opaque with need as they sped, the desperation of wanting to push that last bit closer, uniting. They didn't blink as they held their gaze moving together. She saw his eyes turn from opaque to intense.

Andy drove, all control lost at the feel of her, blowing them both away with a power that shook. As she collapsed over him, he shuttered with a need for her that he hadn't quite satisfied. He gently rolled over, then lifted her breathlessly. With weak arms, he picked her up and carried her to the single bed that doubled as a couch. As she lay dizzy on her back, he took her hands, lifting them over her head and wrapped her fingers along the small headboard. "You should hold on," and took her. Cheek to cheek, he felt tears drip down her face until they both went over again.

Rose lay there with arms overhead, seemingly frozen in time. "Amazing," she breathed, lifeless.

He laid his head on her chest, opening one eye to see her. "I hope I didn't set a standard. A little pent up, you could say." Resting his cheek betw   sighed. "I'm lost in love with you."

CHAPTER 21

Andy remained still as beams of morning light lined the air in the cabin of the boat. He would never let go again. She was his now.

With their legs twined, Rose lay sleeping, using his shoulder as a pillow in the chilly morning. He watched the rise and fall of her back as it moved with the slight sway of the boat. Closing his eyes, he rested his chin on the top of her head. How did this happen?

He was able to tell the moment she woke from the change in her breathing. Brushing the bits of hair from her face, he tucked the short pieces behind her ear. With her neck now exposed, he set his lips on the side of her neck and whispered, "Good morning," then rolled to his side, propping himself on his elbow.

"Mmm." Her eyes lit when she opened and saw him. "Good morning."

He heard her breath catch, just a little, as he crawled over her and walked naked to the small fridge, taking out two bottles of water.

Sitting up, Rose blurted out, "Jeez, I left Grace, Gracie, Grace. I left both of them."

Kissing her forehead, he sat back next to her. "I left the carpenter. They'll live. Today's the Fourth." He twisted the cap off the first bottle and handed it to her.

Rose sighed. "Your folks' party, yes. We should start with food, though. I'm thinking I'm famished." Looking down at her naked body, then next to the floor at her torn shirt, she added, "And I need a shirt."

He let his gaze travel to her breasts. "That would be a shame." He grinned. "I don't remember these."

"I was one of the few that benefitted from the freshman fifteen."

He got up and sauntered to another compartment. He had a small stash of clothes and an extra toothbrush for reasons he wasn't about to confess.

"Thanks." She wrapped their blanket around her and headed to the tiny bathroom with things in hand.

He dressed and waited on the couch with his legs propped on the secured coffee table. Surreal. She didn't seem to take any more time getting ready than she ever had and came out quickly still looking loose and lazy.

"I know an incredible little dive that I remember has the best French toast this side of the great lakes," he said.

She adjusted an earring and smiled. "I'm hungry. Let's do it. Then, we should pick up Charcoal before heading to your folks'. He'll be so glad to see you."

They found the place just before starvation hit. Debating, he argued they hadn't replaced the tables or chairs, while Rose thought they'd rearranged the layout.

Eating dripping French toast, he noticed her watch the owners working behind the long counter. Although elderly and slow, they had a rhythm and seemed to work as a unit, a team. No one but Andy would have noticed the slight change in her expression.

"What's the matter?"

"Nothing." Her eyes softened as she looked at him. "Nothing at all, actually."

"I've got to put in a few hours at work today and I'd like to get to Gracie's pad. That's what Delores and I like to call it."

Rose lifted her eyebrows as she dipped a bite in syrup. "Delores?"

"Mmm, yes. She'll be brokenhearted that I'm two-timing her now. Except, she has had her eye on a man in her Silver Sneakers class."

Rose took her coffee in both hands and propped her elbows on the table, sipping as she listened.

"...worked for me going on three years now. She's a gift. A good-luck charm and is one of the prettiest ladies I know." He picked up his mug and drank. "As I was saying, I'd hoped to finish Gracie's pad soon." He smiled wide. "But I was pulled off the job yesterday."

In Rose's pickup, they rounded the corner onto the cul-de-sac. "Look, the neighbor's flowerbeds are in full bloom. My mother takes care of these over here...blue hydrangeas, yellow day lilies, creeping petunias. This is one of the prettiest times of the year," she said. "Sometimes I miss working in the dirt."

The next thing she mentioned was Dave's unmarked car in the drive. "Uh, oh," she mumbled. "This can't be good." She turned to him sheepishly. "I should see what's up. You don't have to be here for this."

He shook his head at her. "I just got you back." They opened their doors at the same time and walked around to the front of her truck.

"Together then," she said and reached out her hand.

It was quiet as they climbed the handful of porch steps. No barking. No arguing. Rose used her key. Slowly, she opened the door halfway. Stopping, she softly called out, "Mom? Dad?"

They could clearly hear murmuring from the kitchen. With Rose by his side, they headed in that direction.

Sounding annoyed, Rose spoke up, "I know you can hear— holy shit!" Her hand covered her eyes like she'd been blinded by the sun.

Her stepdad stood in his boxers, partially hidden by her mother, who was wrapped in a bed sheet. She was sitting on the kitchen counter with a carton of cookies and cream between them and the oddest expression on her face that Rose had ever seen—even if from between her fingers. Her frigging parents. *Divorced* parents. Eating ice cream. Half naked. In the kitchen. "What the hell?"

"Hello, Andy." Her mother shifted her posture as if that would make a bit of difference. "Charcoal's in the yard, Rose dear. If you wouldn't mind going back to get him, your dad and I could...you know. Get dressed."

* * *

Rose paced as they waited, frustrated with Andy's easy demeanor. He sat on the floor, scratching the hundred-twenty-pound Lab's belly. They both made male purring noises of bonding and macho shit.

Looking up to her, he smiled. "Don't look to me for shock and disgust, my folks are like rabbits."

Men.

Dave came down in wrinkled work clothes, her mother in a coral no-sleeved mock turtle neck and ivory slacks with no-toe pumps.

Andy joined them and they all sat at the kitchen table. This was one of those times she wished she couldn't read him so well, because she could tell Andy was ready to burst out laughing. Traitor.

"Well?" Juvenilely, Rose crossed her arms. "Are you two sneaking the hell around? What the hell happened to your eye?"

Dave and Andy looked at each other in some kind of silent understanding.

Men.

Her mother placed her hand gently on Rose's. "That's a lot of 'hells,' honey." Nodding over to Andy, she just as juvenilely responded, "Hypocrite much?"

Rose looked back and forth between the three of them, then rubbed her hands over her face. "Okay, okay. Andy and me later. You two, now."

Dave interrupted with what sounded like his detective's voice. "It's a holiday."

Her mother looked at him much like Rose might toward Andy if they were having one of their silent conversations, then turned back to her and Andy.

"Yes, it's a holiday," her mother said to them all, "and it looks as if we both have some explaining to do." She dropped her head on Dave's shoulder, then up again. "But you'll need to come by this weekend, then I'll explain. Saturday? Please? It's important. You pick the time."

Rose looked at her through the corner of her eyes. Sighing heavily, she nodded. "All right. Early afternoon. I have a publicity shoot for the new enclosure with Gracie in the morning." She turned to Andy. "So, no pressure for you," she said sarcastically.

Standing in front of the police station, Amanda sighed as Dave ran a hand over her hair and her cheek, then lightly kissed her bruised eye. "I'm so sorry. Some detective. Right under my damned nose."

"Stop saying that. This is on me." She took his hand and kissed his palm. "Me." Then, placed his hand on her cheek. From her small purse, she took out a large pair of sunglasses.

Dave took them from her hands and placed them gingerly over her eyes. "This is the last time you'll ever have to wear these."

She saw something terrifying in his eyes and it made her feel strangely safe.

"He will never lay a hand on you again. Never. Promise me one more time."

"I promise." She reached up to kiss him. "To never keep anything from you again as long as I live." Then deepened the kiss before letting him take her hand and walk into the tall, brick building. She was self-conscious and nervous, embarrassed and ashamed. Those were familiar feelings. Yet, she also carried a newfound strength.

He led her first to the sketch artist, stopping outside the door. "He came in on the holiday as a favor. Can you do this? He's good. He'll help you."

Flashes of Michael's face ran across her mind. "It won't be a problem. I should tell you, though, he changes his appearance. Hair color, style. Colored contacts."

"Yes, we'll go through all that. Get us a face, Amanda."

She gave his fingers a squeeze before parting with him.

Dave went directly to Lieutenant Tanner's office, knocked on the open door before entering the large room and shutting it behind him. Promptly, he sat in one of the smooth chairs across from his boss' desk. Then, impatiently rested his forearms on his thighs.

Dave Nolan and William Tanner went way back to when Tanner was the detective and Dave just an officer. In the nearly thirty years they'd known each other, Dave had never entered his office so disheveled. Not really knowing where to start, he decided on the beginning.

* * *

Rose stood next to an eight-foot, plastic folding table that was set up just outside the main building. The male bald eagle brought in during the night would like the outdoors, she decided. It was drizzling, but the eagle didn't care. Not just cold proof, eagle feathers were nearly waterproof thanks to a gland near their tail feathers that excreted an oily substance. Strangely, she didn't mind the rain either. The smell of fresh rain after the long dry spell was soothing and carried its own unique scent.

The bird was weak, yet could stand. Although, at the moment, he preferred to lie on his belly much like a hen sitting on her eggs. Tearing off small pieces, she hand fed him bits of frozen rat meat.

At the rumble of the engine, her hand stopped inches from the eagle's mouth. Andy. Her heart raced. Adrenaline rose. Andrew Reed. He was hers for good this time. Taking a deep breath, she gave herself a few seconds to take in the thought. She was a little old for running around the building to jump into his arms, so she focused on the bird.

He must have been frustrated that his food dangled just out of reach, because he rose up from his belly enough to grab the meat from her hand.

"Good, boy. You're not too weak to get annoyed with me, now are you?"

She heard the car door shut, then saw him make his way around the corner from the front. She felt like a teenager but made herself keep working. Mature. Professional. Head over heels. He made worn jeans and a faded polo look like he was on a catwalk, and she knew that walk minus the jeans and polo. Looking to him slyly, she nodded.

His responding wink stirred her insides. It didn't take him long to pause at the sight of the bird. Lifting his chin, he walked sideways around to her, then narrowed his eyes at the eagle. She could have sworn they were having a male testosterone moment, staring each other down. After what seemed to be an appropriate length of posturing glares, Andy continued his sideways walk to her. While keeping his eyes on the eagle, he wrapped a hand around the back of her neck and kissed her forehead with the side of his mouth, before turning quizzically to look at her.

Answering his unspoken question, she explained, "Lead poisoning. Bullets. Damned hunters...and I'm not against hunting per se."

"Says the woman who gathers up a loose spider from my boat and sets it free on the dock." This time he kissed her quickly on the mouth. "Hello."

"Hello back." She thinned her lips. "Several grants and conservation efforts come from wildlife and gaming groups. They're useful and appreciated. Hell, Dr. Gray is an avid hunter. It's the careless ones that get to me. And I do mean the ones who could care less. They claim to be humanely saving animals from overcrowding and starvation. Do they aim for the ones that would starve? The sick? The old? Never. They go for the biggest, healthiest buck with the most points they can find, so they can stuff its head and put it over their fireplace mantle."

Andy dared to get a little closer, checking over the bird. "This one's been shot?"

"No, no. Lead poisoning. Some hunters use lead bullets and leave poisoned carcasses for other animals to scavenge and become sick. He should be better in a few days—one of the lucky ones. How much longer do you think you'll need on the aviary? He could use a larger area to get his strength back."

Inconspicuously, he took her hand. "Mmm. I've always loved it when you get riled up. I could be done a lot quicker if you helped me. What are you feeding him?"

She smiled suggestively, tightened her bandana and set back to the feeding. "Ratscicle. Let me finish up a few things. I can find some time in a little while, sure."

The sketch artist wasn't the only one Dave called in on the holiday. He eyed his assistant who sat in his rickety guest chair. Dave pulled over a new whiteboard in front of their current case board. "We might not have much time. He's likely on the run again."

"Who—"

"Shut up and take notes." Dave took out his marker and drew five vertical lines from top to bottom. He labeled the columns: Description, Known Victims, Suspected Victims, Known Facts/Patterns, Suspected Facts/Patterns, and Locations. "This is what we've got: A man approximately five-foot-six; native language Espanola but can speak English without an accent. He's between forty-five and sixty years old. Suspected to use several aliases, one of which is Michael Rainer—"

"Rainer," his assistant interrupted. "I've read that name."

Dave looked up in question.

With raised hands, Nick explained, "I wasn't creeping, just have seen it on your desk. Don't ask me to be your assistant if you don't want me to look through stuff you leave in plain sight. From the looks of it, you've tried that case on and off for twenty years. What's up?"

Conceding, Dave went on, "We have a...description. A sketch in an hour or so. A pattern. Listen to this." Dave took the tape recorder from his top desk drawer. Gathered the strength to listen to it again. "Then, we're making some calls to see which larger cities over state lines have detectives working on the holiday."

"I want you to know that I fully expect to be announced as your favorite son." Duncan worked with his uncle, anchoring two-by-fours to frame a volleyball court in the field behind Nathan's home. With sweat beading along Duncan's lanky back, he eyed the two truckloads of sand that waited to be spread.

The area was measured precisely to game regulation, of course. Nathan wouldn't have it any other way, and Duncan wouldn't have his uncle any other way. As reluctant as a younger Duncan had been about letting him in his life and his heart, Nathan slipped seamlessly into the role of his deceased father. Never replacing him, Nathan made sure that he and Andy remembered their parents. Duncan's father had been Nathan's only brother. Photo albums were left out, home movies were watched and they visited their graves each year on their wedding anniversary as well as their birthdays. And the stories—Nathan could tell a story.

But Duncan didn't need the reminders. He appreciated them, yes, but his memory served him well enough, too much some times.

He worked shirtless, exposing the tattoo he *hadn't* told his aunt about. Hardly stopping his work, he quickly pulled a band from his pocket and tied his hair in a low tail, lifting it from the back of his neck in the heat. The fresh smell of the wildflowers growing along the floodplain of Black Creek wafted in the gentle breeze. He wouldn't trade these times.

Nathan handed him a towel. "Does your mother know about that one?" He gestured to the tattoo.

"Why does everyone around here seem to be more fascinated with the art on my body than on my canvases?"

Nathan lifted his brows while tilting his head. Together, they ran towels along their necks as they watched the small children run through the warm creek with their parents. Teenagers took turns with the two paddle boats Nathan had added to his collection of large toys. The crowd was thin for now, yet promised to turn into one of the larger Reed gatherings.

Picking up a shovel, Duncan spoke up, "I bought some land north of here. Andy agreed to build me a house."

Nathan was bending to pick up his shovel but paused. Duncan noticed he closed his eyes tightly before grabbing it. "Is that so?" Nathan dug the shovel into the load of sand and tossed it toward the edges of the shallow wooden frame. "How much land?"

He smiled at his uncle's attempt to look casual and appreciated his warm, yet guarded reaction. "Just under forty acres. What the hell am I going to do with forty acres?" Bits of sand stuck to his skin as he helped spread it to the perimeter. "Do you really think people are going to play sand volleyball in this heat?"

"Sure, since they'll have you to fill up their water guns after. Where exactly is north of here?"

Duncan wondered how he ever got these jobs anyway. "Three miles from the outskirts of town on the Eighty-Six."

"I know a wood working artist who might be interested in the cabinet and trim work."

Sighing, Duncan looked over his shoulder at him. "You have your own backlog of customer orders, and I have plans for a very big house."

Nathan stopped and rested a hand on the end of the handle of his shovel. "You mean Duncan Reed big? Let me at least oversee the work."

Duncan held out a dirty hand and they shook on it.

Securing the wired netting around the aviary was mindless work for Andy, and that was a good thing, because his mind twisted with the last few days. He gladly ran the changes through in his head. The beautiful woman holding the netting next to him was an added bonus. He made efforts to respect her position here and keep to his work. It took a lot of effort.

The smell of freshly sawn four-bys and the sound of the staple gun helped him focus. Mostly.

Rose in her work mode left no room for play. Everything was serious, intense. Her sleeves were pushed up, her brows were scrunched and her legs were braced. Mmm. Long, lean legs. He knew they must be flexed and defined and...distractions.

He misplaced a staple, making the edge of the frame splinter. "Shit." He looked around.

"What do you need? I'll get it."

He couldn't keep from smiling. She wouldn't be off to get what *he* needed right now. "Got it." Reaching into his tool belt, he pulled out a chisel and pried the staple from the wood as he noticed Rose's assistant coming out the back of the main action center building. She carried two water bottles and a couple of bars of some kind.

"Got your text, boss." She wore tight, white denim capris that showed off both her female curves and the toffee color of her skin.

"Wow." Grace looked up at the enclosure. "Is it done?"

Rose took the water and bars from her.

"Nope. She's got a few more corners and hinges, then I've got some perches and a tree to install." Andy stuck the chisel back in its pocket and reached in another for the staple gun.

"You need anything else? If not, I'm going right back into the air conditioning and back to that cute intern." She didn't leave without Andy noticing her suspicious glare.

"No, thank you." Rose shook her head. "That's all."

Yup. Curt, serious efficient, sexy, his. He finished the corner they'd started, allowing Grace to disappear back into the main building.

He walked up to her and stood close, without touching, until she turned to him. "Mmm. Peaches."

Rose blinked three times rapidly as her chest expanded and released a long sigh.

"I see it's break time. There's a private spot in that storage shed over there."

Rose lifted a brow high, then pursed her lips together. "I am the most upcoming doctor of biology in the Northeast and a respected conservationist. I can't run off midday for a piece of nookie."

Discreetly, he linked the tips of their fingers as they rested at their sides. "I want my break."

CHAPTER 22

Rose chewed on the side of her cheek and thinned her lips. Andy stepped, barely brushing against her, and whispered with lips close to her ear. "If we get caught, you can kick my ass."

Casually, he picked up several scrap pieces of wood and some random tools, placed them in a wheelbarrow and headed for the shed.

The wheelbarrows-as-props barely fit as he wedged a board through the inside handles of the metal doors.

Rose warned him. "Keep your voice down. What if someone hears us?"

He smiled wide and jutted his chin back. "You're the noisy one." The blue of her eyes lit in the beams of light that crept through small seams in the walls.

"Your hands," she purred as she took one and guided it to her, then molded hers around it.

He took, grabbing possessively, and slid his other hand behind her knee, pulling her leg around his back. In the dark, her head fell against him as she hung on behind him with her leg. Her warm lips traveled along his neck and over his collarbone.

She balanced using her lifted knee while grappling under his shirt. They rotated. Something fell over, broke. He traveled his mouth along her silky neck and down her chest, unbuttoning her shirt and letting his lips follow the release of each. She tasted as good as she smelled. Her flesh was as soft as her lips. Flipping the front latch, the material caught. He expelled a long breath he hadn't realized he'd been holding. Pulling back just enough as his eyes adjusted in the dark, he spread the material, exploring her flawless skin in the dim light. He grabbed hold possessively, circled then pulled just enough to feel her quake.

Andy's exploring lips and invading hands covered her, giving her little time to think, let alone keep any kind of professional composure. She let her leg slide down his side to the ground as he released the button and zipper of her slacks letting them pool around her feet. His hand plunged into lace and over warmth.

The sensations of want and need—being wanted, being needed—overwhelmed and took control. He cupped his hand, assaulting, pressing. She felt the first wave of heat radiating from low in her body. He must have known because he covered her with hands and lips. Her forehead dug into his shoulder and moved back and forth. Shaking, she held on to him.

In a low voice, he turned his head toward her ear. "You're making me crazy."

Her smile turned sly. She knew she had him completely vulnerable and stared intently, watching as she opened his jeans and led him painfully slow.

Her legs wavered, but he held her up as they moved together. She kept her gaze locked with those caramel brown eyes that held so much of her in them. She began to tighten, felt him shake and watched his eyes turn glassy.

This was theirs. She matched Andy as they went over together, a layer of sheen giving smooth movement between them. Her mind spun; her body electrified. She felt him hold onto her hips with urgency. The ride down was slow and long.

They stood together, content and as close as possible, joined.

"You've still never said it."

Was that true? Her smile was slight when she opened her eyes to him. Sincere. The beams of sunlight were enough to faintly see the ring of slate blue around the light brown of his eyes. "You take my breath away, Andy. I love you," she said and kissed one of his eyelids. "I love you." She kissed the other. "I love you." Taking his mouth, she locked her feet together behind him and wrapped her arms around his neck, sinking deep into the moment.

* * *

Sunburns ignored, children dragged themselves from Black Creek and teenagers from volleyball to take up water guns and balloons. Those brave enough to go shoeless walked like they were on hot coals over the dry and brittle grass from the field, then straightened as soon as they reached the barefoot grass of Duncan's aunt and uncle's property.

Duncan reclined on a padded, cast iron chair near the hose spigot. He wasn't so occupied with his role of passing out and filling water guns and balloons that he didn't notice the two people still missing from the Fourth of July festivities were Andy and Rose.

He looked around at the space he'd spent most of his childhood. Years of deadheading, trimming and weed-pulling had once convinced him to make a vow never to allow anything but sod in any property he owned. Now, he found himself admiring the balance of greens, brown-tufted grasses and floral color.

In the landscaping plot closest to Black Creek, two personalized garden stones caught his attention, one for Macey and one for Goldie. Cancer took the one and a broken heart took the other. He missed them more than he'd expected.

The memory left him when Amanda caught his eye in the distance, walking over the bridge with...Dave? How many years had it been since the detective had been to one of these? They maneuvered next to each other with subtle body language that told Duncan they were more than divorced parents working to have an amicable relationship for the sake of their daughters. As they approached, swelling around Amanda's bug-eye sunglasses was evident to him but likely wouldn't be noticed by others.

Sitting comfortably, he nodded in greeting before warning the two of them of the teenagers with loaded water guns waiting in hiding. They seemed to have suspected this already as they headed straight for the safety of the house.

Most of the older adults were inside, except for the ones that were too young at heart to realize they were the older adults. His uncle fell into that category. Nathan morphed into a junior high boy each Fourth of July, rolling in the grass and shooting anything that moved with a time-honored tradition.

Even at close to eighty, Duncan's grandparents could be

caught necking if one paid attention. They weren't quite scared enough of getting wet to go inside and mostly wanted to snuggle on the oversized folding chair and watch their grandchildren play.

No one dared to get Duncan wet. He had the hose. Even still, the little ones drew to him like a magnet. Purposely, they teased him until he turned the hose on them for a quick once over in the heat.

Inside, toddlers and infants took late afternoon naps in bedrooms upstairs while their parents snacked, laughed, and told old stories and new jokes. Each table, counter, chair, and couch was occupied.

Due to the line of cars, Andy parked far and walked up the drive. Together, he and Rose moseyed in silence. He pondered over the hundreds of times they'd strolled this paved road together. Mostly, he thought of how similar it felt, yet in reality, completely different. Now, it was absolute and gloriously permanent.

He held the door for her, inhaling the scent of peaches as she passed. She paused in the foyer as he caught up. He felt a familiar sense of teamwork as they moved around each other. Give and take. It took a few seconds for the two of them to realize the crowded room had gone silent. He looked to Rose, looked around his friends and family, then back to Rose. With a thousand-watt smile, he linked fingers with her and walked into the kitchen, holding their joined hands high like a teenage boy who'd just won a bet. Cheers erupted and toasts circled, honoring the two of them. Words of well wishes were offered as relatives bragged about knowing this would happen all along.

It took little time for Andy to notice someone was missing. He asked as a general question to whoever was listening, "Where's Duncan?" It took only a second for him to answer his own question. "Damn it. I'm missing the water fight?" He dropped Rose like an end loader drops a ton of river rock. "I'll get crap for guns." He turned to her and winked seductively before heading back out the front.

He made sure to have a loaded arsenal of filled balloons ready and topped off his water guns. Slowly, he slipped onto his folks' bedroom balcony, readying a bucket of water meant for Duncan's head.

Duncan lifted a brow before pivoting out of the way of the

dropping water and turning the hose up at Andy.

Fights ensued. Grown men shrunk to the maturity of small boys. Getting soaked was a battle scar to be worn proudly. He had mixed feeling playing war with his brother ever since Duncan returned from the Mideast. Hiding behind bushes, running, diving, shooting. Duncan never showed any signs of emotional scars. They split up into teams, planned, scammed, and attacked until their stomachs spoke louder than their egos.

Andy was one of the first inside; clean but soaking wet, he walked straight to Rose, dipping her into a long, dramatic kiss. More cheers and cat whistles burst out as the group settled in for a late dinner. Most took their plates outdoors.

Nathan approached Andy as Rose chatted with the elderly Grandma and Grandpa Reed. "When?"

Andy turned, lifted his brows up and down once. "Yesterday."

"You sure about that? Looks like a lot longer."

"Feels longer. She won't get away this time. I'm going to marry her. It's not official." Smiling now, he added, "But, this will be the last time she's ever engaged."

He shared a chair with Rose as they watched the antics of the people they loved. Several anti-nuclear families were in the mix—himself, raised by his uncle, Rose by a stepdad. All of them were closer than most four-square families. Blood wasn't always thicker than water, he mused.

Children gathered for the fireworks, orchestrated by Duncan, of course. They squeezed in chairs by twos and threes. A small handful of them waited in the hammock underneath the deck. He realized it was time for the next generation to take over that spot. Just as it was time for him and his Rose to move on and make their own family. He thought of the right time and place to ask her as she waved her hand in front of his face.

"Whoa. Come back to me."

He smiled at her and pulled her close in the oversized lounge chair. "Always."

Cynthia worked in Northridge's favorite coffee shop. She was twenty-nine and lamented about still working the Fourth of July shift, turning thirty soon and yet to be married. Although *she* didn't mind being single. It was her two older sisters, and ugh, her mother. If she had to go on one more blind date, she was moving to Montana.

As she locked up, she thought of ideas on how to get out of her birthday party. She could say she was sick or that she wanted to have a quiet evening with family. Sorting through her keys as she walked, she found the one for her Camry just as she saw him coming from the corner of her eye.

Fear gripped her. This couldn't be happening. Think, think, think. Fumbling for her pepper spray, she turned to defend herself seconds too late. It went flying along with her keys as the man grabbed for her throat. He was disgusting, with faint lines of black hair dye dripping down with his sweat. She couldn't scream beneath his tight grip, could barely choke out words.

Her eyes bulged at the look of the fresh wound on his neck. Eyes darting, her efforts not to panic were fruitless.

"I have money," she breathed. "Credit cards. They're yours." Through fear and pain, she held out her purse.

The man looked around as he pulled out a knife, spun her around and led her toward a clump of trees. "I don't want your fucking money."

CHAPTER 23

Dave stood over the body, barking out orders. The ground was damp, and with the lack of grass in the heavily wooded area, it was an effort to preserve the scene. The coroner worked with his assistant, taking his dozens of photos from every angle. The CSI had finished her preliminary dusting and was working on the details at that time. The few pieces of evidence were photographed, recorded, bagged, and replaced with corresponding lettered markers.

The woman's handbag had been discarded several yards from the body and between the location they'd found her and her car. Dave ordered a rookie who looked especially green to take more pictures of the surrounding evidence locations before he lost it and contaminated the whole damned place.

Dave stepped away for a moment, closed his eyes and took a deep breath, taking in the scent of musty dirt, damp leaves and new plastic from the evidence bags. This was his doing, Dave knew it. The woman had been raped and beaten to death by hands that had been on his Amanda.

The officer first called to the scene sat on the back bumper of the ambulance, drinking bottled water while he waited for Dave to question him. Anxious to get to him, Dave was careful to follow protocol.

Pulling out his old-school mini-cassette player, he pressed *record*. "Victim identified as a Cynthia Coleman, age twenty-nine.

She lies approximately one hundred to a hundred-twenty-five feet from the road. Sprawled on top of the dirt and leaves, on her back, between clustered, young trees in a heavily wooded area. Partially clothed with skirt raised, exposing bruising on thighs. Underwear found torn in close proximity to victim labeled as evidence exhibit A. Face heavily battered and listed as probable cause of death. Likely sexual assault determined by both coroner and myself. Purse approximately thirty feet from victim, labeled as evidence exhibit B. Cash and credit cards remain. Victim found approximately forty yards from her vehicle." He looked toward the street. "CSI finishing up with dusting for prints as I speak. Worked at Java Java. Allegedly closed the shop alone last evening. Waiting to confirm with manager as only the owner available at this time of night. We haven't located next of kin as of the time of this recording."

This was no coincidence. He'd been here. It was nearly more than Dave could take. The woman lay spread out and unnaturally twisted with brown eyes frozen wide in death. He guessed she had been dead between four and six hours but would wait for the coroner to confirm before entering it into his voice recording. She'd tried to use pepper spray. It ended up five yards to the back of her vehicle. Dave played the scene through in his head. She would have come from the south, heading for the driver's side of her Camry. From the location the pepper spray was discarded, that would make the assailant left handed.

"Are we synced on preliminary cause of death?" Dave studied the lab tech taking dimensions of a shoe print as he spoke to the coroner.

"Bruising and tears around vaginal opening consistent with forced penetration. And, yes, we are in agreement that the preliminary cause of death is blunt force trauma to the head."

Dave understood the need to be emotionally removed, and wasn't he often accused of that exact thing? This was different. He cringed at the coroner's calloused descriptions. He would get through this with precision, then head to the station to piece together leads and probabilities.

Walking into his office, Dave's aide carried coffee, soda and a file folder. "I see," she said as she gestured to the photo of Cynthia Coleman.

"Yeah. Shit." Dave took the Styrofoam cup.

He stood at his case board scribbling notes. Next to him was the sketch of Michael Rainer taped in the column labeled *Description.* He'd already memorized it. It hung next to the *Known Victims* column bearing both Amanda's and Cynthia Coleman's photos, before and after for both.

"Get out your notepad. I want three extra paper pushers searching police department databases for cases of multiple reports of pending battery and robbery, sexual assault and robbery, or both. Tell them to start with bigger cities this side of the Mississippi."

Dave rubbed the stubble on his cheek. He'd been called to the scene at 2 a.m. He had to leave Amanda with the damned dog. She thought nothing of it. Once a cop's wife, he thought.

"I'm going back out there to ask around now that people are up and before they leave for work." Dave had seen his share of beaten and murdered women. This was different. A small chill made his shoulders shake. "You get busy leading the search over state lines. Any hits you get, fax them a copy of that." He pointed over his shoulder at the rendering of the alias Michael Rainer.

His assistant set the bottle of soda on Dave's worn desk, opened the file folder and started taping up photos in the Suspected Victims column. "No, I meant *I see* that you went out on this call without me. Not that I don't appreciate you taking me on as your aide, but how the hell am I going to learn if you don't contact me when you get a call? And I'm a genius."

Dave walked over and looked at the before and after photos of the new women that were posted in the Suspected Victims column. Each was labeled at the bottom with name, age and city. Pittsburgh; Indy; Washington, D.C.; Chicago; and Milwaukee. "How? When?"

His assistant sat down, crossing one ankle over the other on Dave's desk. "I told you, I'm a genius and while you were reconciling and consoling your ex, I was pulling an all-nighter."

"You're right. I apologize. I should have called. I was...wasn't thinking."

"On account of the situation, forget about it." His assistant nodded toward the photos. "Each of these women had years of scattered robbery and assault reports. The perp fits the basic description. Aliases used so far are Maarten Ricks, Monty

Rodriguez and Miguel Rauel. Initials M.R. Michael Rainer fits." His aide walked up to the Coleman picture, studied the notes underneath. "What makes you think this one's connected if money was left on her?"

"He was angry. Amanda said no to him. Physically hurt him. Emotionally humiliated him." Dave took a deep breath, his mind spinning with plans and strategies. "Catch a nap in the bunk room, then see what else you can come up with."

"This is Jenna Woith, reporting live for WCEL TV, from the Birds of Prey Research and Action Center. We are here this morning to join in the ribbon cutting ceremony for the newly constructed predatory bird aviary."

"This is stupid," Rose said.

Andy could hear her grind her teeth. "This is publicity." He held tightly onto her arm.

"This is a dog and pony show."

Conceding with a tilted nod, he whispered, "You look beautiful."

"I don't look any different than I do any other day. You're all cleaned up. Look at the size of those obnoxious scissors. The frigging mayor is here. Do I have to? This is Dr. Gray's research center."

"You look like a doctor of biology who specializes in conservation. I'm dressed like I own my own building and developing business." He resisted kissing her cheek. "And, yes, you have to cut the ribbon with the scissors. It's ceremony and this is your project, not Paul's."

She stepped out smiling widely, motioning dramatically for him to follow.

The small crowd applauded.

"Thank you all for coming," Rose said with a clear voice as the reporter shoved the microphone inches from her face. Without acknowledging it was there, Rose continued, "What we have here is a place for injured birds to properly rehabilitate and for Gracie the eagle, our newest addition to the center's education animals." She continued articulately and with appropriate enthusiasm citing a summary of Gracie's avian pox and the events of the animal's life that followed.

He thought she was seamless. She presented just enough facts to keep it interesting and impress the audience without losing the attention of those who weren't into this kind of thing and were really just here to make an appearance. Although the catalyst was Gracie, Rose used the present lead-poisoned bald eagle as an example, making sure to emphasize the enclosure would assist all injured birds, not just the one.

She gestured for him to take the lead. "Please give a warm welcome to Andrew Reed, owner of Reed Builders, whose generous donations of both materials and labor made this all possible. Andy?"

He thought that for how much she hated this, Rose could put on a good show. He couldn't resist shooting her a small wink as he took the podium.

He looked at the crowd and noticed the reporter in the front row lifted a brow.

"Thank you, Dr. Piper." He wore his black dress pants, Duncan's Italian shoes, a fitted gray-blue shirt, and a black tie. "It is the honor of Reed Builders that we were able to give this gorgeous animal a place to spread her wings and thrive as much as humanely possible. Gracie is special, and in a way, represents many species, winged and not, that are at the whim of human intervention. Let's cut the ribbon and set her loose!"

Applause rippled as he glanced over his shoulder at Rose. He did a double take when he saw water pooled in her eyes. She blinked twice at him, then headed for the giant scissors. Smiling at the cameras, she cut the ribbon, cheered and then politely directed the group to the outside of the structure.

He helped with the podium and with the nosy Jenna Woith. Nudging her out of the enclosure, he shut the door securely behind them. They watched as Grace and Rose put on their leather gloves, then stepped out with Gracie tethered to Rose's arm. The enclosure was extensive. He had installed artificial trees at each end that would scrape and peel much like the feel of actual bark and branches. In the middle was a large water tank because damn it if he wouldn't ensure the girl would have her chance at fishing. He wished the area could be taller, as it went only up about three stories.

Jenna Woith edged closer and, while keeping her eyes on the bird, leaned toward him and whispered in his ear, "You two make a cute couple. The conservationist and the land developer. That could make a great story."

He stood expertly expressionless.

"You're Nathan Reed's boy, aren't you?"

He'd had years of practice with reporters who tried to crash the house showing his uncle offered his friends and customers every other year.

He turned slightly to look at her with eyes of steel. "We're here for Gracie today." Then pretended she wasn't there.

The euphoric feeling of watching the girl take her first, honest flight surprised him. There was enough room for her to spread her wings and glide momentarily before perching on a protruding branch and screeching loudly. "Ha! Look at her!" He swore she was working the crowd.

Rose and Grace high-fived over success that was a longtime coming.

"This was his doing, wasn't it?" Amanda took the story she'd printed from the Northridge News site and set it on Dave's desk.

He sighed and nodded. "I think so, yes."

"Did you see it? Was it as bad as they say?" She paced. "I can't help but feel responsible."

Dave got up and took her gently by the shoulders. "No more feeling responsible." Then, brushed his thumb over her chin.

"What happens now? What can I do to help?" she spoke into his chest.

"At some point, we'll bring you back in for more questioning. For now, be careful, be safe."

She frowned at him.

"His pattern is to hit and run. He's likely moved on now. Our work will be across state lines. We're gathering his hot spots. I'm working to clear out the women willing to leave and place unmarked patrols at the others. He's going to show up, Amanda. We're gonna get him." Brushing back the hair from her face, he changed the subject. "Where are you headed?"

"I've got a meeting with the M.O.D. at the shelter in Seneca Falls. I may have to work up plans for another can drive there. Then, I'll stop at the Waterloo location to make sure the volunteers for dinner show up. We've been having some issues there." In response to his scowl, she placed her hand on his cheek. "I've done this for years. I can't live in a closet. Won't."

"Don't go home alone." He put up a hand before she could

speak; a pained expression formed on his face. "You owe me that. Go to Jessica's. I'll call when I'm done here. Please."

She had no choice but to nod in agreement. "We meet with Rose tomorrow at one."

"How many speeding tickets have you had?" Rose sat in the small bucket seat next to Andy as he took a corner.

"Not that many. Lately." She loved when he grinned at her from the corner of his eyes. "I don't speed. Mostly. I just like to get to the speed limit as quickly as possible." He winked and tucked her short hair behind her ear.

"Are you sure you want to be here for this?" She tilted her head. "I'm not sure what's up. Mom avoided me at your folks' on the Fourth."

She had watched them that day at the Reed's. She gave them the space they'd requested even though she wanted to pull her mother aside and demand an explanation. Instead, she waited. Seeing them like that had somehow soothed her curiosity. She'd always been able to accept the divorce of her parents. It had been a decision between two grown adults. But seeing them together, knowing they'd always longed for one another, overwhelmed both the daughter and the woman inside her. And now?

"I'm nowhere near ready to let you out of my sight," he answered.

Charcoal stood at the sidewalk, obediently resisting the urge to run into the street, even though he'd clearly heard the familiar rumble from Andy's car around the corner. Older and much calmer now, the only uncontrolled part of his greeting was his tail. It wagged madly while the rest of him waited patiently.

Andy parked along the curb. They got out at the same time. Squatting, Andy rubbed Charcoal's ears before playfully smacking his side. Males postured no matter what species, she thought. The Lab took the bait and lowered his chest to the grass, tail swishing and daring. Andy nearly mimicked the pose, then chased him in circles as they made their way to the front door. "You coming in?"

Rose smiled, knowing he was talking to the dog. Charcoal darted in front of them as if, of course, he'd understood what he'd been asked.

Dave and her mother were waiting in the front room, holding hands together on the couch. They left the loveseat for her and Andy. She felt subtle warmth at the sight of her nestled parents and the familiar scent of home.

They followed their lead into small talk that ranged from the scissor-cutting ceremony at the center to the dog's latest antics. She noticed as her mother wrung her hands.

"There's more to your father and I getting back together." Her mother blew out a breath.

Momentary silence followed the jump into the reason for the meeting.

"It's about your biological father. It's not pretty, and you'll need to decide if you want Andy to be here for this."

Rose was much more concerned with her mother's jittery behavior than any story about some person she never knew. Never did she feel any need to hear about her biological father as some missing-parent adults did. She was surprised at the topic, though. Very surprised and looked to Andy, read the acknowledgement in his eyes, then nodded to her mother.

"I met him in Nicaragua, but you know that." Her mother stammered in a way that was new to Rose. Keeping her gaze on her mother's eyes, she noticed Dave squeeze her fingers as they rested on her thigh. "I was working with Red Cross. We...no, the reason I was there doesn't matter. What matters is that he broke into my trailer and..." Dave slid an arm around her shoulder. "He came in and...raped me. I left for the states shortly after."

"Mom." Instinctively, Rose's fingers covered her cheeks, a painful wince distorting her face. "Oh, Mom. Why didn't you ever tell me?" Rose felt her face drop as realization filled her. "Oh."

Her mother sat very still.

"I'm so sorry," Rose said. "That must have been terrifying. Were you...hurt badly? Did you have anyone to help you?"

"I had you." Her mother smiled warmly. "It was my choice. I healed and learned I was pregnant with you." Letting go of Dave's hand, she straightened her shoulders and folded hers in her lap. "But I'm afraid that's not all."

"If you think I care one iota about who my sperm donor was, let me just say I'm not built that way. Biology is science. Family is love. I wish you wouldn't have held this in for so long, if you felt you needed to tell me."

"He's come back."

Rose's eyes burrowed. She waited a beat. "What do you mean *come back*?"

"I mean he's been here, broken into the house, stolen from me...from us. Dave is going to find him and put him away so he can't hurt anyone ever again, but I need you to be careful. He's a very dangerous man. Very, Rose. Dangerous."

Feeling heat crawl up her neck and over her face, Rose was certain her face showed the instant it all clicked. Call it woman's intuition, whatever.

"Your eye. Oh, oh, your eye. Mom." She stood from the couch and walked to her mother now. Standing, they embraced with awareness.

Rose pulled back, tears dripping down her cheeks. "How long? No. Don't tell me. My birthday. It was my eighteenth birthday." She pressed her hand to her mouth. "That's eight years." She turned away, running her hands through her hair, grabbing hold of large chunks. "No." She spun. "No, not my birthday."

Dave stood and wrapped his arms around her mother's waist, whispering in her ear, "Let her get it out."

"Great-granddad." Rose looked to her mother and saw the answer she was looking for before taking off out the front door with Andy tight on her heels.

CHAPTER 24

Andy woke early, just before dawn. Rose was warm and tucked closely into him. She'd tossed through the night, turning the pillow over more times than he could count. They'd stayed at her place. His was small but still three times the size of her place. She'd given him a solemn tour without moving from the entrance of her studio apartment by simply gesturing an arm to the left, then right.

He figured the Italian take-out calmed her stomach and the merlot her nerves. Very few words were spoken and it seemed to help her get a handle on this new revelation. She'd burrowed into him while wrapped in a tight ball, something he didn't ever remember her doing.

He heard her suck in a breath and knew when she woke. He tightened his hold, felt her shudder then relax.

"I want to go away," she whispered, eyes still closed. "Not run away, go away. I haven't taken time off, not even a weekend, since—well, since high school."

He rotated onto his back, pulling her partially on top of him, then guided her cheek to his shoulder. Running his hand from the crown of her head down to the middle of her back, he responded gently, "You should go see your mom first. She'll be worried."

"Yes." Rose sighed. "He killed my great-granddad. I can't wrap my head around what she's been through. How did I not see it?

Any of it? We all assumed drugs while my mother was scared and hurt." She turned her face into his chest. "I want him in pain. I feel so angry I can't think. I want him in pain and I want him dead."

He held her closer and felt her skin begin to sheen with sweat. This would take time, he knew. A lot of time. Getting away was just what she needed. "She didn't want you to see, purposely hid it from all of you. She's a cunning woman, Rose. It runs in the family."

He lowered to kiss the top of her head before pausing at the reference to family. Her cringe made him realize that she, too, caught the comparison. Sperm donor was easier to say before they were dealing with murder.

As agreed, Rose went to see her mother. Andy had left early to catch up at work and to give her time alone with her mom. Standing in the empty house, she kicked herself for not calling first.

"You're staring." She looked down from the corner of her eyes at Charcoal. He sat with his head cocked and tail wagging. "I guess I could take you for a walk before I go." Recognizing the word 'walk,' the dog circled and whined. She smiled and sighed.

An overnight rain made the brittle grass smell like wet straw. Charcoal kept pace at her side as they left the cul-de-sac. She hadn't taken the dog for a good solid walk in a long time and, as it generally did, actually felt nice to have time alone. As she rounded the corner to the Reeds' street, she saw Duncan loading his rental car.

"Leaving already?" she called as she led Charcoal up the drive.

"I have a project in L.A. but have a few days yet before I need to go. I wouldn't have missed your sister's wedding and I've never had the nerve to miss the Fourth." He squatted down, face-to-face with the dog, and rubbed his cheeks with his thumbs.

She noted how similar the action was to Andy's.

"He's looking well." Duncan looked up, then darted his gaze down the drive and squinted before turning back to the dog and scratching his ears.

"Well, then in case I don't see you." She reached down and kissed him on the cheek. "Thank you for butting into our business. You don't fool me with your hard shell. You have a heart of gold," she said, and then kissed the other cheek. "You'll be missed, Duncan. Don't stay away for so long this time."

He stood as she turned and called over her shoulder, "See you in the grocery store magazine rack the next time the paparazzi catches you with one of your clients!"

When she returned, she let Charcoal outside, checked his water, then came back in to write her mother a short note.

Dear Mom,

Sorry I missed you—

The door opened before she could finish. "Mom?" Rose headed toward the front of the house. "I was just leaving you a note."

Her mother walked in with Dave. "There. Rose is here. You can go now." She turned to Rose. "So glad you came by," she said and hugged her. "He's become my shadow. Not that I don't like it, but I know he can't get much done like this."

Dave looked at Rose, then down at her mother and back to Rose again. "Don't leave her alone." He kissed both of them on their foreheads before leaving for the station.

Rose led her mother back into the kitchen. "Sit, Ma. I'm making you some hot tea."

"Thank you. I feel like I should be doing that for you. You've been working so much." Her mother sat and folded her hands on the table. "So, are you ever going to tell me the story with you and Andy?"

Rose poured water into the teapot and set it on the stove. "First ..." She sat and set her hands on the table. "I know you worry and I see now why you worry, but I want you to stop. I want you to stop and I want to say I'm sorry for—"

Her mother shook her head. "No need."

"Yes, much need. You need to know that I took off because I couldn't get a handle on what you've been through. Still can't. Not yet. Mostly, I want you to know that I don't care about him. I guess I've never told you that before because I don't think of him. I don't consider him my father in any way. He's an ugly man who hurt my mother. For years. When I think about it...I can't help it; I get angry. Very angry."

"Stay away from him, Rosemarie. Don't you ever—"

"No, no. I'm not stupid. Mom, I'm sorry. I wouldn't...I won't.

Ever." Rose shook her head clear, stood to get down two mugs and tea bags, and set them next to the stove. "I need to know." She turned to face her, leaning back against the counter. "Daughter to mother. Woman to woman. I need to know everything."

Her mother sighed and nodded. "All right." Then, walked over and took Rose's hands in hers tightly. "All right, but first I need you to look at a drawing. A police artist's rendering of him. I meant for you to do that yesterday before you ran out."

"It's not going to bother me." Rose held on loosely.

Reaching over and opening the corner kitchen drawer, her mother pulled out a copy of the nine-by-twelve-inch police rendering and held it close to her chest, facing outward.

So, Rose thought, that's the bastard. Blood boiling, she worked to memorize it. "I've never seen him before," she said flatly.

"Take it. Keep it with you." Her mother held it out.

Rose shook her head but held her hand out anyway. "If you want, but I won't forget."

Placing the copy in her outstretched hand, her mother emphasized, "Show it to whomever you can; Andy, your boss. He's a very dangerous man."

Taking a cleansing breath, Rose clasped her fingers around the paper. "Yes. I see that he is. I can take care of myself. Black belt remember...wait a minute. That's why—"

Her mother kissed her on the cheek as the teapot whistled.

"I was speaking hypothetically," Rose tried interrupting Andy's conversation between him and her boss.

Dr. Gray slouched comfortably in his padded office chair with fingers dug deeply into his front pockets, legs straight out in front of him. He nodded as he looked through her to Andy. "This will be a good opportunity for her assistant to get her feet wet without Rose there to pick her up when she falls down. Wart won't like it, but the bird will survive for a few days."

"Gracie." She felt like she was talking to the air. "Her name is Gracie—"

"Thank you, Paul." Andy held out his hand. "I'll bring her back in one piece."

Andy turned to her as if he just noticed she was there, then lifted his brows.

She stood with her arms crossed and head cocked. "What the hell are you doing? I have summer camp field trips, a list of animals that need care and an eagle to train."

"Grace can do it," Andy and Dr. Gray responded in unison.

She turned to head for her office. "I have interns and fundraising—"

Andy took hold of her arms, turned her. "It can wait." He picked her up, setting her over his shoulder.

"Okay, now this is mature." She bounced up and down with his stride.

"I'm leaving work, too, remember? We both need this." He headed toward the main lobby.

She first tried kicking and squirming; it was like trying to bend steel. So instead, she dug an elbow in his back, resting her chin on her palm as he walked.

She closed her eyes as she bounced over Andy's shoulder. What if Gracie wouldn't eat? What if she slides back on her training? What if the interns don't stay on the right feeding schedule for the baby opossums? What if her mother needs her? She sighed. She hadn't needed her through almost two decades of this.

Andy's strong, warm hand effortlessly held onto her thigh as they bounced through the hall. What if she didn't get the chance to be with him like this for weeks? Months? It was only a long weekend.

When they entered the lobby, the room fell silent. Too embarrassed to speak, she worked up her most intimidating glare.

Wes quickly turned and looked the other direction.

"I see you smiling, McGee."

The sun had yet to come up as Duncan sat in the white wicker couch of his uncle's guesthouse. Coffee in hand and feet propped on the matching coffee table, he read the morning news on his tablet. Crickets along with early morning birds and frogs were awake and easily heard, as the house was close to the creek. But, he wasn't really listening.

Lifting the cup to his lips, he inhaled the smell of strong, black coffee as his eyes narrowed. He took his time memorizing the face of the man on the home page of the Northridge Gazette site. The man with Rosemarie's eyes. His gaze shifted momentarily to the clock display in the corner of the screen, then back to the rendering. Time to get your ass up, Andy.

He used his speed dial as he read the article.

A scratchy and clearly irritated voice fumbled with the phone on the other end. "I'm on vacation. Go to hell."

"You need to get over here."

He could hear his brother rearrange the phone and let out a small grunt. "Everything okay?"

"No. How fast can you arrive?" He set the tablet aside and picked up his laptop. He could be much faster with a real keyboard and he had a lot of work to do.

"Shit, Duncan." There was a long pause before Andy repeated, "Shit. Give me an hour."

"An hour then." Duncan hung up and his fingers started moving.

Andy drove the SUV. His aunt would already be up, but the rumble from the Maserati would wake Nathan and his cousins. Dawn had passed and he could see the reflection of the homes all along the perimeter of the still water on the lake. The air was unseasonably cool for this time in the summer and smelled crisp and damp. He took little notice. His mind was on Duncan and what was going on with him.

Walking in without knocking, he found him sitting at the kitchen table flying across the keyboard of his laptop. He recognized his brother's posture. Concentration. If Duncan woke him up at the frigging crack of dawn and made him postpone leaving on his trip with Rose just to help him with hacking, he might very well kick his ass again.

The last time Duncan wanted his help, he remembered, was to look into the files of a client who was dragging his feet in paying him. The dude claimed to be close to filing Chapter Eleven when, in fact, they found records regarding a few million in gold ounces kept in out-of-state safety deposit boxes.

Duncan turned to acknowledge his arrival, and it took only one look for Andy to know this was big. "Sup?" Andy tilted his head up once.

Duncan changed screens and turned the computer to face

Andy. "You didn't show this to me. You should have showed this to me."

Andy turned his head partially away, but kept eye contact. "I told you what was going on."

"But you didn't show me the sketch of him. I've seen him. I think he might have been following Rose."

The muscles along Andy's shoulders tightened reflexively. Goose bumps prickled at the back of his neck. He took the seat next to his brother and listened. His head spun. When Amanda confessed the identity of Rose's father, of how the man had stalked and extorted her for years, he had felt pity and compassion for Amanda. He had felt a sense of need to protect Rose's heart as she worked to sort this out. Amanda made it perfectly clear that the man had no idea of Rose's existence.

But was that wrong? He thought of where she would be right then and picked up his cell. His brother watched clearly with judgment but didn't offer his opinion.

"Hey." Andy stood from the table and paced slowly.

"You should've slept in, but I'd hoped...I mean I figured you'd be at work." He ran his free hand through his short hair. "He's all right, but we're gonna need to leave a little later today." His hand clenched in and out of a fist but he spoke calmly. "Can you meet me in a little while? Say eight-ish?" Andy looked to Duncan who was back at his keyboard but nodding. "I'll pick you up. See you."

Duncan's fingers flew and he still didn't look but spoke up. "Are you ready to go on?"

His head might have been in a fog, but the information Andy had taken in and his option of the next few steps were in perfect clarity and likely matched that of his brother's. "I'm all right. Where are you at on there?"

Duncan finished a few strokes, then turned the screen to face him. "I'm in three internet cafés in three different states. I've got their pass codes memorized, but I need you to look it over."

Andy took lead and started backing up each process to look at the big picture. This was how they worked. Duncan had the memory; Andy had the sense of building. "You've got some holes, here." He pointed to the screen. "Here. And here." Andy worked while his brother got up to warm his coffee and to make Andy a to-go cup. They sat for nearly an hour, Andy working with Duncan over his shoulder, giving suggestions when needed.

"We'll need to move remote next." Andy ran his hands over his face.

"And we need to wait for someone to log in to track their ID and password key strokes."

They spoke at the same time regarding their next stop. "Internet café and coffee?"

Nodding in succession, Duncan copied files to a flash drive, logged off and shut down.

"First, the police station. I'll meet you there. I'm going to pick up a paper copy of the Gazette."

"Okay. I'm going to pick up my girlfriend. I'm sure she'll take this well," Andy said sarcastically.

"Are you sure you don't want to wait until after your trip to tell her?"

"Can't say I didn't think about it, but no. I won't keep this from her. Or anything else ever again."

Tossing a newspaper on Tanner's desk, Dave paced the worn carpet. On the front page of the Northridge Gazette was the sketch artist's rendering of Rose's biological father. "Copies of the profile and the sketch are also both printed and posted on newspaper sites in each of the five cities that have reasonably confirmed case connections."

Together, they turned at the knock on the door.

"Duncan." Dave looked honestly surprised. His first instinct was to tactfully explain that he was in a meeting and to come back later. Then, he realized Duncan had never once stepped foot in the station before. "I'll be just another minute. Would you mind waiting for me in my office?"

Duncan nodded and turned. As he swaggered down the hall, he wondered if he should bother yet with rescheduling his flight, which was taking off at that moment.

He opened a door down the hall with the plastic nameplate reading *Detective Nolan* next to the doorjamb. Walking in, he first scanned the room from top to bottom just as he habitually did when he entered anywhere new. Then, he headed to the case board.

He'd read the article that went with the photo, knew the man had Rose's eyes and was able to fit the pieces together easily enough. His eyes traveled to the other women—all dead and badly beaten, some naked.

"Who are you and who gave you permission to be in here?" Duncan had heard the footsteps before the voice.

Slowly, he turned and saw a uniformed officer standing with a white paper tray that carried a coffee and an enormous soda. The other hand rested on her gun, although he judged it to be more of a comfortable stance rather than a threat. Cat-like, steel-gray eyes kept contact with his, even though he sensed they were looking him up and down peripherally.

Turning back to the case board, he answered, "Duncan Reed to the first question. Detective Nolan to the second."

She walked over and pulled an empty slide across the case board. "Have a seat, Mr. Reed. He's due shortly."

He obliged. "Do you mind?" he asked, referring to the blank sheet of paper he pulled from the printer next to Dave's desk.

The officer shrugged and went to stand near the window, clearly babysitting him. He certainly could have had a less appealing sitter. Casually, he began sketching as he returned the favor and watched her through his own peripheral vision.

Dave turned back to his boss. "We're compiling an extended data search for victims who've reported a combination of more than three robberies with batteries or robberies with sexual assaults over the past decade as far west as Illinois and as far south as Virginia. How much longer can I keep the extra paper pushers?"

Tanner shook his head. "I can't make any promises, but keep what you need for now."

"Nick's gone above and beyond again. We won't be keeping her long. She's gathered more solid leads than the rest of the team put together."

"Yes, I've thought about that. I think an early promotion might keep her around a little longer. She's earned it. I don't want to rush you, but are you going to see about your friend?"

"Oh, shit." He stacked papers and stuffed them into his file. "I'll keep you updated, sir. Thank you for the support and the manpower."

He walked briskly to his office, running the next several steps in the investigation through his head. He was feeling better but not quite on his game. This was personal, and he knew he had to keep it professional, cross all of his Ts and dot all of his Is if he was going to keep the case. He walked in and saw his assistant standing by the window, the case board covered and Duncan with an ankle resting on top of his knee, an elbow leaning on the arm of the chair.

Duncan didn't stand.

"Duncan Reed, Officer Nickie Savage. Officer Savage, Duncan Reed."

"We've done introductions, sir. Mr. Reed here stated that you requested he come into your closed office to wait."

Dave smiled at the public face Nick could turn on a dime. "That's right. He's an old family friend." He turned to Duncan who hadn't moved since he walked in. "What can I do for you, Duncan?"

Duncan pulled out his phone and Dave assumed he was checking a text. "If you could give me just a few minutes, your daughter and Andy are..." The three of them heard her before they saw her.

CHAPTER 25

Andy held the door for Rose. He let her fume, red-faced and breathing hard.

"Bastard!"

"Officer Nickie Savage, this is my daughter, Rosemarie and her...boyfriend, Andy Reed."

The officer gave him and Duncan and once over.

"Yes, they're brothers," Dave answered her silent question.

She held out a hand. "I recognize you from the news," she said to Rose, then offered a hand to Andy.

Dave used what Andy thought sounded like a disclaimer. "Her language tends to be a little more colorful when heated up and not in front of a camera."

Andy placed a hand on the middle of her lower back. She didn't elbow him. That was a good sign.

"What brings you all here?" Dave sat partially on the corner of his desk.

Rose blurted, "Let's let Duncan start. He's the one that saw the bastard."

"In person?" Dave dropped his file on his desk.

"Yes, walking along the street in front of my folks' home."

Andy watched Dave take three breaths, then sat in his chair. "Why don't you start from the beginning?"

Expectedly, Duncan didn't change his annoyingly relaxed

posture. "Rose was walking her dog. She stopped to greet me. I squatted down to rub his ears...the dog's ears that is, when movement from down the drive caught my eye." Duncan looked toward him to see if he had indeed shared all of the details with Rose. Andy nodded.

Visibly shaking, Dave took out a notebook and pen. "Where exactly were you, Duncan? Up by Nathan's house, the middle of the drive, down toward the street? Please be specific."

"Up by the house. I was loading some things in my rental, getting an early start on packing some things for my departure." Duncan looked at his watch. "Which was a half hour ago."

Ignoring the reference to Duncan missing his plane, Dave went on, "Are you sure it was this man?"

Duncan sighed, annoyed, and squinted but only slightly. "I remember thinking the eyes looked familiar. I didn't think too deeply about it at the time, since I had no idea of what you now have hidden behind that whiteboard." Duncan nodded his head toward the covered wall. He rotated the paper in his hand that Andy hadn't noticed until just then. "This is Rose's father, biological father," he corrected in respectful succession to Dave.

Duncan held up the sketch he'd been drawing.

Officer Savage took a step forward, craned her neck, then tilted her head back, looking down her nose at Duncan.

Andy didn't turn his head or his gaze from Dave.

The drawing was definitely of Rose's father, dressed in a light jacket, dark jeans and ball cap, and had a dark wound circled with light markings around his neck. His hair was sloppy, short and black with lighter pieces showing through.

"Bastard," Rose repeated and paced.

The officer interjected, "You drew this just now? You're quite an artist, Mr. Reed. It's interesting how you gathered this much detail from a, what, half-second glance from down a drive that is long enough to have *up by the house, middle of the drive and down toward the street* sections."

Duncan maintained his casual posture, but this time, he turned his head to look at her straight on. "Don't hold back, officer, say what you really have on your mind."

She answered without hesitating. "I'll simply repeat myself, Mr. Reed. How did you gather this much detail from a quick glance such a distance away? How far is it? Twenty-five yards, thirty-five?"

Andy winced as he stood between his fuming brother and his equally fuming fiancée. He watched as Duncan looked at the officer, then closed his eyes as he turned back to face Dave. "Is there anything else I can do for you? If not, I'll be catching the evening plane to L.A."

"Yes, Duncan. We'll need about an hour for questioning." Dave turned to Rose and Andy. "From all of you. We might be able to spark some additional details from your memories."

Duncan looked toward the case board and rubbed the back of his neck.

"You can use the break room to phone the airline," Dave said as he scribbled notes in a small spiral pad. Dave stepped closer to Rose. "I'd like to tell you that I'm making you still take your trip, but I know better."

"Damn right I'm still taking my trip. Bastard. He's not running my life." Andy noted the slight softening in expression. "What about Mom?" she asked.

"I'll keep her close."

Dave rotated to Andy. "I know I can't tell you to keep your whereabouts from your family, but I will ask that you tell them to keep it confidential and don't tell anyone else. No one."

"We'll check in." He nodded as he repeated Dave's words. "I'll keep her close."

Andy nearly had to threaten Rose in order to get her to promise to stay at the action center until his return. She'd calmed down slightly since learning that her father was possibly following her.

He sat with a glass of iced tea in a corner of the internet café, waiting for his brother. He and Duncan always had an interest in hacking, an interest and exceptional talent. Duncan's memory combined with Andy's perspective on building codes and taking them down meant seamless entry into secured databases, internet sites and governmental agencies.

They set rules, of course. They never stole or cheated. That was for the weak and the lazy. They simply surfed for information of use to them or used their talents to *adjust* options, as they liked to call it. They would get information about trouble clients or options regarding appointments. He thought about how, back in the day, both ironically had been fixing their college class schedules from different parts of the country.

Running lines through several public ports, Andy was able to hack into the Systems Department in the Nicaraguan capital city. In theory, they were in Aruba. Much like the dummy desktop they'd used to anonymously log into the cafés, he waited for anyone in Systems to log in to their computer...hopefully, someone with decent security access.

He would then break down the binary code back into the series of keystrokes that made up the ID and password into the data system. And cha ching.

Duncan came in wearing a ball cap. He pulled up a chair next to him in the back corner, facing away from the café's only security camera. Low budget.

"That one's already popped up. ID is pnmartinez. Password is PNbemine 2. I was waiting for someone with better clearance," Duncan said.

"How do you remember that shit?" Andy shook his head. "Let's try her out. We're not looking for dish on a high profile."

Sure enough, there it was. Reports of a series of robberies tied to assault in and around the city of Managua. Then, there was nothing. In clicking further, they saw the face...and the name.

"May I come in?" Andy knocked hard enough to open the cracked door of Dave's office.

Dave rolled his eyes annoyingly as Officer Savage walked directly to the case board and pulled across a blank sheet.

"I have some information regarding Rose's father, biological father." He handed a folder to Dave.

As Dave opened it, Andy recited, "Miguel Ramirez. Born in Managua, Nicaragua, to a Beatrice Ramirez. Apparently, his father, listed as unknown, was white. Miguel is wanted in Nicaragua for robbery and assault. Last sighting was twenty years ago."

Dave's brow deepened heavily.

Officer Savage interjected as she looked over his shoulder. "How did you get these?"

How could he explain that he hacked into a foreign state database? "They were anonymously given to me."

"That's bullshit," she blurted out, then repeated, "How did you get these?"

Dave held a hand out to her, signaling it was time for her to stand down. Andy appreciated it. "It would be helpful to know the source, son."

Andy sighed. No way around it. "I can't tell you that, sir. I'm sorry. There's a picture of him on the back page. He was younger, of course, but it's him." He sat on the edge of Dave's desk. "What now?"

Dave rubbed his fingers across his five o'clock shadow. "Now, you take my daughter far away from here. Keep your phone on you. I'll call if I find out anything." Dave looked to him. "Anything, rest assured. Call when you get there and if you change locations." Dave took out a business card, set the file down and wrote on the back. "This is my personal cell. Don't call reception."

Andy nodded and stood.

Dave held out his hand. "And, Andy...thanks."

"I've spent weeks at your action center," Andy said. "Now, I want you to see my life."

Rose closed her eyes as he closed his hand around hers as he drove. He lifted their joined fingers and kissed the back of her soft skin.

"Buildings aren't just for the rich or the careless," he went on. "They can be formed to be practical, efficient. They can be pieces of art or a combination of both. Certain cultures or religions enjoy specific characteristics that solidify the distinctness between their buildings, creating unity and community."

Rose had always carried an interest in his passions, even though they weren't hers. However, he couldn't seem to keep her from worrying about taking her first leave in eight years or about leaving her mother. Amanda had dealt with this Michael for years. That was rough.

"Roman Catholics traditionally incorporated pointed arches, ribbed vaults and Gothic flying buttresses." He drove while using hand gestures to describe details. "Expertly, the characteristics lent themselves to appeal to emotions. Methodists took a more conservative approach with common Greek Revival architecture, using lancet-arched windows that flanked the entrances."

Rose worked not to let the images, or the blood rushing through her veins, spoil her time away with Andy. Pieces of tension softened as she realized she could never once remember Andy giving himself to her so openly about his work before.

"Synagogues generally contain an ark, called an aron ha-kodesh where Torah scrolls are kept." He lifted his eyebrows up and down dramatically.

She had never thought of it before, but now, she did think about the similarities between churches.

"Some architects, on the other hand, focus their work on whoever is to be the owner. The customer. Personalizing a building to the buyer. That's what I work to do. I love creating...where there wasn't before. Catering to the individuality of the buyer's tastes and practical needs." He looked to her. "Are you comfortable?"

"Quite." And, she was nearly completely cured of any vacation guilt. She smiled, looking down at their hands.

"What is it, then?"

"Nothing, really. I had no idea so much went into design and really had no idea how thoroughly you've learned about it. I guess I could say, however, that Nathan has a plane."

He glanced over as he drove and smiled his thousand-watt smile that forever made her knees weak. "It's not that far now, and I've already used the plane once this year...to get to a protest."

A picture of a knight in shining armor flashed through her mind. Laughing, she responded, "Thanks for that. How are the lots selling?"

"About half sold. It's incredible, really. Since then, I've started to look into other ways to interest the tree hug...to interest the green population."

She turned to face him now, resting the side of her head on the seat.

"I've found organizations that take donations for the purchase and planting of trees in third world countries. Fruit trees, trees that produce syrup and rubber trees. I'm beginning to have customers search me out because they know I'll donate a dozen trees for each one torn down from an excavation."

Her heart softened as she watched him gesture wildly with his free hand as he explained. He'd always been so smooth.

"Everyone wins. I get the business. The tree huggers...sorry...get a clear conscience with their new house. Poor folks get a way to support themselves, not just a perishable hand out."

The term *tree hugger* didn't bother her, but his need to apologize did. "How will we make this work, you and I?"

"As we were meant to. What kind of question is that?"

"Don't pretend like you don't see the vast differences between us."

"Not a problem. We've already begun to piece that together. Were you listening?"

"Of course, I was listening. About the tree huggers," she said flatly and had almost completely forgotten about her worries by this time, about anything but him.

"And about this..." He turned up a drive that was quite literally out in the middle of nowhere. The building at the end was expansive; a waterfall in the forefront flowed beneath the place and away. Visually uncomfortable concrete slabs jetted out from different angles in aesthetic form. Thick wooden beams and natural stone lined the walls and framed the different areas of the...Home? she wondered.

They parked with the other visiting cars. Andy stretched after he opened her door and held out a hand for her. "Come. Let me share a land developer and builder's work that holds a touch of Rose."

They strolled through the home like the tourists they were. She'd never seen anything like it. An actual home filled with serene character, surrounded by an earthy theme. She felt intensely touched he would bring her all the way out here. To a building that was formed around nature, with nature.

"It's called organic architecture. Drama, disagreements and all-out fights went into building this girl."

She was in awe of the structure, the flow and the character. The rooms were immense with shiny stone floors and built-in planter boxes scattered about. Walls of ceiling-to-floor windows overlooked massive cantilevers and one waterfall that seemed to lead into another. All were nestled tightly among a forest of towering trees that were, indeed, in the middle of no where. No city, no interstate. Mostly, she melted into a puddle at the sight of Andy showing off like a proud dad.

"There've been problems with this building." He stepped in front of her. "Water leakage, rotting boards."

She recognized his purposeful metaphorical comparison to their relationship and smiled warmly at him.

Facing her on the front balcony with the sound of the water rushing beneath them, he knelt to one knee. "And the girl still stands. Through the fighting. Through the changes. Because the foundation is solid, unwavering." He pulled a ring from the pocket of his jeans and held it out to her. "Because the ones who love it worked to keep it strong, keep it new." He took her hands in his. "Be mine, Rosemarie. Forever. I don't care if you want to keep your name. I love you. Marry me."

She pulled him from the stone floor, flooded with love and covered in peace. "I've been in love with you since I was old enough to be in love." She held out her left hand. "Of course I'll marry you." The diamond was oval with two smaller on either side. A thin line of white gold twined around the two smaller, joining them to the solitaire. She looked into his caramel eyes. "I don't want to keep my name."

She watched as his eyelids closed hard. He sighed deeply and kissed the wrist of her ringed hand, her palm and around to the ring on her third finger. When he opened, he gently pulled her toward him, pressing their lips together in smooth, drawn out velvet.

"Are you leaving for real this time?" Brie gave Duncan a smile that he recognized didn't reach her eyes.

He sighed and walked to her, wrapped an arm around her shoulders and kissed her on the top of her head. "I'll be back. I've got the house to check on now."

Her smile was slight but this time sincere. "I know of a pair of excellent landscape artists when you're ready."

"I wouldn't have it any other way."

The smile remained but her brows dropped slightly. "I can't believe I never knew, never even suspected."

Duncan followed her subject change. "She made sure of it."

"I'm her best friend, her coworker. And I should have known Amanda would never turn to drugs unless something heavy was going on. How sad and lonely for her. I haven't seen her shine like she is with Dave since, since...well Dave."

"It was Ramirez I saw. I don't know what he wanted, but Rose will be safe with Andy while Dave heats up the investigation." Purposely, he sat and rested his arm lazily on the back of his chair as a way to show his aunt he was in no hurry.

Following his lead, Brie sat next to him and rested her chin in her hands. "You say you really saw him?" She shivered.

"Mmm." He nodded. "Dave's assistant is suspicious of me."

Brie let her hands drop. "What? Why?"

"She thinks I'm involved...that I shouldn't have been able to sketch him in such detail."

She leaned back, contemplating something. It was several seconds before she spoke. "Why don't you just tell her?"

He was sure his eyes didn't reveal his surprise. Surely, his pause was twice as long as Brie's had been. He shook his head ever so slightly to her before he changed the subject and added, "It's better that Andy took the information we...umm...gathered to the station on his own."

Of course Brie would follow his lead. She was that kind of person. She covered her ears and said, "See nothing, hear nothing."

CHAPTER 26

Andy opened the door for Rose to the expansive hotel room. "I wanted the penthouse suite but thought you might spend the night thinking of how you could have used the money at the action center."

A white couch and chairs were arranged in a sitting area on one side, a tall table with leather barstools on the other. A walk-out balcony led to padded lounging chairs. A tray of fresh fruit was arranged and visible through the small refrigerator's clear door. Champagne set on ice near an enormous, round bed covered with a dozen ringlet pillows.

"This is the best you could do?" She ran like a child and jumped on the bed, spreading her arms and legs like she was making a snow angel.

He closed the door, set down their baggage and watched her—the woman who helped the helpless, with love for family, the real woman, the sexy woman with the understanding of every part of him, and with a great spinning side kick. His woman. "I'll call for room service. Requests?"

"Mmm." She shook her head. "You choose. I'm taking a shower." She took out her shower bag and pranced to the bathroom. He heard a loud squeal.

Andy grinned as he put their suitcases in the closet.

Rose stood for a minute in awe. "Holy cow! This is bigger

than my entire apartment!" she yelled loud enough for him to hear.

A glass-enclosed stall held several shower heads at all different levels. Next to it was a Jacuzzi big enough for six people. There were fresh flowers in vases scattered around the room and bottles of water chilling in ice buckets. Everything smelled of floral potpourri. She decided on the shower, turning the water to somewhere near piping.

Tossing her clothes on the floor, she stood naked, reading the controls on the wall for the heated floor and towel bars. With her hand over her mouth, she stifled a laugh and stepped onto the polished tile. The blazing water beat in pulses over every inch of her. Any and all aches kneaded and melted from her body along with most of the tension from her week.

She lifted her arms and placed the palms of her hands on the tile in front of her. The noise of the rushing water encompassed her as it ran over her head and down her back. Inside, she tried to sort out the vast array of emotions sifting between her heart and her head.

Her mother had kept the truth of the murder of her great-grandfather a secret for nearly two decades. Kept her conception a secret for almost three. Rose couldn't keep back the anger and resentment, but it was clouded with wrenching pain for what her mother had endured.

Rose had spent eight years getting over the loss of the only man she'd every truly loved—no. She wasn't going there. Spilled milk. He was hers now. And, she had to admit, the timing was right. Natural. They were both ready, ready and in love. She tilted her head back, letting the water run over her face and down the front of her body. Opening her eyes, she could see her ring through the rush of water, then she heard the door open. Through the heat of the water, an electric chill erupted from the tips of her toes and the top of her head, driving every sensation to her center.

He stepped in behind her. He felt cool against her back, and she could feel he was just as aroused. Twining his hands around her slippery waist, he pulled her against him and sighed noisily in her ear.

She didn't back away from the blast of water and instead let it run over them as he kissed the back of her neck, his glorious hands moving along her wet skin.

"I love you." Her voice was as silky as her skin and it took him under. They fit. She was soft and warm and his.

Taking her firmly in his hands, he squeezed as he pulled her closer. Possessively and lazily, he circled. Her body arched deeply into his hands, the back of her head pressed against his neck. He ran his lips across and down her wet shoulder.

Leaving one hand on her, the other trailed possessively down her silky stomach. He stopped at her lower belly and pulled her tighter. Her wet back molested him. She shuddered beneath his lips and hands. As she rocked back into him, he struggled with keeping a slow pace and continued until he reached her. The crest was instant. Her arms flew up, one bracing against the tile and the other grabbing his hand as he held her.

She cried out, loud and throaty. As her limbs started to give, he held her firmly, but didn't stop. Gently at first, he led her up again. Her body became limp and her arms rose slowly, wrapping around his neck. Inviting. Surrendering. Making it impossible for him to keep focus. He was completely lost and completely in love.

As she reached the next peak, her head flew back into his shoulder, and she shuddered and shook. Feeling like he was holding up a wet noodle, he let her come down, then reached for the soap. Sloppily, she took the bar from his hands, set it down and traded places behind him. Taking his arms, she placed his hands on the tile where hers had been. She looked at the ring on her finger as she spread the soft bubbles up his back, down his arms and around to his chest.

She thought how his muscles, still pronounced, weren't as massive as they'd been when they were younger. He was more defined now. She traced her fingers around the lines of his lats to his abs. She could lose herself in him, in this. Swirls of passion, their future and the intense need she let herself fall into strengthened her desire. Pressing against his hard backside, she reached around and explored the outline of the soapy squares of his six-pack down to his thick thighs. She let her body rub along him.

Andy knew her well enough to know that she wasn't the type to accept without giving back. He felt her against his back, her hands and the moment she found him.

Bracing, he dropped his head between his outstretched arms holding out, waiting until primal instinct took over. He needed to touch her. Turning, he took hold of the back of her thighs, lifted her easily, and hitched her legs around his sides. He waited until she looked at him. Then, watched her blue eyes as they joined.

The blue grew foggy as she let out a staggering growl and dug her fingers into the muscles on his back. Her face was intense, her grip fierce. Hot water sprayed over them as their pace quickened; he rotated her back to the wall.

Without breaking eye contact, he dropped his forehead to hers as she nodded. He grabbed hold of the backs of her thighs as they went over the final edge together. They stood for what seemed like a long and glorious time. Gasping and shuddering, the water ran over them until their breathing returned to normal.

His legs were nearly as weak as hers. So, he used his body weight and the wall of the shower to keep her wrapped around him. He began to lower her feet to the floor, but she grunted and locked the backs of her feet together behind him.

He sighed at the overwhelming feel of her all around him, inside and out. He turned off the water with one hand, then grabbed one of the large, heated towels. He carried her half-covered to the bed. Dropping her gently down, he lay on his back next to her and tossed the towel over the two of them.

With his forearm covering both his eyes, he muttered, "They said forty to fifty minutes."

"Hmm?" Rose lay in the exact same position.

"Room service. They said forty to fifty minutes."

She opened one eye at him. "That was forty to fifty minutes ago."

Amanda went to the station after work instead of going home alone, just as she'd promised. She stayed out of the way, listening quietly as the team waited for a conference call with the assistant to the office of Nicaragua's ambassador to the United Nations.

Miguel. That was his name. After all these years, she knew his real name. Miguel Ramirez.

Silence followed a series of beeps as Lieutenant Tanner, Dave and Officer Savage straightened in their chairs. Amanda assumed the assistant to the ambassador had connected. Dave looked over at her and she took the hint, slipping out to wait in the break room.

Her feelings were divided. Part of her was relieved that his face was broadcasted on news stations and posted in every train, bus and police station from here to the Mississippi. The other part of her was terrified for the very same reason.

He was getting closer. Had he recognized Rose when he was spotted at the end of the Reeds' drive? Or was he simply scouting the area like he did? Waiting for a time when Amanda would be alone...just as Dave was trying to avoid.

It didn't seem long enough before Dave opened his door for her again. She wondered if it went badly but didn't ask. She was only allowed in the room as a civilian consultant and knew not to push her luck.

She listened as they reviewed the call. From what she could gather, the ambassador's assistant wasn't nearly as upset about the breach in their database. There was a local warrant that was very old. What she found interesting was they discovered his father had allegedly raped his mother and, in turn, conceived him. Irony.

He was half white, light-skinned with blond hair. A gringo. She remembered the degrading term from her days in Nicaragua. The consultant psychologist would have a field day with all of that, she thought. All she saw was a weak man who liked to abuse and control women...whatever the reason.

Dave. She sighed. She was forgiven. He was so focused as he used his hands to explain plans to his assistant. Tanner left and was replaced with a handful of paper-pushers. That was what Dave called them. They flipped through a slide show that Officer Savage had created, showing grainy photos of possible sightings in convenient stores, train stations and buildings that were home to other victims.

"Stop." She bolted out of her chair, abandoning all plans to stay out of the way.

The eyes of Dave, Officer Savage and the handful of lower-level officers on the case turned to look at her.

"Go back. Go back, please." There. That was him. She angled her head to be certain, then repeated aloud, "That's him."

Officer Savage spoke up first. "Are you sure? It's barely a profile, Mrs. Nolan. Not a close up."

"It's him. I...I can't tell you...it's the way he's standing...or I guess, walking."

Officer Savage read the date and location of the photo. "Boston, two weeks ago. Apartment hallway."

Amanda wrung her hands.

"Get BPD on the phone. Find out who lives there."

CHAPTER 27

They took the first flight out. Thankfully, Dave included Amanda in her civilian consultant capacity. Lieutenant Tanner had agreed with Dave that the other victims would be more likely to open up to her, especially since Miguel had a history of threatening women if they went to the police. Dave had explained that the lieutenant granted leave and funding for stops at three of the most likely other hits: Chicago, Boston and Pittsburg. He said it made up three flights and two over-state-line trips in rental cars. It was going to be a long two days.

The station in Boston was much like the one in Northridge right down to the smell of the stale coffee. Dave came out of the captain's office at the Boston Police Department. He'd asked Officer Savage to wait with her. Amanda recognized that she would wait without question because he asked her to, but also that it burned her up. "VanDellan, Rebecca." Dave gestured his head toward the stairwell.

Amanda hugged herself as they walked toward the exit.

"Age thirty-seven. Found dead in her apartment at the corner of Washington and Jefferson." Dave read as he walked down the stairs, pausing to wait when they heard other footsteps. "Four reports in the past five years of robbery and assault. The first was a sexual assault."

"Penetration?" Amanda asked.

Dave winced, then nodded.

"So, he kills some, especially when he's been scorned."

"Apparently. We've gotten the okay to view the scene. The captain's sending a local uniform as an escort."

The smell of death still permeated the air. Amanda didn't attempt to cover her nose. The place was small. The woman had lived alone. She wondered if it was because she didn't want to bring this down on the people she loved.

It felt eerie as she stood out of the way and watched Dave and Officer Savage work. They wore gloves but still were careful not to tamper with anything. How many times had he been here? she wondered. How many years? What made him choose her? Would all that be in the police report? She would wait to ask Dave. She imagined the woman saying just the wrong words with Miguel in just the right state of mind, and realized how lucky she was to still be alive today.

Barely, she noticed something warm and wet on her face. Her purse slipped down her arm. The room became louder. The air conditioning? Why was it so loud?

She came to in Dave's arms. He was rocking her.

"I'm okay, really," she mumbled. "I probably should have sat down is all."

"I shouldn't have brought you here. What was I thinking?"

She forced herself upright but knew not to stand just yet. "You did the right thing. I'm all right. I'll sit next time. How much do you think the other girls will tell you without me?" At that moment, she realized Miguel would have used pictures of her grandfather. Certainly he would. She felt light-headed all over again and buried her face in Dave's shoulder.

Andy and Rose canceled much of their plans and decided instead to stay in their room, leaving only when they tired of room service. While sunning on the balcony, they made plans for their future. They lounged in the Jacuzzi and snacked on trays of pretzels and chocolates. Plans ranged from the rest of the summer, the next year, all the way to how many children they wanted. They made love between ideas until their arms and legs could simply fall from their bodies and lie as if detached on the oversized bed.

Andy had come back with graphing paper from a morning

coffee and bagel run.

He sat on one of the leather chairs, sketching designs for their home. She noted that Nathan and Duncan's artistic genes hadn't passed over him. The drafts were detailed, creative and to scale. He wanted big; she wanted small. He wanted wood; she wanted brick. As they had learned to do, they met somewhere in the middle. She had never really thought of choices of rooms, sizes of rooms or roll-out drawers versus shelves. She generally unpacked her few things at the cheapest place she could find.

He seemed to know her wants and needs better than she did. A general area on the main floor was designed just for her to get away. It included space for her tech equipment and a desk facing two walls of windows that looked out to a large area built for any injured animals that needed round-the-clock care. He made a place for Charcoal and any other strays she may pick up. A door equipped with an animal flap for a dog to get in and out led out to the other areas.

As he sat next to her, he propped his feet on her thighs, crossing them at the ankles. She recognized the slight squint he did when concentrating deeply. As if he came out of a zone, he looked over to her, set his graph pad down on his lap and leaned back, clasping his hands on the top of his head.

"I'm in love with you." She stood and walked to him, replacing the graphing pad with herself on his lap. "We're going to be married." She kissed him lightly. "We're going to be married, and you gave me exactly the weekend I needed." This time, she drew out the kiss, meshing lips and tongues, tilting her head to sink deeper.

"How am I supposed to plan for our home when all of the blood has drained from my head?"

She reached toward the coffee table to pick up the pad. "Explain."

He detailed his ideas and made revisions as she described her thoughts and the needs of any animals that may come to stay with them. She found herself as excited as a teenager getting her first puppy. She watched him as he erased and revised, and she thought of how he took her away this weekend, mostly to explain his reasons for his passions. Instead of reluctantly accepting, she'd found herself diving in with him and, oh, it was an amazing fall. She could picture herself in this home he created on paper, living with her best friend, her lover, her husband; and raising their children and teaching them about conservation and building.

She realized he, too, had become not only accepting of her lifestyle but developed his own need to do his part. And, he was in love with the cranky, self-serving Gracie every bit as much as she was.

They never made any mention of the years that had been stolen from them or of her biological father. No one would see anything from Rose except a woman in love, taking an extended weekend away with her lover.

No one needed to know about the private mornings when she wrapped her hands and beat the heavy bag in the hotel gym as if her life depended on it. Without condemnation, Andy worked the weights, allowing her all the alone time she needed.

Rose picked up Grace at Wes' place on her way into work. Still weird, she thought. Grace's toffee skin had a rosy glow. Her dark, shiny hair tied low in a smooth tail.

"You look clean and neat and...not wrinkled. You have a drawer. You have a drawer and closet space at Wesley McGee's apartment."

Grace grinned now, coy and ear to ear. "What if?"

"What if I said that if you give me even one detail, you'll be scooping poop for a month?"

"Well I want details," Grace said. "Lots of details. The knight, eh? I have two words. Yum and yum."

It was Rose's turn at coy. Damn it, Grace was right. "I'm swinging by my mother's. It was too late when I got home last night to see her. She makes a great cup of coffee."

"You're the boss." Grace propped her feet on the dash and rested her head back on the seat.

"Well...it's great to see you," Rose told her.

"Huh? Really. In that case, I'll tell you that Gracie is fed and exercised. How *well* fed and exercised might be a different story. I don't know how you do it. She's all yours."

"Hello?" Andy called as he walked to the door of his office, with his keys in one hand and his briefcase in the other. He sighed at the tall piles Delores had left him, piles he had all but ignored and wondered when he could get to them. When his phone rang, he put his keys in his front pocket and pulled out his phone. He wondered who was calling his private number at this hour.

"It's me."

"What's with the blocked number, Duncan?" He held the phone between his ear and shoulder as he dug his keys back out.

"I found something. Is your computer up, yet?"

He stopped walking. "It's already been up. I was just leaving for an appointment." He turned back and was glad he'd left it on. "Sup?"

"I sent you an attachment. Open it."

"Okay, okay. What've you got?"

"He's in Binghamton."

"You mean Ramirez? He was just spotted in Boston a day or so ago." Andy could hear his brother sigh heavily on the other end of the phone. Waiting for his computer to wake up, he asked, "What have you been up to while I was gone?"

"I've been looking through the Northridge Police Department's computer files on Amanda and Rose. I found him. I'm sure of it."

Andy sat in front of his computer. "How? What?" Damn it, load!

"Hundreds of tips have come through since the wanted posters went up. I've been combing through them."

The still photo popped up. It wasn't clear. The person was walking away, but it seemed like he turned and looked right at the camera. "I can hardly even tell this is a man, Duncan. What time is it out there?"

"Damn it, listen to me! It's him. The eyes." He made a frustrated growl Andy had only heard a few times in their lives. "This picture was taken yesterday. Some single, old dude who lives in an apartment they're watching. He's called in so many times that they aren't listening to him anymore."

Andy dipped his head closer to the screen. "Fuck." He pushed away from his desk and left everything as he ran for the door.

Amanda stood in the doorway watching him. Dave pulled apart the knot in his tie for the second time, grunted and started again.

She slipped between him and the mirrored dresser. Taking the tie from him, she didn't ask but stated, "You got a call."

"It's not that I can't tie my own damned tie. I'm just pissed off, that's all." He paused for a minute. "Yes, I got a call."

"Anything about Michael...Miguel?"

Dave placed his hands on the sides of her face and took a deep breath. "Are you sure you want to hear this?"

She wrapped her fingers around his forearms and squeezed. "Is it Rose?"

"No. No, not Rose." Dave shook his head.

She felt the muscles in her face relax. "I can take anything, then."

"What time is Rose coming by?"

"Any minute now. She called not too long ago and is en route."

She finished with the tie. Dave checked the safety on his gun and placed it in his holster. His phone vibrated at his waist. He looked at the number. Taking her hand to his lips, he kissed her fingers. "We're getting closer. There was another possible spotting not far from the Boston site. I'll call you when I find out." He leaned over and took her face in his hands. "I love you."

She kissed him and stepped out of his way.

Rose rounded onto the familiar cul-de-sac. She'd gone for much longer before without seeing her mother, yet the ache in her heart seared. Should she be gentle? Talk about it? Not mention it? The elephant in the room. She decided to be herself.

She and Grace walked up the familiar concrete path passed the aged weeping willow to the front porch. As she reached to push the door open farther, she heard a man's voice. Next, she heard the sound of Charcoal going mad from the back of the house. Straining her ear toward the screen door, she listened. Her heart nearly beat out of her chest.

"You thought you could beat me at this."

"Please, you can have anything. I have money. Lots of money."

"It was only a matter of time before he left you alone. Not so tough without the Taser, are you, Mandy baby? I bought my own toy."

Rose heard him cock it. She motioned for Grace to call for

help, then crept silently through the door. She worked to control her ragged breathing as she tried to assess where he was, where her mother was. Whimpering came from far inside the kitchen.

"Mmm. You make me hard when you do that."

"You're right. Of course you're right. What can I do, Miguel?"

"You don't call me that!"

Rose peered around the corner just as her mother's head jerked from a pistol whipping and fell to her knees. "Please don't, not now, please," she choked. "You can have anything. Have me."

Rose watched her mother open the front of her blouse as blood dripped down the side of her face. She nearly wretched at the horrifying sight.

Her mother noticed her from the corner of her eye just long enough for Miguel to see the flicker. He had a smirk on his face as he twirled the gun, ready to shoot.

CHAPTER 28

As he turned, Rose jumped with one foot and kicked with the other, sending the gun flying across the room. Miguel used a left hook, but she was faster. She ducked and he lost his balance from swinging at air. She used her weight and momentum to plant her fist in his gut. He swayed but stayed up, clenching his fists. Faking a low kick, he took the bait and went to block as she spun and sunk her heel into the side of his head.

Grace came running in at that time, screaming tirades in Spanish.

Rose was half mad, shrieking with anger. She struck him again, but he wouldn't fall. As he staggered, she caught sight of her mother. The blood, her tears. Her mother's hands clutched her head as she wept. The pause gave Miguel his chance. He connected his fist with her temple. She fell face-first and hit her head on the back of the nearby kitchen chair with nearly as much force as the blow from Miguel. Stars danced in her vision, and she hung onto the kitchen table, trying to sort out the sounds: her mother crying, Grace screaming, Miguel cussing, and Andy...

He'd heard the screams of Grace from the drive, and the sound of insane barking from the dog in back. But the sight of Rose bleeding sent him over a staggering edge he'd never crossed. He didn't slow down when he hit the front door and felt the vibration when it struck the wall after he shoved it out of his way. It took three running strides through their living room to reach the kitchen. He growled much like the dog as he flew through the air and took Miguel from the side. They toppled the kitchen table with Andy, fist and fury, landing on top. Taking Miguel's greasy hair, he used his other hand to punch his jaw hard enough to hear a crack. Miguel bucked beneath him. Andy hit him again, knocking out a tooth and bloodying his lip.

As he pulled back to wind up another punch, he heard a rip from the back of the house—the screen door. Miguel took the opportunity and twisted, spinning sloppily, and staggered to his feet. Running past the screaming Grace, he stopped abruptly at the front door and turned, squinting deeply.

Andy checked on Rose and saw her look to her mother, to Miguel, then back again. Andy knew what she was contemplating. Torn between the same two ideas, he watched as he saw Rose's expression change to astonishment. She stared at her biological father as she lifted her hand to cover her mouth.

Miguel stood at the door and smiled through blood and a missing tooth. "Mi hija," he said. Then, he turned and ran from Charcoal as the dog took off after him.

Rose sat in one of the rough, padded chairs of the ER waiting room. Andy paced in front of her as images of her mother flashed through her mind. Hurt, bleeding, exposed. She tucked her legs up on the seat and placed her hands over the ice pack on her swollen temple and her ears as if that would make the sound of her mother's whimpers stop running through her mind.

Andy paused and sat next to her. "She amazing, don't you think? Refusing pain meds?"

She nodded. "Dave will stay with her and make sure the nurses don't make a mistake. She keeps saying, 'He knows.'"

"They said concussion."

She closed her eyes at the feel of his warm hand on her cheek. "Yes." Rose nodded. "Slight. She's sleeping now."

Grace and Wes walked to the two of them. Grace wrapped her arms around Rose's neck. "We'll stop back in the morning."

She hugged her back. "Yes, hopefully it will just be for overnight observation. We're leaving soon, too."

Rose pulled Grace back and took a deep breath as she grabbed her shoulders. Looking deep into her dark brown eyes, she asked what she didn't want to know. "What does it mean? What did he say?"

Grace nodded in understanding. She placed a hand on the side of Rose's face and said plainly, "It means, 'my daughter.'"

The sun began its descent in the overcast sky as Andy pulled out of the hospital parking lot with Rose next to him. She was staring out the window of his SUV. He reached to twine her limp fingers with his. It was a small gesture of support, for someone so lost in her thoughts. "She's not alone this time, Rose."

"Hmm?" She shook her head a few times quickly.

"Your mother. She's not facing it alone this time or ever again."

"True." She nodded. "Yes, that's true."

"She'll be okay for the night. I imagine she's still working the nurses and Dave to let her out of overnight observation—"

"I want him dead."

"Rose." He had to work to make his voice sound sincere, especially since he felt the same.

"I want him dead and I want to do it with my own hands," she continued flatly.

He didn't respond. Instead, he gave her some time and space and decided to remain as a presence for her. He would serve as a getaway. A distraction.

"Where are we going?" She looked around, then turned her body to face him.

"I want to check and see how far the excavators and cement crews got on Duncan's house while we were gone. It's peaceful there." He brushed the backs of his fingers along her cheek and watched her eyes drop closed. "Come with me."

She took his hand and pressed his palm to her warm cheek. "I never could say no to those three words from you."

As they bumped along the gravel road, he noted the tell-tale construction signs of deep ruts from heavy trucks, slabs of spilled concrete scattered on the drive and large hunks of mud left from the wheels of the earth movers. At the end of the half-mile road, they simply stopped in the center.

"What a muddy mess," she commented as they climbed out of the SUV together.

He walked around and pulled out his tape measure, checking dimensions. "What do you think?" he asked.

"I think I bet it's just what it's supposed to be for now."

"You think right. He wants three stories. The top floor will be small. Slanted ceilings. For his painting. Skylights. He has some good ideas."

He stepped to her and took her hands. "Tell me."

She took a deep breath. "I like it. He'll love it."

As he shook his head in two short movements, he said, "Mmm mmm, there's something you're keeping inside." He tapped the middle of her chest.

She covered her face with her hands. "It's the eyes," she said and pressed her fingertips over her own. "I've seen pictures of them, but..." She set her forehead on his chest. "I have his eyes. I looked into the eyes of that bastard and I saw me."

He laced his fingers through the short pieces of hair on the back of her head. Then, slid them down and took her hand. "Come, I want to show you something."

They climbed back into the SUV and drove farther into the woods until they came to a clearing. He'd measured it as ten acres in diameter. The smell was a mixture of running water, earth, wildflowers, and endless trees.

"The creek is far enough away to keep us safe from flood damage. It would take well water since we're a ways from the city lines, but I could rig up a nice purifier. The view this way is the best, I think." He motioned to the east with the sun at his back. "That would make the kitchen face north, which would be nice so that you, I mean we, could look out the window while doing dishes without the sun blinding us, plus that way my office can be over here." He gestured largely. "Yours over...here with windows to keep an eye on the aviary and dog run. Hell, I can put in a damned chicken coop if you want."

He turned to her just as a tear spilled on her round cheek.

"I should have brought our plans. I didn't think to bring them. Damn it. I'm going to marry a woman who carries a Swiss damned Army knife around like some carry lipstick and I'm the builder with no damned plans." Closing the distance between them, he lifted her hand. He kissed the ring on her chilled third finger, then pulled her into him. "This is part of Duncan's lot. I haven't signed anything with him yet. We can pick another spot closer to home if you—"

"It's perfect." She wrapped her arms around him and pressed her cheek to his chest.

Carefully, he lifted her chin to him, then brushed his lips over her swollen temple. "When I look in your eyes, what I see is someone who brings out the best in everything she touches. I see the best of me."

Near a small tent, he and Rose lay on a thick blanket looking at the millions of stars erupting in the country twilight.

"When did you get camping gear?"

"While you were questioned at the scene...after." He snuggled her next to him and even though they shared a pillow, she laid her head on his arm. "And I don't know if I call a tent, blanket and a pillow actual gear. Brie came to see what the sirens were for and gave me the idea. She's one of the smartest people I know."

"And we'll be able to get home—"

"Before your mother is awake and released. I made sure of it. We have our cell phones. It's a twenty minute drive, tops."

She rolled completely on top of him and surprised him with a long deep kiss. Like a meeting of mouths and minds. "Take me away."

She didn't need to ask for him to know what she wanted, but the sound of it rolling off her tongue was enough to make him determined to do just that.

He drew out the kiss, tilting his head slowly, softly sinking into her as his hands ran up her waist, brushing his thumbs along the sides of her along the way. Running his hands up her shirt, he thoughtfully worked at a mixture of arousal and soothing.

Rotating, he tucked her beneath him just enough to be able to rest on his side and still have his hands on her, all over her, moving gently, carefully. They caressed and stroked as the last of the birds announced their evening departure and the bullfrogs their nighttime territory.

He watched as her eyes rolled back and felt her body slowly unwind.

Each kiss along her throat, her neck was smoother than the last. Her skin was warm and little tremors erupted every so often as he let his hands move over her. He cupped her and found his favorite spot with his lips just under her ear.

Along her collarbone, down to the hollow at the base of her neck, he let his warm lips glide like velvet.

Rose was dizzy in love and felt like an isolated cloud of need. She could get through anything with Andy. He was hers, now from then on. A growing strength and need raced through her. Yet, he continued like a rock, steady and painfully slow. Each button released was followed by warm lips on her skin. Down, down to her waist.

When he spread her shirt open, his awe flattered and aroused her. He paused and dropped his head to her chest. The warm air from the evening blew over her skin, cooling her sheen of sweat. He created, stirred, eased. She lifted just enough, offering. He took her blouse the rest of the way off.

Holding her possessively, he circled. "You're beautiful." He kissed the swell that lifted just over the satin. "You're mine."

She took her turn lifting his shirt off, lightly nipping his shoulder as he held her against him. His hands ran up her back and released the clasp. Pulling the straps from her shoulders, he slipped it off between the bare skin of their bodies. She melted into the feel of her pressed against his chest. The floating feel of flesh on flesh.

They each took their time exploring under the moon and the stars. Andy pulled her legs around him as he sat in front of her. He lifted one over his shoulder, as he preferred to do, then turned his lips and pressed them against the inside of her knee. He held onto her, possessively grabbing with both hands as he traveled from her knee to her thigh. She was there for him and he took her carefully. Watching her completely let go, he let her ride the first easy hill slowly.

He wasn't sure how long they took turns taking each other where no one else ever could, moving together in careful love. When they united, he was just as slow, as long and as careful. Rose expelled a heavy breath as he covered her everywhere, all over and inside her. Hanging onto his back, he could feel the crescent marks she was leaving in his flesh. The intensity of her next peak was followed by tiny tears that dripped down her temples before they went over together.

Spent, they collapsed and lay completely still, twined together inside and out on the blanket in the clearing. They nearly fell

asleep before Rose tapped him. "My legs. Can't move my legs."
He rolled next to her, then pulled the blanket over them.

"Rose."

"Hmm?"

"We're sleeping in our master bedroom."

CHAPTER 29

The air was warm but not as hot as it should be for a late July morning in upstate New York. A swift breeze wafted the scents of Sycamores and Tulip Poplars across the field where Rose stood with the recovered, mature bald eagle. Her temple was completely healed and her mother's had faded to a jaundice yellow. Miguel was leaving a sloppy trail. Rose felt better.

She tried sneaking around the back of the main building at the research and action center but she knew Gracie could sense her and the male.

Although the male ran into some complications and took longer to heal from the lead poisoning than she'd expected, he was fully recovered and ready to be free once again. She drove him out to the spot she'd chosen in a crate on the back of one of the center's four-wheelers. A wild bald eagle would never perch on a human's arm. She rubbed the puncture wound on her hip serving as a reminder of how hard it was to teach even an adolescent eagle to do just that. Five hundred pounds of pressure went through flesh and muscle like butter.

Gracie was learning the hard lesson that if you bite the hand that feeds you, you don't get fed. Eagles weren't pets, and Rose knew getting Gracie to simply tolerate her would take time and work. The sound of her call was heartbreaking. How did animals sense these things? Silently, she said her apologies to Gracie as she parked the four-wheeler.

Dr. Gray and she had discussed the great publicity the center could earn from televising the release of the male. They also agreed that sometimes things were meant to be done in peace. So, instead she waited for Grace to show up with the digital recorder. The recording would be posted on their social network page and website. And, maybe Rose would give a copy to Jenna Woith over at WCEL.

The reporter had been instrumental in getting updates and drawings of Miguel Ramirez onto the local stations, all with her mother out of his sight. Rose wondered how long her mother would be able to follow Dave around before her job was in jeopardy.

Pride swelled in her heart as she thought about how her mother had held up. She'd made it through the hospital stay and stitches without sedatives.

She spotted Andy and Grace as they pulled around in separate four-wheelers and realized that she had her own crutch—her own sturdy, sexy, thoughtful crutch. Glancing down at the ring on her finger, she sighed at the exaggerated turns her life had made recently. The flashes of her own eyes looking back at her from her biological father's weren't as frequent now, although nearly as potent. The shape, the size, the color—there was no doubt that she carried his blood in her veins, and wished she was as certain of her declaration negating the importance of whose sperm created her as she once had.

Wes rode in the seat behind Grace, carrying the recorder and tripod. The grass was still wet with dew as they parked and stepped out to greet her.

Andy held two steaming cups in his hands. Smart guy.

"Good morning." He kissed her softly and long enough to send a chill to her toes but not long enough to cause Grace and Wes to suggest they get a room.

"That's the second time you've said that today." She smiled slyly and pivoted the crate to the open field. Lines of thick trees were almost a hundred feet away but still gave the feeling of an enclosed spot. Narrow trails could be seen, ejecting periodically around the perimeter and into the woods, and looked like oversized mouse holes.

"Almost ready." Grace spanned the view. "Got it. We're ready."

Wes held his camera prepared for action shots.

Andy stood on the balls of his feet with unashamed excitement.

Rose opened the door to the crate and stepped back. The bird walked around on the inside, scraping talons on the plastic as he moved.

She stepped forward, opened the door farther. She murmured, "Come on, boy, you're free."

Picking up a stick, she gently encouraged him to the opening. He grabbed it, jerking it from her hands, then crushed it into splinters. Still, it worked. The eagle walked to the edge of the crate and out onto the trailer of the four-wheeler. Squatting down, the amazing creature braced for takeoff, then spread his enormous wings and lifted to the sky. It only took a few flaps of his wings to gain enough altitude to then use the wind beneath as a glide. Like riding a bike. The vast wing span dwarfed any other species at the center. He soared in a circle before perching on one of the trees just outside the perimeter.

"Are you getting this? Can you still see him?" she asked.

Grace smiled without moving her hands or her gaze. "Oh, yeah."

Wes shuttered shot after shot before they all cheered when he took off over the trees.

Andy decided there was time enough to check on Duncan's house before his meeting with Dave at the station. As he drove through ruts and potholes, he made a mental note to order a few more truckloads of road gravel.

When he reached the top of the hill, the first thing he noticed was the excellent job the framers did with the plywood walls. No fiberboard for this house. The next was the new bike—shiny black, very expensive and very fast. It sat far enough away from the crew vehicles that Andy cocked his head. Duncan was in town? The last thing he noticed was Rose laughing with him around the side of the house.

"Are you here to check on the place or make moves on my girl?" He and Duncan embraced and smacked each other on their backs with two slaps.

Duncan jerked his head in response. "Both if you're not careful. Rose gave me the tour, as well as her approval since we'll be neighbors."

Andy looked around. "How'd you get here?"

Rose and Duncan turned in unison and gestured to the motorcycle.

"Nice." Andy walked over to it. "Wait a minute; you took my girl out here on that? Well, damn you." He shook his head with jealousy.

"I've decided to crash your scheduled party with the detective and the ice princess." Duncan walked into his future foyer. "What are these two-bys here?"

"Front closet frame." Andy rolled up his sleeves and walked in with him. "Ice princess?"

Andy spoke a mile a minute about the house, what they'd finished and what was next. Duncan added few words as he explained.

They made it to the station with time to spare. The front desk receptionist directed Andy and Rose to the conference room, as there wasn't enough space in Dave's office for the five of them—six, actually, with Duncan.

Duncan stepped in front of him and opened the door without knocking. At the look Officer Savage threw him, Andy understood how she earned her nickname. He sensed she wanted to say something, but she sat back instead and let Dave take lead. He could also tell Duncan placed himself strategically close to her and sat defiantly, even more so than he normally would.

"The purpose of the meeting is to update you on the status of Miguel Ramirez and outline strategies to keep yourself as safe as possible."

He walked to a wall of dry-erase boards and pulled a map down over the top. "Officer Savage, will take lead for this update." Dave looked to her and nodded with approval.

She wasted no time with greetings. "There have been a number of unconfirmed and false sightings. However, we believe the reports from Columbus, four days ago, and Detroit, two, are legit, which means if previous patterns continue, the perp is making his way east. Both cities were home to suspected victims that have since been relocated. We assume he spotted the PD surveillance teams and left." She followed in a general pattern on the map.

Amanda covered her mouth with her hand. Rose ran both hands through her short hair. Dave sat expressionless.

"He likes to stalk. Not for the sake of stalking, but as a sort of stake out. He's looking for patterns. Therefore, don't give any. Come and go at different times. Drive different vehicles. Share rides on days when you can. Change your lunchtime routine. Mostly, be aware of your surroundings. If he's near, that alone will serve as a deterrent."

When Officer Savage turned, Andy noticed that everyone except he and Duncan had their faces dropped practically between their legs.

"Holy shit, look at you," she said.

Dave shot up a look at her.

"I apologize, sir, but this isn't helping. I feel if I'm taking lead at his presentation, I must repeat myself. Look at you. The girl," she gestured to Rose, "is knee-deep with the guilt that her mother carried this...this burden for the sake of protecting her. Your ex feels guilty because the perp discovered he has a daughter. And, if I may, sir, you're the worst. The cloud you've been carrying around is bringing you down. Amanda didn't want you to know and she's a smart woman. Everyone made their choices. Bad things happen. How long has it been since you've let her out of your sight? Does she still even have a job? No offense, ma'am. You've been a valuable, on-site source. All this misplaced guilt is doing nothing but clouding the facts."

"And what facts would those be, Officer Savage?" Dave stood and asked her.

Andy watched the woman breathe heavily. Past issues? Or just nervous to be given lead. "The facts are Miguel Ramirez is the one that raped Amanda and produced Rose. Ramirez is the one who has been taunting her. No one else is to blame."

"Nickie's right." Duncan didn't move an inch, only turned his eyes toward her. "Someone's going to slip up if they don't clear their conscience. What's done is done." He stood and walked in front of everyone and right to the map. "And if patterns prevail, he's almost here."

The man that hijacked Carolyn Foster's Honda thought she was dead, lying in the backseat, and she was determined to keep it that way. He'd shot her in the chest, but she was still breathing, still alive. She was cold and, even though she slipped in and out of consciousness, she knew she was still bleeding.

When she would wake, she first cried salty tears of fear that she would soon be dead. Then, she tried to listen to the man's ranting and tried to figure out where he was taking her. He carried on about bus stations and trains and someone named Mandy. When he finally mentioned a woman in Buffalo, Carolyn knew she didn't have much longer.

Holding her breath, she remained as still as possible as he parked her car on a busy street. He didn't bother locking it and tossed the keys on the seat before casually wiping down the steering wheel and door handles.

She waited as long as she could to make sure he was truly gone before opening the door and rolling out onto the sidewalk.

Miguel smoked a cigarette as he walked down the street from the target's townhouse. It had only been six months since their last little visit, much sooner than he would have liked to have seen her, but the last two apartments were empty. Hadn't he shown them pictures of what he did to women who moved without his permission?

He paced nervously, very much unlike him. He was generally smooth, observant and confident. The wanted posters were too much. The fucking train station placed them so far in the building a dozen people could have seen him before he was close enough to see his face, his own face.

He shaved his head and coated himself with skin darkening cream, put in black contacts, but it was still him. "This is Mandy's doing," he said out loud as he paced, forgetting all about the townhouse he was staking out. "No one fights back." He took one last drag, inhaling deeply, before throwing the cigarette in the street. "No one."

He started to walk when he saw an unmarked slow down in front of the place, pull over and stop. Plain clothed pigs got out and walked around to the back. "Fuck." Miguel turned and walked slowly toward the hijacked car. He was running low on money, and it was getting to be a problem.

He would regroup, that was all. He didn't stay out of the light for all these years on accident. He would make more stops, get new women if he had to. Get an extra large stash, then alter his appearance surgically. When he rounded the corner to the car, there were two black and whites and an ambulance. "Fuck, fuck, fuck." Turning to backtrack his backtrack, he saw the unmarked driving slowly, clearly looking for someone—for him.

CHAPTER 30

"We have a probable victim in Buffalo." Dave used the station interactive whiteboard to put up a map of confirmed sightings. "That adds to the one in Columbus, Ohio, and another in Detroit, Michigan. He hasn't made another hit that we know of until this woman." He showed a black and white printout of the woman. She hadn't been beaten but was unconscious. "This is Carolyn Foster. She claims to be the victim of a hijacking and has described and identified Ramirez as her assailant from a photo lineup. She's been shot in the chest. The bullet missed internal organs and was removed from beneath her left lung. This doesn't follow any pattern except the location, but we'll go out and see what she has to say for ourselves."

Each from the group made conscious efforts to abide by Officer Savage's advice.

Amanda did, in fact, still have a job when she returned and knew she would. Homeless shelter manager wasn't a highly sought-after job. She was thankful that was the case. There was chaos, last-minute decisions, changes, and the need to be flexible. Mostly, she loved being part of the reason someone may stick it out another day, helping them find success in some corner of their lives.

Sure enough, the backlog of empty food shelves, gaps in volunteer servers and an employee schedule that looked like a third-grader put it together were just what she needed to make her feel normal again.

After spearheading a couple smoking dope in the back of the building, she took advantage of the outdoor air and had a moment of alone time.

Rose, too, made efforts to change her routine, but animals simply didn't work that way. They had routines, needed routines. She wasn't about to trade places with Grace and put her in danger. She tried to work with someone around whenever she could, something she rarely did.

Keeping an eye on her surroundings, she checked the smaller animal habitats from both inside and out of the main building. An opossum mother and her babies were a more recent addition. She had gotten tangled in a plastic six-pack ring, became infected from the wounds and rejected her young. Rose checked on the interns as they syringe-fed the babies while the antibiotics worked on mom.

The week that had passed didn't settle Rose, but it did allow her time to imagine Miguel with new funds and possibly working on some prosperous illegal gambling deal somewhere far away.

They decided to have a regular girl's night out, one with bridal magazines, mothers, future mothers-in-law, sisters-in-law, and sisters. Rose waited with Brie for the others while they mixed spicy cream cheese dip and arranged sun-dried tomato crackers.

"Did you know your mother and Dave plan to remarry?"

Rose paused and considered. "I guess I expected they would, sure."

"Did you know they plan to make a stop at the law and justice center and grab the nearest person as a witness?"

Rose set down the box of crackers and looked at Brie. "That's awful."

"That's what I said. You know what I think? I think you only get married to your husband for the second time just once in your life."

Rose turned that around in her head as the others arrived. Five women gathered around a giant table in Brianna Reed's kitchen, talking about colors, dates, locations, and of course flowers.

"So, you're thinking fuchsia and sky blue?"

Rose couldn't read her mother's expression with the question. "Dark pink and the color of the sky, sure." Ugh.

"In the fall?"

Oh, Rose got it, now. "I just want to get married." She hated this stuff. Was no good at it. "What colors do you think?" she asked less curtly.

Her mother leaned forward. "This is your day, honey."

"What colors?" Rose asked a little more forcefully.

Her mother and Brie held some kind of secret flower person meeting with their eyes. "What do you think about russet orange and sun-dried yellow?"

"Deal."

"It will look lovely with your hair." Brie was looking at her, judging and deciding. Rose could tell.

They flipped through pages of a magazine that could have been mistaken for a New York City phonebook.

Jessica took her turn to confuse Rose. "What are you thinking regarding table decorations? I liked using the flowers from the aisle guest seats for the vases in the centers of the reception tables."

"Whoa." Rose stood, arms out in surrender. "You and you." She pointed to her mother and Brie. "What do you think about being in charge of the flowers and ...flower stuff?" Next, she turned to her sister and Hannah, who were uncharacteristically quiet. "What do you two think about taking care of the chair thing and reception...ya know, looks?"

As if they'd planned this all along, Hannah and Jessica stood and gave each other a high-five large enough to make someone think they were guys at a pro ball game. As if that wasn't bad enough, her mother and Brie did the same.

Rose set a bucketful of water and three live fish on the trailer behind her four-wheeler. She heard her assistant start up the second four-wheeler that carried the gear for training the new interns. Although Gracie would see the fish no matter how far around the aviary she chose to drive, she purposely took the long way around the enclosure. She wanted Gracie to get a good, long, predatory look at her dinner.

Never once looking at the fish, the eagle followed her with both body and yellowing-eyes all the way around the frame of her aviary. With a lifeless glare, the bird stared her down. Perched on her artificial tree, she waited for her moment. Her posture was clearly that of a challenge.

Stopping at the entrance, Rose turned to face her. "Listen, girl. We can do this the hard way or the easy. Up to you. You're not getting one bite if you come at me." Rose couldn't hold back her smile.

Grabbing hold of the five-gallon bucket, she set her hand on the door and gave Gracie her best threatening posture. They both knew it was fake. Gracie loved the game...and the fishing. Rose loved the eagle. Using her free hand to unlock the door, she shook her head at the sudden, potent, acidic smell. She took in a shocked breath of air, felt the cloth that covered her mouth and turned. Gracie shrieked behind her. In the seconds before Rose collapsed, she looked into the all-too-familiar eyes that matched her own.

"That's too many switches for one box."

Andy tried to explain to Duncan that more than three switches on an electrical plate and even the owners wouldn't remember which went to what. Duncan didn't argue. They arranged and rearranged electrical boxes, leads and tubes that would carry all the wire to the mother box. He convinced Duncan to use an extra dummy tube that traveled up all three stories of the home as a place to run wire for any future changes in heart after the drywallers had finished. Looking around at the work accomplished, Andy warmed at the sight of his cousins joining in the work.

Andy had to admit Hannah had some damn good ideas about hiding extra outlets under cabinets, around the kitchen and along the top of the fireplace mantel. Jonathon, of course, knew his way around a work site; he'd spent plenty of summers working for Andy. James was going to be more of a suit and tie kind of guy but didn't wince at working with his hands. Both twins helped the roofers scatter boxes of shake shingles over the roof.

Miguel had parked the four-wheeler in the back of the cottage. He should have had at least another hour before the girl woke up if he followed directions good enough. He had taken his time checking to make sure the ride was out of sight from the road, all the shades were pulled, and the windows and doors were locked. It didn't matter. She wasn't going anywhere.

He pulled up a wooden chair from the rental cabin's kitchen table, spun it around and sat in it backward as he faced her. Lifting her lifeless head by the chin, he pulled open one of her eyelids. He couldn't tell with her face all limp like that. The timing was right, though. How could Mandy have hidden this from him all this time? Fuck.

Slapping Rose a few times firmly on the face, he tried to rouse her. He'd been waiting for this, anxious. Sighing deeply, he let her chin drop back on her neck, stood up and walked to pour himself a shot of gin.

Rose sat with her hands tied behind her back and then to the back of a chair. She was awake, could hear a voice, but wasn't lucid enough to piece everything together. Sheer instinct told her to play dead, or in this case, unconscious. She had vague memories of being dragged through dirt, her feet bobbing over a threshold and her head hitting a doorjamb. The mountain of a headache told her the memories were real.

She smelled musty wood and floor cleaner mixed with the smell of cigarette smoke. Her nose burned like she'd been breathing in lacquer, but her mouth wouldn't open. It felt like it was sealed shut with cotton. The voice was unfamiliar and the man wasn't speaking English. Where was Grace when she needed a translator?

At that moment, her mind cleared. Grace. She was supposed to meet Grace behind the action center to help her with Gracie and the new interns. She could feel the duct tape covering her mouth. The rag, the man, her father—it all came together and made her dizzy with bubbling fear.

She worked to keep her breathing slow and kept her head down. How long had she been like this? Surely they knew she was missing by now. Her neck ached enough for her to think she had been in that position for a significant amount of time.

"When do you go back? The folks like it when you stick around." Andy sat on the dirt with his forearms resting on his lifted knees. Through the opening to the window for Duncan's front room, he could see his cousins in a heated debate. He grinned.

Duncan leaned against a tree, sipping from a bottle of water. "Soon. I've nearly finished the first portrait. Not bad, if I say so myself."

"You just did. At least stay for some grilling with Hannah and the twins. They leave for college in a couple weeks," Andy said.

Andy's cell phone rang. He stood up to dig it out of his pocket. Not recognizing the number, he almost didn't answer, but something sent a chill running down his back.

Rose waited until she heard him moving around in the room next to her. She opened her eyes slightly, trying to judge her surroundings. Miguel must have been in the kitchen. She opened her eyes completely and saw she was in a small cabin. Recognizing it as one of the models a few miles from the center, her mind began swimming through scenarios. They were a long way away from people.

She was alone. She was alone and drugged and tied to a chair with the man who raped her mother. Bile rose to her throat. Her fear turned to an ice that gripped her arms and legs. How did they get here? Who would know?

Hopelessly, she tried to maneuver her secured hands to one side of her or the other. She could move them about a foot before the rope caught. Shifting her hip, she worked to get to her pocket. Her phone was missing, but her father must have stopped searching after he found it because her Swiss Army knife was jabbing her hip. She could just get her thumb inside and reach the compact knife.

Miguel was ranting. She could hear him pacing. Every so often, he slammed down a bottle. She had worked the knife to the edge of her pocket when the sound changed to soft, approaching footsteps.

"Andy Reed," he answered his phone with brows creased.

"Oh, Andy. Son of a bitch, get over here. I called 911. I called and they're com—"

"Slow down. Is this Grace?" Her accent apparently accentuated when she was excited. Andy was already slinging his leg over the seat of Duncan's Suzuki as his brother climbed on behind him.

"Yes. Yes, I'm sorry." She took a short breath "Please come. To the center. It's Rose. She's missing."

Andy stopped before turning the key to the ignition. "What do you mean, 'missing'?"

"She would never leave the door open to Gracie's enclosure. Her phone. It was in the grass."

Andy wasn't sure what else Grace said. He hung up and flipped the bike out of neutral. The door left open was enough for him. He spun out of the drive with the gears ringing at a high pitch as he raced down the gravel drive to the highway with Duncan hanging on in back.

Dave drove in focused silence with the hidden lights blazing from his head, tail and back window brake lights. Nick sat in the passenger seat as if he hadn't just taken the last corner nearly on two wheels. As Rose's dad, he called Amanda to let her know. As detective, he called for backup.

Nick turned and yelled over the noise of the engine and the siren. "Get the dog."

He didn't let off the gas. "What?" he asked in frustrated disgust.

"The dog. Get the dog. It knows his scent. It hates him. Do you remember? If he's taken her somewhere, the dog might be able to follow."

"Damn it." He darted his eyes as he considered. He sure as hell hoped she was right. He checked the back mirror, then did a screeching u-turn.

CHAPTER 31

Rose let her chin drop back down on her neck while she stumbled with the small knife between her thumb and forefinger. Miguel walked from the kitchen straight to her. She hung on to the knife between two fingers as she smoothed the shift of her body back to a centered position, pretending she was stirring to wake. "Hmm." She forced herself to breathe deeply and lift her head with eyes half open.

Looking at the floor in front of her, she saw a leg wearing khaki carpenter pants swing over a turned chair and Miguel Ramirez plop down in front of her.

"Good morning, my daughter." He lifted her chin, looked into her eyes. "Yes, there it is. Like looking in a fucking mirror." He was so close, she could see the deep, tanned crevasses in his face. Every piece of stubble.

His breath reeked of days-old cigarette stench. Mixed with the smell of sweat and liquor, she nearly wretched. Terrified to move, she silently flipped open the small, smooth blade.

"Yes, look at you. How'd Mandy do it? She's a smart chick; I always knew that." He got up from the chair and stepped backward, tilting his head and leaning from one side to the other. He looked her up and down.

She closed her eyes tight in disgust and despair.

"Yes, yes. Your kind is always pissed...at first." He smiled, showing yellowed teeth. "And then comes the begging." He began walking back and forth in front of her, turning his head, keeping his eyes on hers as he paced.

"She'll have to die now, of course. Has she told you how this works? It's simple, really. Cross me and I kill the ones you care about. Then, I kill you. Some women need a little photo brigade to help them...get past the mad. It will help you, too. I promise. You'll take some wonderful photos. I'm thinking lying next to your mother will do nice. Our dear Mandy. What do you think she'll say when I bring her here to find your body?"

Rose squirmed and shook in the chair, moving it several inches and nearly dropping the knife on the wooden floor.

Miguel threw his head back laughing, sat down backward in the chair in front of her and ripped the duct tape from her face.

Duncan hung onto him even when they reached the parking lot to the action center. Smart. Andy hardly slowed. He jumped the curb and headed straight to the back along the side with the bird's enclosure.

He stopped, but didn't turn off the bike. The aviary was empty. The door hung open. He heard Gracie screech almost immediately. She perched in the branches over one of the half-dozen trail entrances around the field.

Revving the engine, he took off in her direction.

"Are you sure you know what you're doing?" Duncan asked.

"No!" Andy yelled with insane grief over the sound of the engine, the wind and the rough terrain.

"This isn't a dirt bike, Andy."

Gracie flew away as they approached. Duncan pointed to tracks in the dirt on the trail. "There," he said.

"All the trails have tracks from bikes and four-wheelers," Andy yelled.

"Trust me," Duncan yelled back. "Go."

The trees were thick and branches slapped Andy's face as he strained to see through the leaves a sign of a vehicle. Knowing this was a long shot, he convinced himself he'd find her before it was too late.

Rose worked the ropes as she listened.

"You know my father was white." Miguel smiled inches from

her face. "Came to my country to help after a hurricane. He raped my mother and left her there. She was rejected when she birthed a white baby, birthed a gringo."

She could feel his breath. It made her sicker than the chloroform. "If you're looking for sympathy for why you do what you do, you're looking in the wrong place," she whispered. "*Both* of our mothers were raped and left. I didn't feel the need to grow up a mental case. You chose your path." She reared her neck back, then head butted him with all she could as she shook her hands free. "I chose mine, you fucking bastard!"

From far away, Andy saw the cabin and the four-wheeler. He first thought they were too close to the center. It could have been anyone's place, except that all the shades were drawn and the windows and doors closed. He pointed.

Andy cut the engine, tossed the bike on its side as he and Duncan jumped off and ran toward the cabin. He could hear moaning and knew it was the right place. He could feel it. Worried that the man had a gun or knife to Rose's throat, he crept around to the back door.

"Get up." Rose clipped her knife shut and tucked it back in her front pocket.

Miguel rubbed his forehead, shook his head clear and then looked up. "Why you little whore." He charged.

She knew she couldn't afford to let him reach her and dodged. He was slow and predictable, but she wasn't nearly a hundred percent. "Like I've never heard that line before, you murdering—" She spun and clipped his face with her heel. "—coward." As her body was still turning from the kick, she took him full force through the underside of his jaw just as the back door to the cabin burst open.

Dave's tires skidded to a stop in the front of the center. He bolted from the car and followed Grace to the back.

"Andy flew by on a motorcycle a few minutes ago. He went that way." Grace waved her hands wildly toward the woods. "He went in there."

Charcoal scrambled out the window from the back of the unmarked car. He let his nose do the investigating. Running to catch up with Dave and Nick, he quickly caught a scent.

Growling low, his black fur stood on end along the back of his head to the center of his back. With nose near the ground, he took off across the field.

Miguel staggered and steadied, swinging madly. He regained his balance and struck.

Rose jutted her head back, but still took a partial blow to her right temple. She was still able to block the return jab with her forearm.

Andy stood watching them. She looked like a madman, screaming and cursing. He fought the urge to step in. She needed this.

Duncan ran in seconds behind him, but Andy put an arm out and shook his head.

Moving lightning fast, Rose ducked and struck, then struck again. "You raped my mother!" She spun, using momentum, and planted the backs of her knuckles to the side of his face. "Fucking bastard. You hurt her!"

Andy heard the crack of bone and wasn't sure if it was Rose's hand or Miguel's face, or both. Then, he heard a barking dog.

Miguel lay on the ground but still had enough in him to slide his legs under Rose's feet before collapsing on his back.

Rose rolled, straddled his chest, striking his face again and again as she sobbed.

Dave came up behind her and took her gently by the shoulders. "Come on, honey." He grabbed hold as she fought and kicked before turning to bury her head in his chest. He wrapped his arms around her and rocked her as they stood.

"Dad."

"It's all right. I'm here. It's over."

Nickie stood over Miguel with Charcoal snarling in a 'stay' at her side.

"Good boy." Duncan patted his head.

Miguel was conscious, barely. Shrugging a shoulder, Nickie flipped him, not so carefully, onto his stomach and cuffed him.

Duncan reached to help her heft him up.

"I've got it, Mr. Reed."

He looked at her. "Of course you do," he said and pulled him up anyway. They led him out back together.

Rose tucked her arms between herself and the only father

she'd ever known. He stroked her hair and soothed her as she sobbed. Turning to see Nickie on her way out and Andy standing patiently, Dave eased Rose over to him and let them have a minute alone before they sealed the place.

Andy inspected her temple, looked into her eyes and pulled her hand between them to check her knuckles. Broken, he knew. Barely touching the skin, he kissed them.

She looked up to him. "You're here."

He tucked her hair behind her ear and smiled down at her. "Always."

EPILOGUE

A soft, warm breeze ruffled the deep reds and bright yellows of the autumn trees. The hydrangeas and daisies had been trimmed back with asters and sedum taking their place as the prominent color of the Reeds' backyard.

The arbor blossomed with a mixture of bright lavender chrysanthemums and yellow helianthus. The lines of white clothed folding chairs were adorned with their own mixture of the flowers created by Brie and her mother.

At the end of the white runner Rose stood with a skintight, sequined dress that hugged her to just above her knees. The neck was haltered and cut low enough to show hints of her fleshy curves. She thought it was about time to show some cleavage. Small ties of baby's breath and miniature mums twined in her short locks of hair with scattered, sparkling gems throughout.

In one arm, she held a dripping bouquet of yellow satin ribbons and rows of tight-fitting flowers. In her other arm was Dave. They watched in front of them as James and Jonathon finished ushering guests in their tailored charcoal tuxes and coordinating boutonnières.

Dave covered her hand that held onto his arm as the wedding march began. She smiled wildly as cameras flashed and guests stood. And then, she saw him. Light brown hair cut short in a fitted tuxedo that couldn't conceal his physique. Her best friend waited to take her hand, the man she'd been in love with since she was old enough to know what being in love was.

They walked the aisle reverently before Dave kissed her cheek and handed her to Andy, then stood on the other side of the pastor and turned to face the guests.

Everyone, including her and Andy, turned their attention to her mother who stood at the end of the runner on Nathan's arm. She was so similar to her that they could be taken for sisters, eyes or no eyes. Her mother's dress was more conservative, yet just as fitting with a high waist and long train. Lace covered the strapless bodice and gathered in the back. Her mass of red hair wound tightly on her head with bits of beads and flowers, matching Rose.

So much the same and yet so different.

The crowd remained standing as cameras continued to flash before Nathan kissed her cheek and gave her to Dave. On one side were Andy and Rose with Duncan and Hannah standing as best man and maid of honor. On the other, Dave and Amanda stood with Nicole untraditionally standing as best man and Jessica as maid of honor.

They turned first, couple facing couple, nodded to each other and then faced the preacher.

"We gather here together..."

Turn the page for an

excerpt from

DARK
VENGEANCE

The Black Creek Series
Book Three

R.T. Wolfe

Duncan walked into the apartment of the man he knew was involved in the attempted murder of his aunt.

Detective Nickie Savage handed him gloves and told him not to touch anything. Twice. Even with the gloves.

Nickie was thorough, he had to admit. Although he didn't want to admit anything about her at that moment. The detective was proving far too inquisitive, too smart and too complicated.

Working with three local officers, they leafed through every book in the apartment, and carefully removed each desk, dresser and kitchen drawer for anything stored in the back space before calling it a wrap.

Not once did Nickie mention their prior discussion. He wasn't sure what to think about that, except it made him all the more aware of what he'd dug up on her. His aunt was the only person alive who knew about his...issue. Not even his uncle or brother had any idea.

Then, one day, out of the blue, his aunt had asked him why he didn't just tell people. It was the same question the detective had asked just a few hours ago.

Duncan rubbed his hand along the back of his neck. What was Nickie going to do with the information? She had no proof, of course. But the way she avoided eye contact with him was disconcerting. Disconcerting yet damned intriguing.

Nickie, the detective with long, honey wheat hair, black, worn-leather boots, snug slacks and a badge.

Her movements looked rehearsed. Write in her notebook, place item in evidence bag, write on the bag with a marker, write more in her notebook. Rinse and repeat.

The locals working with them were actually careful and rather neat. Savage even more so. Their search was not at all like the movies where dresser drawers are overturned and mattresses cut. Duncan looked around the man's open living room. The place hadn't been ransacked but it was definitely disheveled, and it gave him a sort of satisfaction.

The only thing missing was the tower and monitor Nickie confiscated, along with some files and papers Duncan wasn't privy to know about...yet. He had all the pass codes he needed to get that information.

Nickie rested her thigh on the corner of a computer desk, and cocked her head at him. "You never hacked into my past."

He couldn't decide if it was a question or an accusation. "Yes I did...do a search on your past. You know that. As you did on mine." Curious, he lifted a single brow to her, waiting for what she was getting at.

"No. No, you didn't. Not my missing year."

Well, shit. Now he wanted to. But he had rules. No stealing. No cheating. No hacking into someone's life without permission, or at least due reason.

His sudden curious-as-hell status probably didn't count as due reason.

"No. I didn't," he said flatly.

She stepped to him, grabbed the collar of his shirt with both hands and raised herself up until her lips just brushed his. Her scent was so close, he could nearly taste it. Lavender. He was used to women throwing themselves at him but this was profoundly different. She was different. This was more of a challenge than a kiss. Like a threat. After a much too short meshing of her soft, full lips, she pushed away.

"Oh no you don't." He took hold of her shoulders and pulled her back to him. Going from zero to sixty in seconds, he parted her lips with his tongue and dove in. She tasted as smart and sophisticated as her scent. He sensed her chaos and his confusion. What he *didn't* feel was what he was accustomed to;

bony hips, pencil thin arms and breasts that were four sizes too big for a body. Nickie was fit, toned, soft and all woman.

Their arms circled each other in a dance of reason. Heat built. Their knees tucked between each other's. He ran a hand up her arm.

As their mouths tangled, he slithered his hand into the locks of honey, lacing his fingers through the smooth waves. This shock on his system was something he never allowed.

She pulled away and this time locked her elbows, arms outstretched. She took two, deep sexy breaths and licked her lips. "Show me what you found, Duncan. Then, let's grab a bite to eat before we bag us an ex-fireman."

DARK VENGEANCE
available in
print and ebook

MEET THE AUTHOR

Its not uncommon to find dark chocolate squares in R.T.'s candy dish, her Golden Retriever at her feet and a few caterpillars spinning their cocoons in the terrariums on her counters. When R.T. isn't writing, she loves spending time with her family, gardening, eagle-watching and can occasionally be found viewing a flyover of migrating whooping cranes.

R.T. enjoys hearing from readers. You can contact R.T. through her website: www.rtwolfe.com